HEART OF ASHES

Hearts of the Highlands
Book One

Paula Quinn

Books from Dragonblade Publishing

Dangerous Lords Series by Maggi Andersen
The Baron's Betrothal
Seducing the Earl
The Viscount's Widowed Lady
Governess to the Duke's Heir

Also from Maggi Andersen
The Marquess Meets His Match

Knights of Honor Series by Alexa Aston
Word of Honor
Marked by Honor
Code of Honor
Journey to Honor
Heart of Honor
Bold in Honor
Love and Honor
Gift of Honor
Path to Honor
Return to Honor

The King's Cousins Series by Alexa Aston
The Pawn
The Heir

Beastly Lords Series by Sydney Jane Baily
Lord Despair
Lord Anguish

Rulers of the Sky Series by Paula Quinn
Scorched
Ember
White Hot

Hearts of the Highlands Series by Paula Quinn
Heart of Ashes
Heart of Shadows
Heart of Stone

Highlands Forever Series by Violetta Rand
Unbreakable
Undeniable

Viking's Fury Series by Violetta Rand
Love's Fury
Desire's Fury
Passion's Fury

Also from Violetta Rand
Viking Hearts

The Sins and Scoundrels Series by Scarlett Scott
Duke of Depravity

The Unconventional Ladies Series by Ellie St. Clair
Lady of Mystery

The Sons of Scotland Series by Victoria Vane
Virtue
Valor

Men of Blood Series by Rosamund Winchester
The Blood & The Bloom

PROLOGUE

Bannockburn, Scotland
The Year of Our Lord 1314

C AINNECH MACPHERSON, SECOND Highland commander to King
Robert the Bruce, smashed his shield into an English soldier's
chest, knocking him to the ground. Cainnech dropped his shield, put
his boot on the soldier's belly, and lifted his spear in both hands.

He looked down into the eyes of his enemy. His stomach should
have twisted at what he saw. But it didn't. He'd seen it thousands of
times before. Killing another man was a nasty task that took its toll on
the soul. One either learned to live with it or hesitate and die.

He brought down his pike into the soldier's chest.

A warm breeze passed over him. It reeked of blood and piss and
purpose. Comforted by the familiarity of it, he yanked his spear free of
bone and chainmail and freed his axe from his belt. He swung it
upward while he turned on another soldier coming up behind him. His
axe caught the soldier under the chin, splashing blood across Cain's
face and giving deeper color to the glacial blue of his eyes. His gaze
raked over the battle going on around him. The English forces were

dwindling. Their cavalry was trying to make their way toward the hill.

He left his axe where it had landed and bent to take the dead soldier's sword from the man's fingers. He used it to hack several more men out of his way until he had a clear line of vision to Father Timothy waiting in the mist.

He followed the priest's gaze across the ferocious melee from whence he'd just come, toward the woods where Thomas Randolph, the king's nephew, brought his schiltron, or shield wall, out of the trees.

Cain took a moment to appreciate their perfect formation and to enjoy the surprise on the faces of the English as the Scots hemmed them in.

He took it all in, glad to be a part of it. He'd waited long enough. It was time to win Scotland's independence…and his own.

He picked up a shield and pounded his sword against it, then shouted for his men to make formation.

They fell in smoothly, killing everyone in their way, and formed an impenetrable wall, weapons pointed at the English.

Cain took his place in the front line, eager to fight, to show the English the monsters they'd unleashed.

Pushing his shoulder against his shield, he prepared to give the order to move when he saw Father Timothy shoving his way to the front.

"What the hell are ye doin' here?" Cain demanded.

"I am here to help," the small, bald-headed priest replied calmly against his shield.

It was the same thing he'd said sixteen years ago when he'd found a seven-year-old Cain huddled against the tree from which he was tied.

"I dinna need yer help, old man. Now get back to the—"

"Ye should give the order to move now, Commander," the priest offered in a softer tone. "The men are waitin'."

Cain scowled, knowing the priest was correct. This wasn't the time to argue. His men were ready and awaiting his order. "Move!" he shouted. "On them! On the English! Ye!" He turned to Father Timothy. "Go back! Dinna let me see ye here again."

He didn't wait to see if the priest obeyed him or not. Every man in his regiment obeyed him. They trusted him with their lives—and somehow he'd always managed to keep them alive.

They charged as one living, moving entity, four hundred strong, decimating Edward's infantry.

Cain yanked his sword free from over two dozen men before he found a moment to turn to the one who would likely get him killed.

"What d'ye mean by disobeyin' me, Father? I told ye to go back!"

"I obey the good Lord. Not ye, Cainnech," the priest answered, unruffled by a glare that was said to stop the hearts of the English.

"Oh?" Cain asked, tightlipped. "And the good Lord wants ye to fight? To kill?"

Father Timothy's brown eyes were large as he smiled, exposing old, yellowing, but straight teeth. "Some are called to carry out His judgment."

Hell! *Again*, this wasn't the time to argue with the old fool! Cain respected King Robert and he'd give his life in battle for any one of his men. But he'd cared deeply for only one person in the last sixteen years. He wasn't about to let Father Timothy put his life into the hands of something or someone Cain could not see.

Without wasting another moment, Cain went to Father Timothy, grasped him by the back of his robes, and pulled him into the fray. He made certain nothing came too close to the priest while he swung his sword and hacked away at the English with one hand.

Covered in the blood of his enemies and dragging a sword-wielding priest behind him, he set his course toward the hill and joined forces with Thomas Randolph's men to drive the English cavalry into the marshes. The Bruce's regiment took the English from the south, where the English king retreated.

"Aye, run!" Father Timothy shouted. "If ye know what's best fer ye, ye will never come back!"

Cain glanced at him and then continued on toward a clearing in which to collapse without falling on a body—or into the marshes.

They'd won. They'd beaten the English before, but nothing like today. Cain hoped England's King Edward was watching when King Robert brought down his battle axe on Sir Henry de Bohun's helmeted head, striking him dead.

Cain smiled, and not for the first time that day. Robert fought like a savage and Cain was proud to call him teacher.

But hell, he was exhausted. He just wanted to rest for a wee bit.

"God has given us victory!" the priest rejoiced.

Cain shook his head and held up his axe.

"What d'ye think 'twill be like tomorrow?" Father Timothy came up beside him and asked excitedly.

"I'll let ye know when 'tis over."

"Come on now, Cainnech." The priest joined him sitting in the grass.

Father Timothy never called him Cain. He claimed the weight of such a name created its own beast. Cain disagreed. Being raised in the English army, by the men who'd killed his family, had created it.

"This is it. We're close to independence. I want to be a part of the victory."

"Ye are already a part of it," Cain assured him. "Ye advise the king. Who else d'ye know who can say such a thing?"

"Ye," the priest told him. "Ye advise him, as does the king's brother, his nephew, the—"

"All right," Cain held up his hand. "Never mind any of it. I have a few moments to rest and ye're interruptin'. Let me put this to ye bluntly, Father. Ye willna be joinin' me, or any of the men on the field tomorrow. I will tie ye to a tree if I must. I willna have ye fightin'. If anythin' were to...I consider ye my..."

"Son," the priest said softly, taking pity on Cain's stumbling tongue. "Tomorrow is goin' to be an historic day. God has shown me."

"Ye see?" Cain yawned and closed his eyes. "Historic days usually involve many dyin'."

"We will not die, Cainnech. I must help ye find her first."

Cain opened his eyes and looked up at his friend's filthy face. "What are ye talkin' aboot?" He leaned up on his tired elbows. "Her who?"

"God has not revealed her name but we must find her."

Cain scowled at him. "Why?"

Father Timothy shrugged. "Somethin' to do with love, I suppose."

For a moment, Cain thought his friend was trying to be humorous. But when the priest remained sober, Cain blew out a short chuckle and shook his head. Love? Never. He wasn't meant to love. He was born to fight, to kill. He was brought up on the battlefield, unperturbed by the blood of Englishmen drying on his skin. From a young age, he'd watched the blood of loyal Scotsmen pouring out into the dark grass. He'd wanted to fight with them, for them. It fueled the only passion left in him. To kill.

"Are ye and yer God mad?" He lay back in the grass and closed his eyes. "What place is there in the ashes fer love?"

CHAPTER ONE

Northumberland
Four years later

THE WAIL OF bagpipes dragged across the shallow strath and carried along the crisp night breeze to the battlements of Lismoor Castle.

Aleysia d'Argentan closed her eyes and pulled her cloak closer around her in an effort to drive out the cold. But it was no use. The Scots were coming. They would be here by first light.

She'd always known it was only a matter of time before Robert the Bruce sent his men to the village of Rothbury. She had forfeited her brother's estate for not acknowledging the Bruce's kingship. She never would, even if it meant giving up her life. Robert the Bruce and his savage army were murderers and nothing more. They killed her dear brother, Giles, at Bannockburn. She hoped they all burned in hell.

But first, they were raining terror down on most of Northern England. Most recently, they'd besieged and blockaded the town of Berwick, one of King Edward's most strategic locations.

They'd waited like snakes in the grass for the right moment to attack Berwick Castle a pair of months ago, securing lands and villages around it while they waited, killing anyone who opposed them. They didn't fight like civilized soldiers, and poor Edward didn't know how to combat them.

She opened her eyes. The bagpipes had stopped. She dragged her gaze across her land. It was dark. Almost the midnight hour. To the south, she could just make out the ribbon line of the River Coquet dappled in the silvery light.

To the west, the village was bathed in moonlight, its inhabitants gone from their homes. She'd met with them all over the last several weeks to discuss her plans and to have them swear by her brother's good name not to stay and try to fight the enemy. They were to leave that to her.

Eyes fastened on the dark land before her, she didn't breathe off rhythm when she heard the light fall of footsteps behind her.

"Is everyone out?" she asked softly without turning.

"Yes, my lady," a man's voice sounded behind her. "Matilda and Miss Elizabeth left after much weeping."

Aleysia sighed into the wind. She had wept over losing them, too. The people of Lismoor and the villagers were the only family she'd had since Giles brought her here along the English border twelve years ago from Normandy. But the time for weeping was over.

"All of the staff are gone," the man continued.

"And the guards?"

"They have reluctantly left, my lady."

She pried her fingers off the edge of the stone wall and turned to her dear friend and one of the six older guardsmen who'd first served her father in Normandy.

"And what are you still doing here, Sir Richard?"

He bowed his head, illuminating his crown of silver hair in the moonlight. "Forgive me, my lady, but I promised your brother I would always protect you. A few Scots will not change that."

Oh, she would not smile at him. She must remain strong and resolute to her task. Of all her father's knights, she loved Richard the most.
But she could only do this alone. She'd been training for the last four
years, and long before that when the great Sir Giles trained his men
and she watched and practiced everything he taught in secret. If her
friend remained behind because of her and perished, she could never
live with herself.

"My dear Sir Richard," she said, her voice imbued with the tender-
ness she felt for him, "we have been through this more times than
either of us can count. You know my wishes. You also know that I can
do this—"

"With respect, my lady, some traps set in the woods and surrounding grounds will not be enough to keep them out. I will not—"

"You forget the skill you and the others have taught me?" she cut
him off. Her green eyes sparked with pride. "I am an expert archer.
You said so yourself. I can protect myself with a shield and defend
myself with a sword. Besides, if they manage to get inside, I have
planted weapons throughout and have poisoned all the wine and grain
in the kitchen." She knew she couldn't fight a battle with hardened
warriors and win. But there were other ways to kill a man.

"Aleysia," the old knight blurted. "I never agreed to you doing this
alone! 'Tis madness! I must insist that you leave with me."

"And give up all to them?" she asked softly while a breeze blew her
dark hair across her face.

"You will have your life."

Would she? What would she have left? She would lose everyone
she loved. She would be forced to live with her cousin Geoffrey in
Normandy, only to be married off in the first month.

No. This was her home. She would rather die than give up her
knights, and Mattie and Elizabeth, not to mention all the villagers. No,
dammit. She was master of her ship. She liked it that way. She was
prepared for this, confident in her prowess and abilities. But she knew

Richard wouldn't leave her.

"Perhaps, you are correct," she said, looking off into the distance with a slow sigh. "What can I do alone against savages? What can any of us do? I…I do not wish to see my brother so soon."

She sniffed and looked away, mostly to keep him from seeing the satisfaction in her eyes when he agreed in his gentlest tone.

"I knew you would come to your senses, my lady. 'Tis best. I will bring your things to the doors."

"Thank you, and Sir Richard?" She waited while he paused to look at her. "If Giles were here, he would agree that you have taken the very best care of me."

"I will continue to do so, my lady."

She listened to the tapping of the knight's boots growing fainter as he left the battlements.

She felt terrible for deceiving him, but it couldn't be helped. She would leave Lismoor with him and find an inn where she would pay the innkeeper to lock Sir Richard in his room, or she would bar his door herself. Hopefully, by the time he found her, she would have killed their enemies—one way or another—or died trying.

Emboldened by her purpose, she looked out toward the forest, where, with the help of the villagers, she had set hundreds of deadly traps.

Let them come. She was ready. She was waiting.

Turning from the wall, she made her way back inside the keep and met Sir Richard on the stairs. She didn't look back as she walked out of Lismoor.

She would not be gone long.

A LIGHT BLANKET of dew covered the ground and Aleysia's painted, hooded face. Dawn was about to break and, with any luck, Sir Richard was still asleep in his bed, unaware that she was gone.

From her carefully plotted vantage point perched high in a tree, she could see in every direction. How many would come? How many could she possibly kill by midday? She carried thirteen arrows and her dagger. Once she cut the ropes, she wouldn't have enough time to miss—so she wouldn't.

She tried to remain calm, but the silence was too loud. Over the past four years, she'd prepared for everything. She'd even learned to climb trees. She hadn't been able to train for being completely alone though. She knew she would be, but she couldn't prepare for the haunting echoes of life around her. She hated the Scots for driving out her beloved villagers and her dear friends. She had no choice but to let them go. She would bring them all back when this was over. But she had to be quick. It had already been almost a pair of months that they had been away. Some stayed with family, others with friends. They couldn't impose much longer.

With the thought of victory firmly emblazoned in her mind, she listened to the quiet, instead of trying to drive it out.

According to rumors from Berwick, the Scots liked to attack at first light. From the sound of their pipes last eve, they were close.

Would the Bruce send more men after she killed these? Would it ever end?

Her eyes caught sight of a flock of birds rising from the treetops not far away. Such an occurrence was not a usual sight. She tensed on her perch, slowly releasing her dagger, watching.

She waited with her heart slamming against her ribs. Listening to her breath, trying to slow it down. This was real. There was no way to practice for it. An army of Scots was coming! She couldn't panic.

She heard the sounds of horses and underbrush being trampled.

The waking forest went still as they appeared through the trees along the winding path that led to Rothbury.

Aleysia quickly determined that there were at least twenty men. Not a large army as she had feared, but enough to make her task a challenge. Besides that, they were Highlanders, the most savage of them all. The traps *had* to work.

She didn't move. It wasn't time.

She surveyed the men, trying to determine who was the leader. It didn't take long to find him once she spotted the priest keeping pace beside him.

A priest. She almost huffed. She should shoot that Judas first for standing with the Scots.

If she did, she was sure the man riding at his side would immediately fall into action.

Patience, Aleysia. Let the traps do their work.

She watched the one who had to be the leader. He rode at the head of the group. He was a big man, with straight, broad shoulders, clad in a gray cloak over his Highland plaid. His knees were bare and his hair was long and as dark as his Scottish soul. He exuded confidence in the subtle tilt of his shadowed chin, the straightening of his spine.

For an instant, Aleysia forgot to breathe as he set his frost-filled eyes around the forest.

Don't look up, she prayed. She prayed also that her cloak, dyed to match the colors of the trees, was enough to conceal her if he did.

He didn't look up but as if sensing something were amiss, he paused his mount, stopping Aleysia's heart. The priest stopped with him. Thankfully, some of his men continued onward.

Her dagger was sharp. Just a few cuts and the first rope snapped. Aleysia smiled as it released a set of small swinging boulders with sticks sharpened at both ends tied together with rope.

She quit smiling soon enough and almost lost her morning meal when the boulders met their marks and struck two riders in their heads. It was more brutal than she ever imagined and her determination faltered. But what she'd done was necessary. She hadn't trained for four years just to go soft over death or killing when the time came. People were depending on her. She'd promised to bring them all back when it was safe again.

The thought of her friends spurred her into action. She drew back her bow and let her arrow fly into the chaos below. She hit three men before the rest realized they were being fired upon. A shout went out and shields were raised.

She took the moment of them not moving and hiding for cover to run across the thin planks she and her friends had hammered high amid the branches, connecting one tree to another.

Cradled between two thick branches, she paused and squatted. She was ahead of them now, watching them making their way forward, slowly and cautiously.

The leader held up one hand to slow his regiment and used the other to hold up his shield. She'd have to take him down but she didn't have a clear shot yet. Just a bit closer. He was leading them. His eyes were on the ground and everything around it.

He heard the cry of a horse as it stumbled over a hidden trap to his left. His face went dark in the filtered morning light as he turned to watch the rider launch forward from his saddle onto a bed of sharpened pikes placed in the ground.

The men around him leaped back even while their leader ordered them to be still. Aleysia wanted to put an arrow into him but he protected himself well with his shield.

She climbed away instead to another group of branches, where she had a clearer angle of which rope to cut. She picked one that freed a long, sharpened pike from another nearby tree. It swooped down and went straight through a man's chest and carried him off his horse.

"Nobody bloody move!" the leader shouted from his horse. "I will kill the next one of ye who disobeys my order! Off yer mounts! Fall in behind me! Slowly! Eyes open!"

They all dismounted and moved into a straight line behind him, leading their horses at their sides, trusting their lives to their commander's eyes.

Aleysia waited while he led them closer to the set of traps—closer to her, until they were once again in range.

She wanted them to believe they were the ones tripping the traps. It kept them from looking up. The leader was clever, making them dismount since most of the traps were set for the height of a mounted man. He would note if spiked boulders were flying about when his men walked in his footsteps. He'd start searching the trees.

So she let the men pass beneath her without cutting any ropes. She readied her bow and nocked an arrow, though, while the last of the soldiers were led away.

She took the last man and the soldier in front of him down quietly before anyone knew. Without waiting for them to discover that their comrades were dead, she followed the rest from her canopy as they reached the meadow of arrows. So named for the one hundred arrows nocked and ready to fly, ready for weeks. Was it months?

Pity that all but one of the arrows would be wasted, as they were set out *across* the wide field. They were meant to kill many, but because all the men traveled in a single line behind their commander, only one arrow would matter—the first one—aimed at the first in line.

The more she looked at him, the more convinced she became that he was the most dangerous, the most savagely alluring man she'd ever set eyes on. It was almost a shame that he had to die.

She shook her head to clear it of any more thoughts or judgments about him. She wanted him to die. She wanted them all to die. They weren't taking her home, her land.

She snatched an arrow from the quiver over her back and raised her bow. She was tired of waiting. If she took away their leader, her traps would take care of the rest of them.

She pulled back on the bowstring and watched him through one eye as he turned in her direction. Her fingers trembled for an instant before she released her arrow. It flew. He moved his head an instant before the arrow went through his eye.

But not completely in time to avoid the metal tip grinding against his left cheekbone.

Aleysia's eyes opened wide. No! How could she miss?

She went still as fury flashed across his icy blue gaze. He found her in the branches. Blood dripped down his cheek. He didn't reach for his wound but slammed his shield to the ground and reached for his bow and arrow instead.

She pulled another arrow from her quiver and nocked it but he was faster. His arrow flew…and so did Aleysia, through the trees, over planks and thick branches, on a path she'd traveled over many times before, until she was gone.

CHAPTER TWO

"**D**ID YE SEE that?" Cain didn't wait for anyone to reply before he moved for the trees. Had his eyes deceived him? How could a man travel through the boughs with such agility and speed? Was this some sort of sorcery? No, the bastard was real and responsible for killing nine of his men—for almost killing him. He lifted his fingers to the blood on his face.

Cain was going to catch him and kill him…slowly.

"Cainnech, careful!" Father Timothy called out.

"I think I hit him," Cain called back. "Amish!" he shouted to his second in command. "Keep the men still."

He looked overhead at the web of branches. There didn't appear to be anyone else. He needed to be certain, and to have a closer look at the assailant's perch.

Slinging his bow over his back, he reached the tree and used his axe to begin climbing.

When he reached the desired branch, he pulled himself up and looked in the direction of where his arrow should have landed. He spotted it jutting from the trunk. Attached to it was a piece of cloth torn from the bastard's cloak. He yanked the arrow free and replaced it in his quiver and then examined the cloth. It was dyed in the colors around him.

Clever, he thought as he lifted his gaze for the first time to the branches around him. How many more of these enemies were there?

He went still as his eyes began to focus on the ropes tied to branches. They were everywhere. Everywhere he looked. The bastard was cutting them as he and his men moved beneath him. If he hadn't tried to kill Cain and missed, he would not have been spotted and fled.

They never would have made it through the forest.

His blood went cold. This was too elaborate. There had to be more than one person here. He squinted into the branches. Would he even see them? He barely saw the one who shot at him. He listened for any sounds of things moving in trees. There wasn't any, not a single bird stirred. He should have been listening for such sounds or the lack of them earlier. Nine of his men might still be alive.

He looked down at Father Timothy and shook his head. So much for an easy siege. According to the priest, Lismoor had no guard, no lord. It was the reason he'd volunteered Cain and his men to the king. Take Lismoor for the Bruce and then go to Whitton for some rest. This wasn't supposed to be difficult.

Now it was war.

He climbed down to tell the others what he found. "The ropes must be cut to release the traps. With the bastard oot of the way, there shouldna be any more trouble." He stopped for a moment to accept a small cloth from Father Timothy and pressed it to his bloody cheek. "I dinna think there are any more of them."

A low murmur rose from the men. Father Timothy spoke what they were all asking.

"One person did all this? Cainnech look." He stepped over something and called out to the men to stand behind the trees. When they did, he hacked at something in the deep grass and arrows flew. At least a hundred soared outward into the meadow.

Cain paled. He knew it seemed impossible. "We'll see," he vowed. "Keep yer shields raised and yer eyes on the ground. I will meet up with ye all at the edge of the forest." He turned again for the trees.

"What do ye mean to do?" Father Timothy called out to him.

"I mean to see where this leads. If it leads to a village or a castle, I mean to take it and draw the assailant oot."

"Cainnech, we dinna take villages," the priest gently reminded.

Cain stopped and turned back to him. Aye, Cain had sworn never to kill villagers. But the priest knew he had a black heart. It went along with the name, though Cain had never known the story of the murderous son of Adam and Eve until Father Timothy had read it to him when he was nine. "Father," he said, his voice resonating with authority. "I will know who is responsible fer our men's deaths." He already knew who was responsible for their lives. He was. "And then I will put an end to his."

He didn't wait another moment but climbed back up the tree and moved cautiously away.

On his way around branches and planks, he surveyed the ropes and how they led through the intricate web of branches and leaves to the other side of the woods, where spiked boulders and long, sharp pikes hung waiting for release. The culprit may have been alone today, but he'd had help building all of this, planning it all as if they were expecting Cain and his men. How? Who was it? An English general he'd defeated in battle? Who lived in Rothbury?

He would find out soon enough, he thought as he came to the edge of the forest. He stood in the branches and looked down at a village spilling over the strath and a small castle on a hill in the distance.

He peered down at his men and then took one last look around for the culprit before he climbed down and joined the others.

"I dinna know which way he went," he told them, "but, mayhap, someone in the village knows."

Without waiting for anyone to object, he leaped onto his waiting mount, led to him by Father Timothy, who opened his mouth and then shut it again when Cain rode away.

The villagers were going to help bury his men whether they wanted to or not. He'd kill any who refused, or refused to help him find the assailant. He didn't care what Father Timothy believed about attacking villages, or that he quietly agreed.

Someone was going to pay.

He was the first to arrive in the village, the first to notice that something didn't feel right.

No one was here. Had the village been abandoned? Were the villagers hiding in the forest?

They searched every house, narrowly avoiding a dozen more traps that were set off upon opening doors.

"I should burn it all down," he ground out when Father Timothy brought his horse close. "It may draw him oot."

"It might if there were people inside," the priest remarked calmly. "But this place is deserted, Cainnech. It has likely been this way fer the last four years."

"Why d'ye say that?" Cain asked, his interest piqued. What did Father Timothy know?

"Sir Giles d'Argentan," the priest said, looking around.

"Ye said he was dead," Cain reminded him with a clip of annoyance in his voice.

"He is. The Norman knight served under King Edward and gave up his life at Bannockburn rather than flee with the king."

"Aye," Cain remarked. "I know the story of England's hero. Are we certain of his death? Does he have brothers wantin' to avenge him?"

"Aye, we are sure. Commander Lamont's regiment took him down. As far as his kin," Father Timothy told him, "he has no brothers. I know little aboot him, but whoever is responsible fer what happened today knew we were comin'. He must have heard Duncan's pipes last eve and planned his attack."

Cain his shook his head. "This took time to plan and put together." He narrowed his eyes on the village. "There were people here and they helped. Fer that, they will now lose their homes."

"Cainnech." The priest turned to him, his large, brown eyes, pleading—and filled with determination. "Ye have agreed to go to Whitton to pray fer yer sins. Will ye add more to them now?"

Cain laughed softly to himself. How much more proof did Father Timothy need before he would admit the truth? "Yer God obviously doesna want to hear from me, Father."

"Ye are still alive, so I would disagree," the priest replied quietly, turning back to the houses before them. "Dinna burn the village, Cainnech. Do this fer me. I ask little of ye."

Cain cast him his darkest scowl. The priest told the truth. He usually did what he wanted without asking. This time he did ask though—and for what? To save some abandoned dwellings to appease his God, who seemed bent on killing Cain?

"Verra well," Cain murmured, then gritted his teeth with disgust at his own heart and the softness in it for the old man beside him. "But ask no mercy from me when we catch this bastard."

He turned his horse to face his men. "To the castle!"

They followed him to the fortress on the hill, its keep and high, seemingly deserted battlements set against the backdrop of darkening clouds.

They approached the curtain wall slowly. If anyone were inside, they had to already know the Scots were here, yet Cain and his men met no opposition. There were no traps attached to the stone archways leading into the inner bailey, no guards patrolling the walls. Like the village, the castle appeared to be deserted.

A few of his men muttered things about ghosts and crossed themselves. Even Father Timothy seemed uneasy.

They climbed an outside staircase next to a short, stone walkway that led to the high, square keep. They came to a set of heavy doors and on Cain's command, they burst through them and into the keep's great hall. They immediately made formation, shields up, axes and short-swords held before them at the ready.

Cain looked around. The walls were bare of tapestries. Tallow candles were impaled on tall, vertical spikes and held in loops secured to the walls. Bowls of oil lamps were suspended in rings and from stands, and a hearth was built against a hooded wall. None of it was lit. Dismantled trestle tables were stacked in the rushes.

The fresh rushes.

No ghosts here. Senses piqued, Cain broke up the men into four groups to search the entire castle, including the small towers, and secure it.

"If anyone is found," he commanded while Amish lit their torches, "bring them to me."

"D'ye mind if me and the men bring him back in more than one piece?" his second asked. The men behind him nodded and chimed in about what they wanted to do to the man who killed their comrades.

"Bring anyone ye find to me alive and able to answer my questions," Cain warned them. "If anyone ye find is guilty of killin' our men, ye can all have him and bury him in as many pieces as ye like. Until I speak with them, ye will lay a hand on no one. Is that understood?"

The men all nodded and had a look at their shields or around at the bare walls—anywhere but at the raw strength in his gaze. They knew he would let justice be carried out for their fallen friends. He would face a ghost to do it.

With nothing more to say, and even less time to lose, Cain set off toward the northern end of the keep with his group.

If their forest assailant lived in this keep, chances were there would be a sign of him. Like the fresh rushes. He wanted to catch the bastard.

Nothing would stop him.

Rooms connected to other rooms through narrow archways and short stairwells. Each bed in every room they entered was nearly stripped bare. Dust had settled on empty chests and trunks and basins were dry. There was not a sign of anyone to be found.

Save for the last chamber they entered. It was the main solar, where the lord of the castle usually slept. The quarters were divided by a wood partition into a bed chamber and a sitting room. The bed was one of the finest Cain had seen and certainly nothing he had ever slept in before. Carved wood with four posters, it was set high off the floor, with hangings draped from a frame suspended from the ceiling beams. Like the others, almost every linen and item of clothing was gone. But there was no dust on the furniture and atop a tall, polished wooden chest was a hair comb.

Cain held it up and uncurled a long, dark hair from its alabaster teeth.

He looked at the hair and held the comb up to his nose. The faint scent of some kind of flower filled his nostrils.

"Father," he said in a low voice and looked up from the hair. "Did d'Argentan have a sister?"

DEEP IN THE belly of the keep, in the dungeon where once were held enemies of the king, a small door concealed in the wall began to move. It had been moved many times before.

A silver head peeped into the dungeon. "My lady?" Sir Richard whispered, exiting the small doorway. "My lady, where the hell are you?"

CHAPTER THREE

C AIN STOOD ON the high battlement wall of Lismoor Castle, formerly owned by the d'Argentans. Now, it had been claimed by Cain for King Robert. He spread his gaze over the strath to the village drenched in the golden light of the setting sun. Was their enemy hiding in one of the houses? He should have burned them all down. He still might.

The search of the keep and the surrounding area had turned up little. The assailant had not been found. That didn't mean he wouldn't be. But tomorrow was a new day. Cain wouldn't have his men wandering about in the dark and stepping into a trap—or whatever else the culprit had waiting out there.

Where was he? Who was he? Was he even a he at all? It couldn't be a lass who had waged war on his men today—running and leaping through the trees, almost killing him.

Father Timothy didn't know of any women related to the deceased previous owner.

Cain shook his head at himself. What was he thinking? A lass. He was a fool. An exhausted one. That was why he was allowing his thoughts to ponder madness. He laughed softly into the cool, heather-scented breeze.

How long had it been since he'd even spoken to a woman? Six months? Over a year since he'd lain with one. Hell, he didn't have a permanent bed. Most nights, he slept beneath the stars close to where he would be fighting the next day. He'd given up comfort and desire for familiarity.

He closed his eyes as the haunting echoes of men crying out in death returned yet again to plague him.

He was seven years old during the battle of Falkirk, when Edward I and his troops defeated the Scots, led by William Wallace. He watched the slaughter of his countrymen as the Scot's bowmen and finally the schiltrons, armed with their shields and long pikes, were killed. When he had to walk among the dead and dying and drive a post into the bloodstained ground to mark an English body that needed retrieving, he vowed to avenge his kin and his countrymen someday.

And he had. He'd killed thousands of English since that day, including the men he had lived with for eight long years. His homestead in Invergarry was once again his. Berwick was back in the hands of the Scots where it belonged. He'd helped Robert win his wars. He'd taken back his home and killed the men who had taken it from him. Was it enough? Enough for watching them kill his father...and later, his mother? For seeing them carry away his wee brother Nicholas? For watching Torin run before they took him as well? He longed to be free of the English, free of the shackles, though they were made of memories and not iron.

Was it enough for all the years of beatings and being ordered about? Of defying an enemy army with just a priest at his side?

"Commander?"

Cain turned at the sound of Amish's voice. His second was holding an old man by the collar. An old man Cain did not know.

"Who is this?" he asked softly, turning to fully face them. He knew immediately this couldn't be the one who fled through the trees today. The man was older than Father Timothy.

Cain didn't reach for his axe. If the stranger made a move, he'd be dead before he drew his next breath.

"He is—"

"I am Richard," the old man said, straightening his shoulders and gathering his mettle, "the steward of Lismoor."

Amish yanked the man by the collar to silence him. "He was found exitin' the dungeon."

Cain raised a curious brow. "There is a dungeon?" He crooked his mouth at the steward when Amish nodded. "Perfect."

He pushed off the wall and closed the gap between them. The man looked up at him with faded, guarded, blue eyes. The mettle he'd gathered moments ago shrank until he finally looked away.

"Richard, the steward of Lismoor," Cain said in a deep, deadly voice. "Ye will spend the night in the dungeon. In the morn, ye will be handed over to my men to do with as they please. After that, whatever remains of ye will be scattered aboot the village—or ye can sleep in a bed tonight and yer life will be spared." He rested his hand on the steward's shoulder and led him to the edge of the wall. "All ye have to do is tell me what I wish to know."

"I will tell you what I can, Sir."

"And also what ye canna." Cain tossed him a smile tinged with malice and led him around the perimeter of the wall. Richard wasn't the man he was looking for but, perhaps, the assailant was out there watching the castle, seeing a man he knew in the hands of his enemy. Perhaps, he might try to do something about it.

"Whose steward are ye?" he asked.

"Sir Giles d'Argentan's, Sir."

"He is dead. Is he not?" Cain asked, walking him around and looking out over the land.

"He is. Everyone has left, save me."

Cain turned to face him, his brow arched in doubt. "Everyone?"

Richard did not blink. "Aye, everyone."

Cain's smirk grew wider. "Then 'twas ye in the trees this morn?"

A faint glint of fear mixed with anger shot through the steward's eyes. He knew something.

"No. 'Twas not me," he told Cain in a remarkably steady voice. "'Twas Alexander de Bar, my lord's cousin. He came here after Bannockburn. He took care of the villagers. They accepted him as their lord and did as he asked in exchange for his protection."

"What did he ask them to do?"

The old man glanced toward the village. He likely didn't realize that regret and guilt were shadowing his eyes.

Mayhap he did because he blinked back to his stoic expression. "He asked them to help him construct traps, and then he asked them to leave."

"And his guard?"

"He had no guard, Sir."

Cain listened while the steward told him about this cousin of the d'Argentans who had taken over Lismoor with Edward's consent, and his passion for revenge against the Scots.

When the old man was done, Cain knew many things about de Bar and one thing about the steward. He wasn't being truthful. Richard wanted him to believe he was so loyal to the d'Argentans that he'd remained on at Lismoor to see to everything after his lord was killed. Judging by the ease with which he spilled everything he knew about de Bar, Richard held no loyalty to him—so why was he so afflicted that he had to struggle to keep his composure? It was as if he were protecting someone else. But who? Who else could have done this if not de Bar?

Cain didn't have much to go on save a sweetly fragranced comb and a long hair, both found in the main solar in the keep. He didn't know what he was thinking. He refused to believe a lass had anything to do with such a savage day.

He heard a sound behind him and turned to see Father Timothy stepping out onto the battlements.

"One more question before I decide what to do with ye in the morn," Cain told the steward. "Does de Bar have a wife? A sister?"

Richard's weathered face visibly paled. "No, my lord. There are no women here."

Cain drew out a short sigh and motioned to Amish. "To the dungeon then."

He waited until his second came close to the wall before he handed Richard over so that if anyone was watching from the village or the forest, they might see their loyal friend in danger. It was a long shot, but the steward was protecting someone—a lass?

Cain lifted his hand and rubbed the back of his neck, a habit born from waking on the cold ground, and dismissed the ridiculous idea of a lass once and for all.

Whether de Bar or someone else, Cain hoped the culprit was just as loyal and this might lure him out.

He watched Father Timothy stop Amish and his prisoner to speak to them and then finally come forth.

"Try to get a confession oot of him later," Cain said and turned back toward the darkening landscape.

"His confession goes from me to God and no one else," the priest said stubbornly.

Cain flashed him an impatient scowl but he didn't press it. He knew about the rules of Father Timothy's service, for the priest had taught him much from the Holy Book and had hoped Cain would someday swear his life to God.

But when Cain finally left the Bruce's service, he wasn't going to swear to anyone else. He would live out his life alone, back in the Highlands, free of the English, free of everyone.

"Duncan saw to yer wound then?" the priest asked, narrowing his eyes on Cain's cheek.

"Aye, 'tis nothin' of concern."

"Come," Father Timothy urged. "We'll speak of all this at the table. I am hungry."

Aye, they all were, but wary of falling into a trap, Amish and his hunters had returned with only a few fowl and half a dozen hares. "'Twill not be enough."

"Thankfully," the priest informed him, "Duncan discovered a few casks of flour and oats and young William has been bakin' bread. I told ye 'twas a good idea to bring him—what is it? Why are ye—where are ye hurryin' off to?"

"To the hall," Cain called out. "Our enemy is clever, Father. The grain Duncan found is likely poisoned."

Father Timothy made a quick sign of the cross and then followed Cain to the great hall.

The aroma of roasted hare and freshly-baked bread made Cain's mouth water as he strode into the hall. The men were settling into their seats. It didn't appear as if anyone had eaten yet.

"Men!" he shouted, commanding their attention.

Someone's grumbling belly echoed in the silence.

"Take yer bread from yer trencher and put it aside. Dinna put it to yer lips. It may be poisoned."

He squared his jaw at the murmurs of frustration and disappointment in their eyes. They were hungry. He would find a way to see them fed.

"And the wine we found?" William asked.

Cain stared at him for a moment, remembering the lad was likely barely a score years old. They didn't know for certain. They had picked him up in Berwick two months ago, after he'd escaped his English master. He'd been badly beaten and hadn't had much to say. Father Timothy took him under his wing, as he had Cain.

Cain didn't blame young Will for not suspecting anything nefarious. The lad knew nothing of war, only its aftermath. But the others…he raked his gaze over them. "Dinna drink the damned wine until I know fer certain that 'tis not poisoned."

"How will ye know?" someone called out.

He told them about the steward, keeping it brief, then scooped up a hunk of bread from the table, along with a cup of wine and left the great hall.

CHAPTER FOUR

ALEYSIA CRAWLED ON her hands and knees through the narrow tunnel, praying as she went that her dear Richard was still alive. If he wasn't, she would find a way to kill them all.

She'd been too far away earlier to shoot her arrow at the bastard commander while he dragged Sir Richard around the battlement wall. He'd wanted her to see, perhaps draw her out into the open.

But she went underground.

The tunnel wasn't overly long, about thirty feet, beginning behind the castle at the edge of the forest and leading to the dungeon. She'd had it built in case all else failed and she was thrown into the small iron prison. This was her escape route.

The entire length of the tunnel was reinforced with wood planks around the sides and overhead to help prevent collapse. There was no light, for it was nearly impossible to crawl on one hand while holding a torch in the other. Equally difficult was a cloak, no matter how short, so she'd left hers behind.

She didn't mind the pitch black or the cramped space. She'd made herself get accustomed to it by entering it every day the moment it was finished.

She wasn't afraid. She'd stopped being afraid a few months after she learned about her brother and the terror of the wild Scots coming for Lismoor and killing everyone had settled over her. And then she had done something about it.

The last four years changed who she was. She'd come to Lismoor as a lady. Now she was a warrior.

When she came to her destination, she pressed her ear to the thin, wooden door painted to look like the stone wall of the dungeon.

Silence returned.

Was Richard inside? She couldn't wait a moment longer and pushed on the door.

Cautiously, she entered the dungeon, looking for a guard on duty as she moved. She found one beneath the only source of light, in a chair by the doorway. He looked to be in a deep sleep, which didn't surprise her. It was long after midnight. She glanced quickly at the cell but could not see inside. Her knight had to be there or a guard would not have been posted.

The enormity of what she had to do hit her and though her breath turned to mist in the cool air, she broke out in a sweat. Could she kill a man while he slept? Shove her dagger into his throat? Dear God…she couldn't hesitate now. She had to save Richard.

She licked her dry lips and lifted her dagger. Something near the guard's belly caught her eye as she moved forward—the torchlight flashing against metal. An arrow tip. The rest of the shaft was inside him.

What? This was one of the men she'd shot with her arrows. He…he was already dead! Her heart drummed so hard she feared she might die right here with him. She took a step back and hit a wall. Of hard muscle. She spun around but before she completed the turn, strong fingers closed around hers and squeezed her dagger free.

Once he'd eliminated the threat of her weapon, he spun her around the rest of the way to face him and yanked her arms behind her back. He held both her wrists in one of his large hands and pressed her against him.

"A lass."

His voice was like ancient thunder reverberating through her blood. His breath, caught slightly on a thread of hesitation and urgency, was warm along her cheek.

She made the mistake of looking up. Torchlight flickered across the cool, sapphire surface of his eyes as they roved over her features. His hair was dark and long, worn pulled back at the temples in the style of the savages she'd heard about. Despite the rugged beauty of his visage bathed in the golden light, he was a Scot—bold, arrogant, and untamed.

"Your keen perception is startling," she bit out, fighting to keep her teeth from chattering. It was one thing to practice. Nothing had truly prepared her for being captured by her enemy, for finding terror and warmth in the circle of his indomitable embrace.

She had to think! Remember what she'd been taught. She looked away from him, as if that would somehow make him less real, and pulled back her knee.

She caught him in the groin. He went down on one knee, pulling her with him. She'd hoped he'd let her go but the beast was determined to hold on.

She drew back her knee again and, this time, caught him in the jaw. He reeled backward, finally letting her go. She didn't waste a moment to escape, save to run to the cell. It was empty. Richard wasn't there.

She had no choice but to leave without him. For now.

Without looking back, she ran and leaped for the doorway to the tunnel.

She looked into the darkness with a hopeful heart. Could she truly make it out? She should have killed the man while he was down. But this was a trap. He'd used Richard to draw her out of hiding. If she killed him, his men would kill Richard—if her friend wasn't dead already—and then come after her.

She plunged into the darkness but the Scot caught her by the legs and heaved her back. She clung frantically to the wood planks, almost pulling one free in an effort to escape him. She kicked as his hands rode up her thighs to her waist, until he finally pulled her free and latched on to her wrists.

He flung her over on her back and climbed atop her. She closed her eyes, though she couldn't see him in the dim light. Would he rape her before he killed her?

"What do ye know aboot the traps in the trees?"

She expected a knife in her neck, not a question. She opened her eyes and swallowed what felt like her heart.

"They were built to kill the Scots," she told him the truth without regret.

"Who built them?" he demanded in a guttural whisper.

What had Richard already told him?

"Where is he?" She tried to fight his weight on her, but it was no use. He didn't budge. Was that armor beneath his léine or solid muscle? "What have you done with Sir Richard?"

"*Sir* Richard?"

Before she had another moment to think, he yanked her up by her arm and pulled her toward the cell. "I will have the truth."

"Oh, will you?" she challenged and with her free hand, pulled a small dagger from her bosom. She swiped at his face but he bent backward as if he could see in the dark. Bastard.

He snatched her wrist and bent it backward until she dropped her dagger and cursed him.

"I'm going to kill you," she vowed tightly.

"Doubtful."

He pulled open the unlocked door to the cell and tossed her inside, and then slammed the grate shut and locked it.

"Where is Sir Richard?" she demanded, clinging to the metal bars.

"If ye want to see him again," the bastard commander snarled, returning to the torch and the dead soldier beneath it, "ye'll tell me who is the one responsible fer killin' my men today."

"I am," she said boldly. She didn't care if it was foolish. It felt satisfying telling him.

His jaw tightened, drawing her eyes to its strong, square cut and shadowy contours.

"And who are ye?"

Both Aleysia and her captor turned at the sound of another male voice. The priest. Aleysia scowled as he stepped into the light.

She sized them both up. She had to. She would most likely have to kill them at close proximity. It was best to know exactly what she'd be up against.

Of course, she didn't want to kill a priest. If he even *was* a priest. How could he pray to God and be on the side of savage Scots? If she had to kill him, she would.

He was thin in his dark robes, and short in stature, barely reaching the bastard commander's shoulders. He looked to be about twenty or so years younger than Richard. If it came down to her or Richard's life, taking the priest wouldn't be too physically difficult.

She made the sign of the cross and mouthed a quick, silent prayer. When she opened her eyes, the priest was coming toward her with another fiery torch. Had he been holding it when he entered the dungeon?

He handed it to her through the bars and waited while she lit her cell.

"Ye were sayin'?" the priest went on. "Ye are...? And by the way, Commander MacPherson, ye will make certain Alan is buried tonight." He looked at the dead man in the chair and shook his head. The commander didn't reply or even acknowledge the order.

Prideful, she thought sourly and squared her shoulders. "I am Lady

Aleysia d'Argentan, servant of King Edward, sister of Sir Giles d'Argentan."

They were silent for a moment. They shared a brief, unreadable glance before looking at her again.

Torchlight bounced off the top of the priest's bald head when he returned to his friend. "Ye will fergive us fer not believin' that 'twas ye in the trees this morn. We know 'twas Lord de Bar."

"Who?" Aleysia asked.

"I believe her," her captor said, his features chilled with ruthlessness and an utter lack of mercy.

Aleysia met his frosty gaze head-on, ignoring his powerful stature, his chilling beauty...and the arrogant tilt of his dark brow. She, too, could be ruthless and merciless. Why she—

One corner of his mouth tilted up just a bit and sent a fissure of alarm down her back. She looked away from him for a moment to clear her thoughts. He frightened her but she would not cower. Not now. Not ever.

What about this did he find humorous? Was he mocking her confidence? He claimed to believe she was responsible for the traps and for the deaths of his men. Why would he smirk at her challenging stare?

"You do not believe I can kill you, as well," she said, doing her best to sound as confident as he.

"From a tree, mayhap. Not if I stepped into that cell."

Would he?

He was long and muscular, but not overly so. Authority and danger oozed from every part of him. He was going to be harder to kill— though she'd had the chance twice now and let it slip through her fingers. She was awaiting the best moment.

"Ye canna tell the men," the priest said, jarring her from her thoughts.

"They deserve to know. 'Twas their comrades who fell by her

hand."

"First of all, Cainnech," the priest said with more command than she expected to hear in his hushed voice, "she is a lady. Ye canna give her over to the men." They both looked at her and she swallowed, knowing what the men would do to her. "Second, her brother was held in high esteem by the English king. She must be offered to him before she can be dealt with by ye."

"Why?" the commander muttered. "Since when do we give a damn aboot what the English king thinks?"

"Since Robert does not want these wars to go on much longer. And third, we dinna kill ladies."

"Who says?" The commander set his flinty gaze on her.

She smiled. Let him try. Hopefully, he and his men would be dead by morning if they found and drank the wine. She didn't let herself hope that one of them cooked with the grain.

"I've told you what you want," she reminded him. "Now tell me, where is Sir Richard? Does he live?"

"Fer now," the commander said blithely and bent to haul the dead soldier over his shoulder.

"I will have my home back," she promised, tilting her chin.

When he straightened, he openly mocked her with a smile that was anything but merciful or humorous. "I will decide what to do with ye both in the morn."

He said nothing else to her, mumbled something to the priest and left the dungeon.

Fool.

She set her gaze on the priest. The commander might be finished, but she wasn't. "How do you serve God and Robert the Bruce?"

He came closer to the cell. When he spoke, his voice was soft and soothing. "The Lord is no respecter of persons. Besides, is it wrong to want to be free?"

Of course not! She thought. It was what she was fighting for! Her freedom from being sent to Normandy or to King Edward and given in marriage to a man she did not love, to live under his rule. She would rather die.

"Your cause has little to do with freedom and more to do with killing everyone in your wake. To pillage and rape and to kill innocent people. The Scots are savages."

"Cainnech hasna killed innocent people, nor has he raped anyone," the priest defended. "He is lost, but he is a good man."

Lost in what way? Did he not mean to come to Rothbury? Why was he telling her what kind of man the commander was? What did she care?

"I am Father Timothy, by the way." He smiled, showing off a full set of teeth.

"Well, Father Timothy, I am going to kill your Commander Cainnech MacPherson. First chance I get."

CHAPTER FIVE

CAIN SQUATTED AT the open hole his men had dug for Alan MacRae, and lowered him down.

He hadn't wanted one of his men sitting around in the dungeon waiting for an arrow to the guts while he laid in wait for the assailant. Since Alan already had an arrow in him...

Cain would bury him before the sun came up. It would give him time to think about what to do with Miss d'Argentan.

A lass. The Norman hero, d'Argentan's sister, for hell's sake. What was she doing running through trees, creeping through tunnels, stopping his breath with her courage and beauty?

He reached for the shovel and jammed it into the pile of soil prepared earlier. He tossed the dirt onto Alan's body and cursed Aleysia d'Argentan to the farthest reaches of hell. She deserved to be tossed over to his men, yet he protected her locked away in a cell—and no one knew she was there. Again, thanks to Alan.

Cain shoveled more dirt down upon his soldier. Alan's eight countrymen were buried nearby.

She had done it. He believed her. She was small and spry enough to leap through trees. But what convinced him was the hatred giving fire to her gloriously large, green eyes, the resolute dip of her mouth, her braw promise to kill him.

He'd never killed a woman. He did not want to do so now. What was he going to do with her in the morning?

He should give her to the men. He'd promised he would. But the thought of them touching her made him question his decisions.

She was protecting her home as he would have done. Alone.

The memory of her long raven locks tangled around his fingers sent a warm thread down his back. Her body, soft and unyielding beneath him, had tempted him to keep her there longer.

Aleysia. She smelled of the forest…and something floral and light. The solar above stairs was hers. She'd sent everyone away and stayed behind, most likely with *Sir* Richard.

Cain looked toward the rear tower, where his men were keeping guard over the old knight. He'd made himself useful when he refused to eat the bread or drink the wine. He blamed it on de Bar.

What was to be done with them?

Miss d'Argentan launched an attack on his men. He still had difficulty believing it. But he understood why she did it.

He finished burying Alan MacRae, said a prayer he no longer believed, and returned to the keep—to her room.

He entered and looked around. He imagined her sitting by the hearth, mayhap thinking about the day. Standing by the window, wondering if her traps would work. Lying in her bed.

His gaze slid there. Hell, he was weary. He pulled his léine over his head and sat at the edge of the bed to yank off his boots. He'd sent many men to their maker. But he found that the thought of killing a lass and an old man sickened him.

He lay back on the mattress with only his plaid wrapped around his waist and closed his eyes. He didn't remember falling asleep or how long he was sleeping when the cool tip of a blade at his throat and a soft feminine whisper at his ear awakened him.

"This time I will not fail."

Cain took a split second to appreciate her bold courage and the fact that she escaped the damned dungeon.

Moving faster than she could blink, he disarmed her and pulled her close. "If ye wanted to kill me, lady, ye wouldna have waited until I woke up."

"I do not usually kill men in their sleep," she bit out, struggling to be free of his grasp.

"Yer first error."

"One I will not make again."

He liked where she was. He'd like to keep her there, atop him, beneath him. He didn't care which. He liked the scent of her, the sound of her, staring into her eyes and seeing something familiar within the fire that once possessed him.

She was English, or she might as well be.

He should take her dagger and kill her with it. But madly, he enjoyed battling with her. Still, he couldn't have her going around trying to kill him. He couldn't put her back in the dungeon.

Strengthening the fortitude he'd honed at war, he pushed her aside. And with her dagger clutched tightly in his fist, he left the bed.

He pulled his léine back over his head, tucked it and her dagger into the plaid wrapped around waist, and yanked open the heavy door. He stepped halfway into the hall and called out. "Amish!"

Let them take her. She deserved her punishment.

He waited a moment and then called again, giving his second a chance to wake up and get his arse moving.

He saw a figure moving down the hall, coming closer and using the wall for support. Who the hell...William! The lad held out his hand to Cain and then crumpled to the ground.

Cain's blood froze. Poison. He almost turned back to go deal with her once and for all, but William was in trouble.

Running to him, Cain knelt at his side. The lad's skin was cool and pale. Hell, even his lips were white. His dark hair was damp with perspiration and clung to his skin.

"Will?" Cain gave him a gentle shove and then let himself breathe when the lad opened his eyes. "Did ye drink the wine, lad?"

"Aye, Commander," Will said weakly. "Forgive me."

"We'll speak of it later." Cain tried to sound stern, but it felt like his heart was beating in his throat. He wasn't one for friends. Friends died. But Cain wanted more for William than an early death on the battlefield.

He fit his arms beneath Will and lifted him. When he turned for the room, he caught his prisoner tiptoeing away from the door and going in the opposite direction.

Hell, he couldn't chase her now.

"Miss d'Argentan," he called out and waited for her to stop and turn to him. "If ye run, I will give the order fer Sir Richard's death."

She stared at him for a moment, as if she were trying to decide if she believed him or not.

Finally, she moved her arse and stormed back inside the chamber. Cain followed her, carrying Will with him.

"Ye're responsible fer this," he hurled at her, his gaze darker than the deepest corners of the dungeon while he laid Will on the bed. "If he dies, ye die."

"What ails him?" she asked, trying to appear unaffected by his threat.

"Yer wine is what ails him. He drank some."

"How much?"

He shook his head. He didn't know and the lad was no longer conscious. "What do we do?"

"I need to boil mulberry leaves in vinegar." She moved for the door.

Cain leaped in her path and blocked her. "Ye think me a fool?"

"I want to live," she said, looking up at him. "So either accompany me to the kitchen or get out of my way."

She stared at him while he thought about what to do. He couldn't let her go alone. She'd run and continue being a threat. He didn't want to leave Will. Where the hell was Amish?

"What has happened?" Father Timothy appeared at the door, took one look at William, and ran to the bed.

"He drank the wine," Cain told him as the priest began praying over lad. "She claims to know how to prepare an antidote. I am takin' her to the kitchen." He pulled on his boots and headed for the door. "Ye remain here with him."

Father Timothy nodded and shooed them away.

"Will yer remedy work?" Cain asked her as they hurried to the kitchen.

"Aye, 'twill work."

He looked at her, but when she returned his glance, he looked away.

"He is young…innocent of bloodshed. He was a servant to a master who took pleasure in beatin' him."

She was quiet for a moment, then repeated, "'Twill work."

They reached the kitchen and he waited while she prepared the mixture, pacing while it boiled.

"You still have not told me where Sir Richard is," she said, turning to him.

He stopped pacing and stared at her. "I need not tell ye anythin'. 'Tis yer fault William is in this condition."

"'Tis your fault for coming to my home and thinking to take it."

"I *have* taken it."

Her full, beguiling lips curled slightly upward. A gleam of fire sparked across her eyes in the torchlight. "For now."

He almost smiled back at her bold, but foolish confidence. He let his gaze take her in from her dirty boots to her waist-length glossy black waves. Her legs were long in her woolen breeches. Her waist was narrow and her bosom, humble in her tunic and snug-fitting bodice. She dressed like a warrior, ready for a fight.

"Where are yer guards? Why did ye send them away?"

She returned her attention to the pot and stirred the mixture with a wooden spoon. "Sir Richard and five of his friends are my guards. They were loyal to my father and to Giles and they are loyal to me. I sent them all away, but Richard refused to leave. He is innocent of what happened this morn."

Cain leaned his hip on the chopping table and folded his arms across his chest. He watched her. He knew he shouldn't but he couldn't take his eyes off her. Her beauty was sublime and deadly. Like the allure of a siren, it was designed to weaken men and bring them to their deaths.

He knew it but he kept watching.

She'd killed his men and William was dying.

He kept William in the forefront of his thoughts. He liked the lad. At first, they'd thought him mute for he spoke to no one. But Cain had heard him crying out a name in his sleep—a name he called out every night after that. Julianna. He never spoke of her during the day, or about what had befallen them. Cain didn't let the men push and Father Timothy made certain they obeyed. Over time, he began speaking more and even laughed, but he was shy and obedient and he never spoke of Julianna.

Cain clenched his jaw and pulled his gaze from her.

"'Tis ready," she said and poured the mixture into a cup. "We must wake him enough to drink it."

Cain nodded and took her by the elbow to lead her out of the kitchen.

"You said I would die if he died," she reminded him while she kept her eyes on the hall ahead. "Will I live if he lives?"

"I havena yet decided."

Why hadn't he? What the hell was wrong with him? If it were

anyone else, they would have been turned over right away to his men. She deserved to die.

But damn it, he didn't want to add killing a lass to his many sins. And why did this particular lass have to be so hauntingly beautiful that killing her would be like rolling up the sky and the stars and tossing them into the fire?

Father Timothy mentioned her being returned to the English. Cain would write to Robert and ask what should be done with her.

Aye. That's what he would do. Let the Bruce decide. But until then—

"Father Timothy tells me you are called Cainnech."

"Cain," he corrected.

She furrowed her brow and cut him a quick side-glance. "Why would you prefer Cain?"

"It fits better."

"I see."

Aye, he thought, let her see the truth then. He was an unmerciful, unrepentant killer, just like his namesake.

"I told Father Timothy I was going to kill you," she said boldly, tempting him to smile. If he wasn't such a superior warrior, he might be worried by her confidence.

"And what was his response?" he asked as they neared the chamber.

"He said I would have to go through him first."

Finally, Cain smiled.

CHAPTER SIX

I F SHE LIVED through the next few days, Aleysia never wanted to see the Scottish commander smile ever again. It made her forget her name and all her carefully laid out plans. She didn't abandon them. Never that.

It was almost as dangerous as seeing him asleep in nothing but a plaid around his waist. The sight of him, illuminated in the candlelight, had made her feel like she had too much wine. He had slept on his back, one muscular arm tossed over his head. His broad chest was lightly dusted with dark hair. His belly was tight with muscles. There were at least a dozen scars covering him, including the one on his cheekbone, left by her arrow. It did nothing to lessen his handsome features. She had stared at him too long.

Oh, but when he disarmed her and pulled her down atop him in her bed, she had been less afraid of him and more afraid of his effect on her.

How could she find him more alluring than any man she'd ever met? Awareness of him ripped through her as she doubled her steps to keep up with his long strides. His height and the breadth of his shoulders cast her in shadows.

Why hadn't he killed her yet? She told herself she hadn't killed *him* yet because she needed him to tell her where he was keeping Richard so she could escape with him.

She looked down at the cup and thought of a way to bargain with the Scot.

They entered the room to a waiting Father Timothy and another brutish-looking man with bright red hair and beard and two long scars running down his face.

"D'ye have the mixture?" the priest asked, leaping to his feet when he saw them.

Aleysia held up the cup.

"Good, good," Father Timothy reached out to take it and shot a furtive glance to the commander. "I told Amish aboot Aleysia, Richard's granddaughter."

"Uhm," the commander mumbled and moved to the bedside. "How is he?"

"He comes back to us and then leaves again," Father Timothy told him and then turned to Aleysia. "Ye can give me the mixture." He moved to take it, but she pulled away. "Come now, Miss. We canna waste a moment."

She looked at the commander when he turned to see what was going on.

"Where is Si—my grandfather?" She held the cup at an angle, letting a drop spill. "Bring him to me or I will let this cup fall."

The commander stormed toward her in two giant steps. He seemed bigger suddenly, infinitely more deadly than she could imagine. His lips were tight, his nostrils flared.

She backed away but he kept coming.

"Ye make demands while this lad's life hangs by a thread?" He didn't wait for her to answer. He didn't try to grab the cup before she made good on her threat. He simply stared her down with a glare that made her kneecaps weak beneath her. "If ye dinna feed that antidote to William before yer next breath, ye willna see daylight!"

She was surprised the walls of the chamber didn't crumble around them at the force of his voice. That her blood didn't freeze from his frigid glare.

She believed him. He would kill her. She should have stabbed him when she had the chance. She'd panicked. She'd hesitated. And now, she had to save one of them.

She brushed past the commander without another word—and with all the strength she could muster to move at all—and went to the bedside.

She looked down at the victim of her poison. William. He was quite beautiful in his slumber, with lush black lashes resting against his pale skin.

"He needs to be roused so he can swallow the mixture," she said, keeping her gaze on William, rather than look at his commander again.

"Cainnech," the priest said, "hold him up and I'll try to rouse him."

The brutish commander pushed past her and moved to the head of the bed.

Climbing into the bed, he sat behind the lad and fit his arms gently beneath William's arms. He sat the young man up, leaning William's back against his chest.

Father Timothy came to sit at the edge and began trying to rouse him.

When William's lids fluttered open, Aleysia stepped forward and held the cup to his lips. "Drink this," she said.

He looked up at her with dark gray, glassy eyes and smiled. "Julianna."

Aleysia glanced at the commander behind him and noted the slight change in his expression. Compassion warmed his gaze, but just for a moment, before he tightened his jaw and pushed it away.

But he did care—at least about William. He wouldn't have threatened to kill her if he didn't. It piqued her curiosity about the lad. What was it about him that pricked the commander's heart? Who was Julianna?

He is young...innocent of bloodshed. A servant.

"Aye, William," she said softening her voice. "You must drink this now."

He pressed his lips to the cup and drank a little then started to drift off again.

Aleysia placed her fingers to his cheek. "Come now, William, drink this for me."

He drank more, slowly, but finally the mixture was gone.

"Now what?" the commander asked her over William's head.

"We should see an improvement before dawn."

Cain moved away from William and laid him back down so he could rest properly. He stood up and walked around the bed, passing her without a word, and went to stand with the red-haired Amish.

"I'm goin' to speak with Richard the steward. Stay ootside the room. She is not to step oot of it. If she tries to leave, kill her."

"Aye, Commander," Amish said.

Aleysia shot them both a murderous look.

The bastard commander closed the gap between them in two strides. "I will bring yer *grandfather* back to have a brief word with ye. But if ye try to escape before we return, ye will both die. D'ye understand me, lady?"

She thought about where two knives were hidden in this room and how she'd like to fetch them and ram them into his guts. "What if I do escape and come and kill you?"

He looked as if he wanted to smile. But he didn't. Instead, he let his gaze slip down her body, pausing at her feminine curves beneath her breeches and léine.

She felt her face begin to grow flushed, but he didn't see.

He started to leave, but then stopped and flicked his gaze between her and Father Timothy.

He pointed to the priest. "Come with me."

Father Timothy didn't argue. They both knew how dangerous she was.

He obviously cared about the priest. She doubted it was her soul he was trying to protect when he commanded Father Timothy to follow him.

She watched them depart, leaving Amish to guard the door. What could she do now but wait? Richard's life depended on her remaining where she was.

She looked down at William. A bit of color had returned to his face. A good sign—for the other side, at least.

She left his side and went to fetch her hidden knives. She took one and hid it carefully in her bodice.

This time, she wouldn't hesitate.

CHAPTER SEVEN

C AIN SAT ATOP one of the trestle tables, his boots on the chair in front of him in the great hall. He lifted his cup to his lips and waited for Amish to arrive with Miss d'Argentan.

"If you have harmed her—" the old knight began.

"She has not been harmed," Father Timothy assured him.

"Yet," Cain added, setting down his cup. "Yer Miss d'Argentan has boldly confessed to everythin' and has much to answer fer."

"How many did she...?"

"Nine, and one more who clings to life." Cain felt his anger rising. "Pray that he lives," he ground out through clenched teeth.

"Did she act alone in her crimes against the king?" Father Timothy asked him.

The knight lifted his chin and bristled in his chair. "He is not her king or mine."

Rebellion. It was what got people killed—proven by the deaths of thousands so far. This English knight knew it and he didn't seem to care. He was loyal until death to Edward and to Miss d'Argentan. He had even come up with an elaborate tale about the nonexistent Lord de Bar to protect her. A quality Cain couldn't help but admire.

"Nonetheless, she is our enemy, as are ye," Cain told him.

The knight looked away.

"How did she do it?" Cain asked him.

"She practiced every day for the last four years."

Dedication. Another trait Cain admired.

"What drives her?" he asked. He expected the answer to be hatred over the death of her brother. He understood hatred. It killed him when he was a child.

"Fear drives her. And loyalty."

Cain leaned forward and inclined his head to the knight. "Fear of what?" But he already knew the answer. "Us."

Sir Richard nodded. "From the moment she learned of her brother's death, she was fired up with this maddening need to prepare for the day when the Scots showed up at Lismoor. She swore to never surrender the castle or the land to her brother's enemy."

"Who helped her?" Cain asked.

"Everyone," Richard told him and reached for Father Timothy's cup instead of the one Cain had given him.

Cain watched with a smile lifting one corner of his lips. The knight didn't trust him. Good.

"I had helped make some of the weapons, as had my brothers. Everyone who lived here, as well as all the villagers helped in the building of the traps and the walkways. But that was all any of us did. She insisted from the beginning that the war was hers and hers alone. When news had come of the siege on Berwick, she sent everyone away to ensure none were harmed."

"How could she have hoped to defeat us on her own?" Father Timothy asked after a sip from Sir Richard's cup.

"She could have done it," Cain admitted in a quiet voice. "The traps were everywhere I looked. We likely wouldna have made it oot of the forest alive. She is brave."

"She is headstrong," her knight added, unwittingly sharing a slight smile with Cain.

Cain's eyes caught sight of her entering the hall with his second.

Hell, she was pleasing to Cain's eyes. This lissome lass in her breeches and boots had rained havoc down on his men. She was doing the same to his senses. How could he think her so alluring after all she had done? She'd tried to kill him! More than once! All he had to do was tell his men the truth and he would be done with her.

Her wide, worried eyes found her knight and she hurried forward.

"Sir Richard!" she cried reaching them. "What have they done to you?"

"Never mind me, my lady!" he said, taking her hands in his. "Have you been harmed in any way?"

"The beast still lives," she said, slipping her frosty, green gaze to Cain. "If he had touched me, his innards would be spilled in the rushes."

Cain found himself aching to smile at her.

Her eyes shone with a fire that had been fanned for four years. He remembered being filled with the same passion. He knew what it did to the soul when the fire was extinguished and the heart lay abandoned in an empty shell, dead and yet alive.

What did he care what happened to her heart? Or her body if his men discovered the truth? She was his enemy. He would allow her some time with her guard and then lock her up someplace she couldn't escape.

"Release him!" she demanded. "He has done nothing!"

Cain guzzled down the rest of his whisky, then looked at her. "Prove yer claim and I'll release him."

Her lips tightened as she drew in a deep breath readying for a fight. His bemused gaze dipped to her hands balling into fists. "How am I supposed to prove my claim?"

He shrugged his shoulders and looked into his empty cup. "That is yer dilemma, not mine."

"It will not be a dilemma once you are dead."

"Commander." Amish stepped forward. He'd heard the lass' threat. Cain didn't want him hearing anything more. What had changed? He had been ready to give her to his men just a short while ago. She'd lost her home. He understood the pain of that. He'd lost his, as well. He'd lost more than that.

"Take the steward away," he told his second.

"What? No!" The lass grabbed hold of the knight's arm when Amish began to lead him off, and turned to glare at Cain. "I have barely had time to say a word to him!"

Cain pushed aside the urge to give in, the temptation to drag her into his arms, to his bed. He had to keep in mind the heavy blow she alone had dealt his men. He wouldn't betray them by bedding the wench who took them from the earth. "Mayhap, ye should have spent less time flappin' yer tongue at me." He flicked a warning glance to his second. "What is he still doin' here?"

Amish yanked Richard by the arm and Father Timothy hurried to stop her from going after them.

"He willna be harmed, my lady," Cain heard the priest tell her.

She fastened her eyes on her friend as he was pulled away and then turned her gaze on Cain.

"Back away from me, Priest," she warned without taking her eyes off Cain.

He raised his brow and quirked his mouth when she produced a dagger from somewhere in her bodice.

"Ye think to fight me, lady?" he asked, pushing off the table.

"I think to kill you, Highlander," she replied, holding her dagger out before her.

Father Timothy moved forward. "Miss d'Argentan—"

Cain held up his hand to quiet him, then crooked the same hand at her, motioning her to come forward. "Let me see just how determined ye are."

He expected her to rush at him swinging. Instead, she flipped her dagger in her hand, caught it by the end of the blade, and flung it at him.

He had just an instant to move out of the way and another to regain his balance. Their eyes met, locked in a moment of surprise, stubborn determination, and trying to guess what the other would do next.

Her gaze slipped to the left. Cain strode forward, and then took off after her when she sprinted toward a candle stand along the eastern wall. She reached it before him, grasped for something attached to the stand, and produced yet another dagger.

"Stay back!" she warned, then swiped the blade at him when he kept coming.

"Ye canna win," he told her while he fought the urge to pity her, to admire the hell out of her for thinking to hide daggers everywhere.

Hell, he didn't know what to do with her. Nothing about her was harmless. She had knives planted everywhere, hidden keys, poison wine and grain, and traps all over the damned forest. She deserved the worst punishment. But he didn't want to see her suffer.

"Even if ye somehow kill me," he said in a softer voice than he'd planned to use, "ye still have to get past the rest of my men. Give me the knife, lady."

He reached out for it and she swiped again. He caught her wrist easily and pulled her hard against him. He looked into her eyes, momentarily mesmerized by her extraordinary power of will, glowing like a flame from within. "That will be enough of tryin' to kill me."

Pressed to him, her breath felt warm against his chin, her body, soft and unyielding. "I have not even begun to fight you."

Part of him looked forward to it.

"Ye tempt me to toss ye to the wolves." He plucked the dagger from her fingers and wondered how many more there were hidden about.

"'Twould be better than spending another moment with you," she insisted, struggling to break free. "Now, let me go!"

He held fast, doing his best to ignore the desire to dip his face into her inky hair and take in her scent. She wasn't his. He didn't want her to be. There was no place in his life for affection, especially not for a dangerous enemy. But he couldn't help his fascination with her. She was intelligent, independent, and passionate. Even if her passion was to hate him. She'd feared losing her home to the Scots, and she had. He couldn't do anything about it without defying his king.

With a measure of reluctance, he released her. He watched her back away and, for a fleeting, mad moment, he wanted to pull her back. He ground his jaw. This had to stop. He should not spend any more time with her. Yet, if she continued to be a threat to him, he would have to keep her close.

"If I say I believe ye aboot yer knight, will ye quit tryin' to kill me?"

She quirked a skeptical brow at him. "Will you set Sir Richard free?"

He drew an inward sigh. What the hell was wrong with him? Why was he about to promise the knight's safety? He turned to Father Timothy with a look of uncertainty he hadn't felt in years. The priest offered him a gentle smile in return.

"I suspect he willna go far withoot ye," Cain finally answered her, "so he will be confined to the keep."

She looked as if she might argue, but then thought better of it.

Cain breathed.

"We have a bargain then, lady."

Her hesitation when he tried to escort her out of the hall made him close his eyes and clench his jaw.

"What about my castle and land?" Her smoky voice rolled across his ears like a sorceress' whisper.

She was either the most courageous lass he'd ever met, or the most foolish.

"They now belong to King Robert." He opened his eyes but looked away. "I have already written to him and had the missive sent today. There is nothin' I can do now."

"Then we do not have a bargain," she said, furthering his misery.

"Verra well then. Come." He took her by the elbow and pulled her back to her chamber, where William lay sleeping or dead in her bed.

Cain hurried to the bed, dragging Miss d'Argentan behind him. Father Timothy reached the bed at the same time, and leaned down to listen to William's chest.

The priest looked up and breathed out. "He lives and his color has returned."

Cain's shoulders relaxed from around his ears. He let his prisoner go and bolted the door.

"Why do you both care so strongly for him?" she asked.

Cain tugged at his léine. "I told ye. He is innocent. He is—"

"What are you doing?"

Cain turned to her after he pulled the léine over his head. "I am goin' to get some sleep. I suggest ye do the same."

"Here?" she asked incredulously.

"Would ye prefer I put ye back in the dungeon, alone with at least five guards? Ye have proven yerself a clever opponent, but I think five men are enough to keep ye where I put ye."

She bit her lip. His gaze dipped there. "Father Timothy will move the partition and sleep in that chair. Aye, Father?" he asked the priest as Father Timothy added more wood to the hearth.

"Aye, Son."

"Ye have nothin' to fear from me," Cain told her.

She cut her glance to the priest, and then returned it to the long, smooth muscles of the commander's bare arms. "I do not trust either of you. Where will you sleep?"

Cain pointed to the floor in front of the door.

Her gaze on him darkened. "You mean to use your body to keep me here?"

He nodded, staring into her eyes. Images of lying naked in bed with her flashed across his thoughts. He pushed them away. She was his enemy. She had killed his men—had almost killed William.

He let his gaze slip from hers and settled it on the lad in her bed.

"Where am I to sleep?" she asked without waiting for his reply to her first question.

He yanked off his boot. "Anywhere ye want. In bed beside William. In Father Timothy's lap. I dinna care." He pulled off the other boot and turned away from her. "I am goin' to sleep."

He expected her to fight back, threaten to kill him in his sleep. He would have told her she wouldn't be the first to try it.

But she remained silent as he sat on the floor and propped himself against the door. He almost smiled with relief and closed his eyes.

They opened a moment later when she sat on the floor beside him. Hell.

Chapter Eight

"WHAT ARE YE doin', lady?"

"I am going to sleep."

"Here?"

"Would you prefer I stay awake and tell you what I think of you?"

Aleysia was glad when Father Timothy blew out all the candles. She thought that in the dim light of the hearth fire, she could ignore the raw sensuality the commander exuded and get some sleep.

But she was wrong.

He appeared almost magical in the soft, golden light. Like some god of war, fallen from the heavens and landing on the floor in her chambers. She could easily retrieve her other dagger but she realized she didn't want to kill him.

He was keeping her safe from his men. He was willing to let Sir Richard go free.

Why?

"I would prefer ye to sleep somewhere else."

His deep, gruff voice sent little fissures of warmth through her blood. Though she did her best not to think on it, the memory of being held in his strong embrace when she had tried to kill him in the great hall made her a bit breathless. Why had he shown her mercy yet again?

He had disarmed her five times already in the space it took her to blink. He was quick and strong, and infuriating.

And quite honestly, she found it difficult to take her eyes off him. His dark hair was pulled away from his face and fell over his broad shoulders. His eyes were closed so she let her gaze rove over the dips and crests along his arms and chest, all dusted with dark hair. His belly looked to be made of beaten iron. A battle-hardened man. She was tempted to run her fingers over his scars and ponder how many times he had come close to death.

She disgusted herself for finding him so distracting.

"Why are you protecting me from your men?"

She almost bit her tongue. She hadn't realized she was speaking her thoughts out loud until he opened his eyes again.

"Yer brother was England's hero." His frosty gaze settled on her. "King Robert is involved in talks of final peace with the Archbishop of York. I dinna wish to jeopardize everythin' he's done by killin' the sister of Edward's favored knight."

"I see," she said quietly, relieved that at least he wasn't planning on killing her in the future. "But taking my home will not jeopardize it?"

He sighed audibly and folded his arms over his chest. "Go to sleep."

"How can I sleep when my home has been taken from me?" she put to him. She wasn't surprised when he didn't answer. "What would you know about it? You do not understand and, so, there is no further point in speaking to you."

She didn't wait to hear what he had to say but rose from the floor and went to sit at the edge of her bed.

He left her no other choice but to devise a new plan of action to kill him—him and all his men.

She didn't look at him again. It was too dangerous. She set her drowsy gaze on William instead. Would the commander truly have killed her if William died? She hadn't wanted to risk it. Besides, if the young man was truly innocent, she didn't want him to die.

Who was Julianna? His beloved, judging by the way he looked at Aleysia when he called her by the girl's name.

She studied him in the soft light. He was quite handsome and free of scars. His hair was dark and curling, now that it was dry, over his brow. His square jaw and dimpled chin were cut almost to perfection beneath a plump, pouty mouth.

She yawned and, when she finished, she saw that he was awake and looking at her. Looking through her. His eyes were the color of lightning across a summer sky; they pierced her like arrows and made her want to look away, lest he see her most hidden thoughts and desires.

But there was something in his gaze, as well, that made her smile at him.

"Who are you?" he asked and pulled himself up. Seeing Father Timothy and his commander asleep on the floor seemed to comfort him. He relaxed and looked at her again.

"I am Aleysia. Richard's granddaughter," she told him softly, careful not to say too much. "You drank poison wine and I knew the cure for it. We helped you drink it."

He nodded, and then grasped his head with his hand. "I remember. I think. You saved my life."

She maintained her smile, though he did not return it.

"You are English," he said, keeping his voice low and neutral.

"French," she corrected. "And you are...?" She wasn't certain. The commander had said William was a servant. But to whom?

He squared his shoulders and tilted his chin. "I am a Scot."

A proud one, no doubt.

She shrugged her shoulders as if it didn't matter to her one way or the other. "You sound English."

"I was…was raised in the home of an English family," he said, giving in to her prodding.

His tone lost its neutrality and quavered on a wave of emotion.

He wasn't raised *by* them, but in their home. Aleysia saw the image of a child in her mind. A dirty, uncared for servant who was beaten by his master. Her heart softened on him.

"You called me Julianna," she gently reminded him.

He stared at her, but it wasn't her layers he was peeling away. It was his own, falling away at the mention of her name.

"Who is she?" Aleysia whispered while his breath stalled. "Your beloved?"

"Aye." A quiet declaration.

Aleysia's eyes filled with tears. "Where is she now?"

"With her father, the Governor of Berwick, if she still lives."

Martin Feathers, Governor of Berwick. Aleysia knew little about him. Giles had had some dealings with him years ago and mentioned him having servants.

She closed her eyes and tried to slow her racing, breaking heart. How terribly tragic! William loved his master's daughter! She opened her eyes to see a tear falling from his. "Forgive me," she said and wiped her nose. "We do not have to speak of this anymore." She did her best to smile again and reached out to pat his hand. "You certainly have earned the affections of these two." She motioned with her chin to the commander and the priest, snoring in his chair.

"Have they found Lord de Bar?" he asked, looking hopeful for the first time.

"Lord de Bar?"

"Aye, your grandfather confessed his name to the commander."

Dear Richard, Aleysia thought, he had tried to save her.

"No," she lied and looked away. She wasn't sure why, but she didn't want William to know it was she who had almost killed him, killed men who were likely his friends. "But you must promise not to eat anything made with the grain."

"I promise."

She yawned again and closed her eyes. "And stay out of the forest."

She didn't remember saying or hearing anything after that.

She was awakened several hours later by a gentle shove. She opened her eyes to find herself sprawled out across her empty bed and the commander standing over her. They were alone.

He held up a small loaf of bread.

"We found grain in one of the villager's homes. Is it safe to eat, lady?" He brought it to his mouth and stared down at her with a hint of warmth softening his hard features. And then it was gone again.

Aleysia rose from the bed and said nothing to stop him while he took a bite. She hadn't thought about poisoning the villagers' grain! She'd remedy that the first chance she got. "You risk your life on the hope that I will save it? You are a fool."

"Not entirely," he corrected and held the bread out to her. "Richard ate the first loaf."

She pushed him out of her way and then whirled on him. "How did you know I had not poisoned *all* the grain?"

"I didna know. I know now. Richard will be tastin' all our food first until the Bruce answers my missive aboot what to do with ye both."

Oh, she wished she had stabbed him. Every moment she spent with him made the thought of it easier. She would not hesitate again when she had the chance.

Her belly rumbled. She hadn't eaten since before the attack. She swiped the bread from his hand and bit into it.

"Where did ye send the villagers?" he asked while she chewed.

"Away."

He looked mildly annoyed by her defiance, but his voice remained steady. "This grain willna last. We need the farmers back."

"They are not coming back until you are dead. I promised them safety from you."

"I willna harm them."

She laughed. "Why should a rabbit trust a snake?"

His gaze on her sharpened, making her skin feel warm. "Ye are no rabbit, lady."

"No, Commander, I am not," she told him, doing her best to ignore the effect his full attention was having on her. "And I will not send for my people until Lismoor is rid of you."

"Verra well, then," he said with a shrug that stretched his léine across his chest. "I shall offer their homes to others."

Her eyes opened wide with surprise and anger at his audacity. "You most certainly will not offer their homes to others! You took my home from me! Do you think I will let you take theirs, too?"

Oh, she shook with fury. She'd failed. She'd failed her friends. Now they were going to lose their homes because of her. She felt tears filling her eyes and hated him all the more for it.

"I will..." She clenched her teeth and closed her eyes to gather control of herself. "I will send for them, but I want you to swear upon the Holy Book that none of them will be harmed."

She thought she saw him smile. It faded before she could define it, but it seemed laced with regret.

"Verra well."

He gave in easier than she thought he would. She wasn't prepared for it and didn't know what to say.

"Let us go find Father Timothy now," he continued, and turned for the door.

She'd failed. She was bringing them back to a castle filled with wild Scots. She wanted to weep, watching him leave the room.

She bent quickly to the feather mattress and lifted the corner. She retrieved the knife she had hidden there and slipped it into her boot.

CHAPTER NINE

CAIN TURNED TO make certain his captive was behind him and not preparing to stab him in the back. When he didn't see her, he clenched his jaw and hurried back to the room.

He barged into her chamber and found her combing her long, loose hair over her shoulder. She turned to him, her large, anxious eyes belying the brief smile she offered him.

"I will just be a moment."

He knew she was up to something but, at the moment, he didn't care. All he could do was stare at her while she ran her alabaster comb through her long, raven locks and think about how beautiful she was. Would the other men think so when they saw her?

He'd written to the Bruce about her but it would take time to hear back. What was he to do with her until then?

He was sorry he'd listened to Father Timothy and come here. It wasn't the first time he'd had regrets. After his men died, he'd wanted to throttle his friend for volunteering them for the siege. But last eve, when the lass told him he didn't understand what it was like to lose his home, he wanted to tell her about his parents, his brothers, his life.

It made him want to run, to leave Lismoor and never look back. If he hadn't written to Robert already, he would have fled.

What had come over him to make him want to share pieces of his life with her? Why did he feel like hell…a monster for doing his duty?

She plaited her hair into one long braid hanging over her shoulder and tied it with a piece of twine.

She held the bottom edge of her bodice and wiggled in it, straightening it on her body. "There," she said, turning to him.

"I have to use the garderobe."

He nodded, beguiled by the way she moved, the way she looked. Who was she trying to impress?

He held out his arm to clear a path for her and breathed her in when she passed him and left the room.

He followed her out, and waited outside the door while she stopped in the garderobe.

He'd stayed awake listening to her speaking to William last eve. She'd been direct yet gentle and managed to get the lad to open up a little about his past and the mysterious Julianna. He'd been the servant of the Governor of Berwick, and was in love with his daughter—who was likely dead.

Losing a loved one was difficult. That was why Cain made certain to stay clear of loving anything.

"How is William this morn?" she asked him, leaving the garderobe.

"He is well."

Her smile lit the hall. "That is good news."

"Aye," he agreed. She liked the lad. It made Cain happy for some ridiculous reason. "Yer potion saved him."

"As I told you 'twould," she replied with her nose to the air and moved past him.

He followed her. "He is in better spirits than I have seen since we found him."

She paused in her steps and looked up at him. "Found him?"

"Aye, we were leavin' Berwick and found him on the road tryin' to get back to the castle."

"For Julianna," she said softly.

"The governor's daughter."

"Aye, is that not the most tragic thing you have ever heard?" She wiped something from her eye and continued walking.

Cain could think of a few things that were more tragic than that. But he didn't say so. Let her pity the lad. It might keep her from killing the rest of them. "Aye, 'tis tragic, indeed. I can find oot what became of him and his family after the attack." Why was he volunteering for this? Why couldn't he stop? "Mayhap we can find her."

She stopped again and turned to him, surprise and delight lit her eyes. "Aye, mayhap we can."

Should he smile back? He was tempted to. Was he giving her too much?

He was about to take her to the great hall, where she would meet his men. He had lied for her. He'd told them Sir Richard's elaborate story of Lord de Bar to keep her safe. He'd done it for the king and for the peace Robert sought. He would continue to keep her safe no matter how many times she tried to kill him. When word regarding her came, he would see her off and get on with his life. He couldn't wait.

She went back to walking without him. "Where is Father Timothy?"

"In the great hall," he told her, turning left after she did. He caught up to her in two strides. "Stay close to me or someone may try to grope ye."

She tossed him a cool smirk. "You must be so proud."

He climbed the three stairs that led to the great hall's inner entrance, and then went inside.

She stayed close and followed him when he leaped upon a table.

He didn't have to shout or even speak at all. In fact, he looked at her and counted their breaths before they had everyone's attention. It took five breaths for his men to take notice of her.

"Who is this, Commander?" someone called out.

"Are ye sharin'?" called another.

"Nae!" he shouted back. "I am not sharin'." He waited a moment until they realized he was serious and they settled down. "That means if any one of ye touches her, *touches her*, he will meet me in a fight to the death. Is that understood?"

He could feel her eyes on him, surprised by his threat and warmed by it. He kept his hard gaze on his men while they nodded and murmured their agreement.

When they were quiet again, he continued. "This is Aleysia, granddaughter of Richard the Steward."

Every eye turned to Richard standing next to Amish and smiling at Aleysia.

If they knew...they should know the truth. They deserved to know. "She saved William's life last eve when he became poisoned by the wine. She is to be treated with dignity. I have given her the solar to use while we are here."

When they heard about William, their smiles softened on her. Still, these bastards were hungry for a woman, and this woman would likely kill every last one of them.

So he didn't let her out of his sight after he bounded from the table. He reached for her and she stepped into his arms. He looked into her eyes, painted golden green in the sunlight splashing through the windows.

For a moment, unlike any before it that he could remember, he forgot everything else. All the death. All the hatred, more rancid than what it produced, was burned up like dried leaves in the fire of her eyes.

He wanted to pull her in while he lowered her feet to the ground. He wanted to kiss her and discover how she tasted.

She stepped away when he let her go. He closed his eyes. What the hell was he thinking? If there was nothing else, she fought on the side of the English! Hell, he'd betrayed his men for her.

He drew in a deep breath. Why was his heart beating so hard he wasn't sure he could take a step without collapsing? He felt ill. The bread—? No, Richard appeared sound and well, as did everyone else.

Could they hear his heart battering against his ribs? Did they notice him breathing as if he'd just sprinted here from the village?

He wiped his brow and took a step. This wasn't love suddenly hitting him hard.

This was the fear of it. Fear of losing control over his decisions based on what his heart wanted. He'd learned every day when he was a boy to control his desires to kill the English soldiers who killed his family. Fear of stirring the ashes and finding an ember of something so painful he had to forget his family to survive it. Of letting his heart wander deeper into the abyss, where he would lose it completely.

"Aleysia, greetings!" William's voice jarred him back to the present. He forced himself to turn and was grateful to spot Father Timothy coming toward them. If his God was listening, Cain needed strength to see this through and get her out of his life as quickly as possible.

"William! You have recovered nicely," she sang, reaching out to touch his arm.

"Aye, thanks to you. I am in your debt."

"No, Will," Cain heard himself saying. He didn't want the lad beholden to the woman who tried to kill him in the first place. "There is no debt. Now, excuse us, we need a word with Father Timothy."

She stiffened when he grasped her elbow and pulled her toward the priest.

"Why were you curt with him?" she seethed on the way.

Had he been curt? He was tempted to turn around and look back at the lad.

And then he came to his senses. Since when did he care about whether or not he hurt the feelings of one of his men? He cursed under his breath and pointed to the way out when he reached the priest.

They stepped off the stairs and into the corridor.

"Brute," she ground out and yanked her arm away. "What is the matter with you?"

That was what he wanted to know. He doubted she had the answer, and he wouldn't ask Father Timothy in front of her.

"We need yer Holy Book," he told the priest, ignoring her question. "I need to swear on it."

As he'd suspected, Father Timothy didn't appear pleased, but he finally nodded and waved his hand. "Come."

He led them to the keep's small chapel and waited while Cain took the Book in his hands.

"Now what?" he asked, turning to her after he swore. "How will ye bring them back?"

She closed her eyes while she inhaled a deep breath. He knew she didn't want to do this, but she was going to have to trust him. They needed people to farm the land. They needed whatever livestock they had brought back.

"I expect you will not be letting me out of your sight," she said with a spark in her eyes and a snap in her tongue. "So prepare to climb a tree or two."

The priest smiled. Cain did not.

"And I'll need arrows."

The two men exchanged a skeptical glance.

She slapped her palms on her thighs. "How else do you expect me to contact them?"

"How many d'ye need?" Cain asked her, feeling as if he were giving in yet again. What kind of madman gave his enemy weapons?

"Three. And I also need three strips of blue linen or wool."

"Why?"

"'Tis a code," she explained. "Blue for safe. Red for unsafe. Anyone could be coerced into penning that 'twas safe to return when 'twas not. Besides, many of the villagers cannot read."

Cain nodded, but he was busy marveling at how thoroughly she had planned everything out. "What if red is fer safe, and blue fer unsafe? How would I know if ye wished to deceive me?"

Her eyes shone in the candlelit chapel. "I do not wish to deceive you, Commander. I wish to kill you. Do not forget that. As for the villagers, you can throw me to your dogs if they do not begin returning in a few days."

She dared threaten him again, and with amusement in her eyes! She had courage and confidence to do so—or she was completely mad. Keeping her close was more necessary than ever. Truly, she hated him.

Why then, was he tempted to pull her back and kiss her saucy mouth when she brushed past him? Damn him. "How d'ye know I willna throw ye to the dogs anyway?"

She paused and turned to look over her shoulder. She smiled as if she knew something he did not.

She was deadly. That was all he needed to know.

CHAPTER TEN

T HE FOREST WAS alive with the calls of ospreys in the distant trees
and red squirrels leaping from alder to birch and elm. Below, roe
deer and smaller critters scurried away from the two people walking
the narrow planks and branches above them.

Aleysia trudged onward with a lowered head. She didn't need to
see where she was going. She'd practiced this run thousands of times
over the years. She knew it well. She hated herself now though. She
wanted to bring the villagers back to their homes, but not with the
Scots here. She'd wanted the commander to swear on the Holy Book,
and he had. But she still didn't believe that her friends would be safe.
And what about Mattie and Elizabeth? They resided in the castle! They
would return with the rest. She didn't have a colorful ribbon to
indicate that only some should return.

Oh, she lamented on the way, what was she to do? She couldn't
get rid of the commander long enough to plot anything. He walked
close behind her, keeping up when she leaped from one branch to
another, being a constant distraction. She'd thought about sending red
ribbon, but they'd been away for two months. They had little. They
needed to come home.

"Ye truly prepared to take on an army alone," he said now, his voice a rich blend of deference and astonishment. "I have never seen such dedication in any man I know."

She stepped out onto a thick branch and turned, wrapping her arm around the trunk to face him. She liked his words and the liquid, lilting way he said them. She liked more than that about him. She wished she didn't. Lismoor was hers. She wasn't giving it up. She couldn't.

"What other choice was I given?" she asked him when he stopped walking. "I learned about what your armies did to the villagers in Berwick. My people are not fighters and I would not have them perish under a Scot's blade."

He stood on a plank a few inches away, tall against a backdrop of leaves and blinding rays of sunshine. He carried on his broad shoulder a quiver of arrows, a bow, and a sword. He moved to block the sun. His gaze on her was potent, taking in every angle, every shape all at once.

She took in her fill as well, noting his fit, ready body with appreciative eyes. He was her equal. A man she would consider giving herself up to. Pity he stood in the way of her home and her freedom.

"My men had no part in what took place in Berwick," he said with disgust while he took a step closer.

She moved away, sure-footed and quick. She paused, squatting in the cradle of two branches and watched him hop closer.

"Nonetheless, your arrival has robbed me of every choice I have ever made and will make in the future."

He looked like he might offer her some more pretty words, but he closed his mouth and reached out his hand just before she jumped.

She landed on a lower branch and clung to the trunk for a moment, thanking God for making branches like steps, and that she hadn't missed the first one. She had to do it again. She didn't want to. Her heart pounded like a drum in her ears.

She heard the commander somewhere above and she let go of the trunk. She jumped again, closer to the ground.

The bastard fell and hit her on the way down. Or perhaps, she reasoned when he landed on his back with her on top, unscathed, he meant to fall.

She looked down at his face, scrunched up in pain, and didn't waste a moment to examine him up close, but leaped up and ran.

She stopped after a moment when she realized he wasn't behind her. Had the fall hurt him more than she realized? Why did she care? She didn't, but if he was injured, it might be the perfect opportunity to kill him.

She turned and looked back and saw him lying on the ground where she'd left him. She returned slowly, taking cautious steps while her heart thrashed against her ribs. Was he already dead? Dying? Could she stab him until he stopped breathing? She took her dagger from her boot and moved closer. Tears filled her eyes and her hands shook. She had no idea it would be like this. Shooting a man with an arrow was bad enough. This was different.

She came upon him. "Commander?"

Perhaps God saw fit to kill him in a fall and save her the trouble.

He didn't answer or open his eyes.

She crouched beside him and poked him in the side. "Cainnech?"

She saw him open his eyes. She had a split second to leap away. But relief startled her and he caught her before she could flee.

In the space of her next breath, he disarmed her, pulled her down, and rose up atop her. He held her wrists over her head and gazed into her eyes, at every inch of her face and smiled, just a little.

"Ye came back."

"To kill you," she let him know, staring back. She prayed he couldn't feel her heart pounding against his.

"Ye dinna want to kill me, lass," he said on a low, seductive growl that made her blood boil.

It was true! She hadn't wanted him to be dead. She didn't want to kill him. How could her own heart betray her this way? How could she want to kiss his succulent mouth? If she did, would it stop her from telling him that he was correct? She was a traitor.

His breath stole across her cheek. She closed her eyes, clenching her teeth to keep from sighing with delight. His lips scored her chin, her jaw. She became more aware of his weight and dominance, making her forget her promises and her plans.

And then, just as quickly, he bounded away.

"I dinna know what ye are doin' to me," he had the audacity to say, "but I demand that ye stop it now!"

"Are you accusing me of enticing you?" She threw back her head and laughed, not waiting for his answer. She stood up and wiped herself off. "You were the one on top of me, Commander." She looked around for her knife or something to throw at him.

"Then I think it best if we keep a good distance from each other."

"I agree. Farewell." She pivoted in her boots and began to walk away.

"Miss d'Argentan."

She stopped at the power in his voice.

"I canna let ye go."

"You mean you will not," she called out without turning. "You are the commander. You can do what you wish."

"And ye know the moment I free ye, ye'll be comin' after me."

She turned and quirked her mouth at him. "Not if you leave Lismoor."

He didn't smile, but his gaze on her softened enough to make her heart pound. "Ye can stay here, lass," he said, moving closer. "No one is throwin' ye oot. The villagers will be safe, safer than before, because their land belongs to King Robert now."

"No!" No, it wasn't too late! She hadn't lost everything! She rushed toward him as he reached her and pummeled him with her fists. Surprisingly, she caught him in the jaw before he closed his arms around her. "I will not lose my home!"

He held her while she fought against him. She didn't want to be pressed so closely to him and not hate him as she properly should. She managed to rotate around so that her back was pressed to him. His arms, just tight enough to hold her, hadn't budged. "I canna leave," he breathed into her hair. "The king ordered this and sent me. He knows I am here. He knows aboot ye. If ye manage to kill me, he will send someone else. A bigger army. Ye will die, lass. Everyone will die."

"No!" she cried, "King Edward will not allow this!"

"He has done nothin' aboot Berwick. Think ye 'twill be different with Rothbury?"

Dear God, was this truly it? Was her fight over so quickly? Was she just supposed to give up now?

"I will harm no one," he whispered against her ear. "Ye have my word."

She closed her eyes and bit her lip to keep from weeping. What if she killed him and his men and the Bruce sent more? What kind of war had she started? How long would it last?

The commander vowed not to harm anyone and, so far, Sir Richard seemed well taken care of. In fact, she'd seen him laughing with the Scots. And…she hadn't been treated poorly, even after she tried to kill her captor several times.

The commander. The man who brought this all upon her, who looked at her with eyes of steel one moment and oceans of regret the next. His confidence was sure. The shelter of his presence was, she would admit, oddly comforting.

He might be her best option, but she couldn't give up.

She stopped struggling and rested her head on his upper arm. "'Tis my home being taken," she told him in a quiet voice. "My life that is going to change. I will never give up, and I will never forgive you."

She moved out of his embrace when he loosened his hold on her. She didn't look at him. There was nothing more to say.

He followed her back up the tree. They remained quiet while they traveled through the boughs and across planks until they reached the crest of a wooded hill.

From their vantage point, they could see in every direction.

She took the bow he offered her and an arrow with a blue ribbon secured to the tip. She nocked it and aimed.

She would never forgive herself for bringing them back now. But even if she was able to kill these Scots, more would come.

Defeated, she let her arrows fly, one toward the east, one toward the west, and one toward the south. When she was done, she turned to him and wiped a tear from her eye.

They returned to the keep in silence. She wasn't surprised to find it being searched for daggers. They hadn't found them all, but the commander seemed a bit more at ease with her. He even left her alone with Richard in the great hall while he spoke with red-haired Amish and some of the others at a table on the far end.

"You did what is best, my lady," her old friend told her.

"Did I?" she asked softly and looked at him with teary eyes. "If Matilda and Elizabeth do not die of fright, they will never forgive me when they see what I brought them back to."

"You cannot win this, my dear," her knight told her—probably for the thousandth time over the last few years. When it came to fighting for Lismoor and Rothbury, Richard had never been the one to go to when she needed encouragement. He'd wanted to take her to Normandy as soon as he learned of Giles' death.

Normandy might be safer for her than the English border, but she was a d'Argentan and, like her brother, she would never flee from a fight.

She looked around at the few soldiers who were lingering at the tables with their whisky. "I could have won if it 'twas just them. But he is correct. The Bruce will send more. It seems all is lost."

There had to be something. Something she could still do.

The priest joined them with a friendly smile and a tankard in each of his hands. He offered one to Richard. Aleysia took the other, assuming it was for her. She took a deep drink. She shivered in her spot and squeezed her eyes shut while the fire burned. Pure Highland whisky. She thought her eyes might have just changed color.

She coughed into her hand and looked into it for blood. There was none. She set the empty cup on the table beside them, and then held on when the room moved.

"Fergive me, my lady," the priest said steadying her. "The whisky wasna meant fer ye."

Aleysia took a moment to wait until her vision cleared. "Father, do you hear the commander's confessions?"

"No," he replied, surprising her. "He doesna go to confession."

She raised her brow. "You are friends with a heathen?"

The priest nodded and softened his smile. "Who else will point oot to him the goodness of God when he canna see anythin' but his past?"

His past? Her interest piqued, Aleysia darted her glance to where the commander sat with his men. He was hard and well disciplined. He demanded obedience from his soldiers and, as far as she could tell, he had it. How many men had he killed in battle? What else had he done? What was so terrible about his past that he couldn't see beyond it?

"I'm sure he will tell ye aboot it if he sees fit."

In other words, the priest would tell her nothing else. Not that she had asked.

She shrugged her shoulders. It made the hall spin in circles. "Everyone has a past—" she paused thinking of Normandy, "—or a future they wish they could change. He is no different."

"What aboot ye?" the priest asked her.

"Future. What...ehm...what will happen to the people who live in the castle, my staff, my friends, Sir Richard and the other knights?"

"They can stay on if they wish," Father Timothy told her.

"Cainnech doesna want to remain here. He only needs to stay until the king chooses who will permanently hold Rothbury and Lismoor in his name."

He'd taken her home and he didn't even want to live in it. She felt a rush of heat wash over her and knew her blood was boiling. He told her she could stay—but with who? She would have to wed whoever it was. Robert the Bruce would be a fool not to require it.

She looked across the cavernous hall and let her scorching glare burn into him.

The bastard thought to marry her off! He thought she should be grateful! She hadn't realized it when he'd first mentioned her staying even though her land had been seized by the Scots. Her choices were to leave and be married in Normandy, or stay and marry someone worse.

She cursed herself for not killing the commander when she had the chance—many chances. The more she thought about it, the angrier she became. She muttered an oath and rolled up her sleeves.

He met her gaze and rose from his seat. His unblinking stare almost shook her to her core, but whisky fired her temper and kept her from running when he charged toward her.

He reached her in less time than it took his men to realize what was going on. They remained looking confused, as did Sir Richard and Father Timothy, when the commander took her by the arm and pulled her away.

"Come with me," he growled and dragged her out of the great hall while she pounded on his arm.

"Let me go! I will not marry him!"

He stopped on the three small steps and spun her around to look at him. "Who? What are ye sayin' and what d'ye mean by comin' at me in front of the men?"

"I did not come at you!" she argued, feeling quite dizzy. She pulled on her arm to no avail.

"Ye were aboot to," he corrected. "I willna have ye—"

He stopped and easily avoided a fist to his jaw. She swung so hard she nearly fell over.

His arm was there to catch her. He said something that sounded indulgent but she couldn't be certain because everything went black.

CHAPTER ELEVEN

C AIN CAUGHT HER in his arms before she crumpled to the floor.
"Miss?" He knelt on one knee and supported her limp body in his
arms with the other. What the hell was the matter with her? Why did
she appear so small and fragile in his big hands? What should he do?

"Father!" he called out into the great hall.

He fixed his gaze on her again. "Lass, wake up." He gave her a
slight shake.

Where the hell was the priest?

When she didn't respond, he gave her cheek a soft slap, and then
felt rather sick for doing it. He might be one of the most feared
warriors in the kingdom, but he didn't strike women.

"What happened, Cainnech?"

Thank God. Cain looked up into Father Timothy's concerned
eyes.

"She fell faint. I attempted to awaken her to no avail."

He waited while his friend bent to have a careful look at her. His
gaze slipped to Sir Richard standing in the doorway watching, a bit
pale, remnants of anger fading from his eyes. He'd seen Cain slap her.

"She is fine," the priest concluded. "She is in a drunken stupor.

Carry her to—"

"A drunken what?" Cain's voice bounced off the walls as he rose up on his feet with the lass in his arms. "Who is responsible fer this?"

"I am afraid I am," Father Timothy confessed meekly.

"Ye?" Cain shouted even louder—so loud that the priest looked down to see if Miss d'Argentan was still unconscious.

She was.

"And ye." Cain turned his angry glare on the knight next. "Where were ye whilst he was gettin' her drunk?"

Richard balked. "He was not—"

"Cainnech, I wasna tryin'—"

Cain was already halfway down the hall by the time they both finished what they wanted to say.

When he reached her bedchamber, he pushed open the door and carried her inside.

He set her on her bed and tried not to look at her overlong. It was dangerous. Distracting. For she was as beautiful in her slumber as when she was shooting him with arrows.

She and her friends had done much and had sacrificed four years of their lives to keeping the Scots away. Now, she had to call them back to a conquered castle.

Hell, why did he give a damn how hard it must have been for her?

She'd told him that his arrival robbed her of her choices and, in that sense, he was a threat to her independence.

To his surprise and dismay, he understood it all.

She stirred up compassion and guilt in him. He didn't want them. All he knew of them was that they caused his belly to ache and his decisions concerning her and her knight to be lenient.

But, he thought while he returned to the door and kicked it shut, he wouldn't let her pierce anymore of his armor.

He hadn't forgotten that she killed nine of his men. God only knew how long she would have gone on trying to kill him. His men had found over one hundred daggers, kitchen knives, and crudely made blades hidden throughout the keep. Hell, he couldn't help but smile, returning to her bedside.

He had never met anyone like her.

Mayhap she was mad. Mayhap he was, too.

Someone banged on the door. Cain left her side to open it.

"Commander," Sir Richard came barging inside with Father Timothy close behind. "'Tis not to the benefit of Miss d'Argentan to be alone in a bedchamber with you. Her future would be damned."

Cain knew he was correct. He hadn't thought much of her future. Why would he? Now that he did, who was she so upset about marrying? "Verra well, but I canna trust either of ye to keep her safe, even from herself." He knew his words struck them hard. He didn't care. They deserved to suffer as she would suffer when she woke from her *drunken stupor.* "Bring William to me."

When neither of them moved, he turned his most lethal glare on them. "Go, or I will have ye both put away in the dungeon."

He watched them both hurry out. Sir Richard left the door open. Cain didn't close it after him. He thought about asking them what they were discussing that made her so angry, but he decided to wait and ask her instead.

He dragged a softly cushioned chair to the side of the bed and sat in it. After a moment of shifting uncomfortably, he decided that if the priest was going to sleep in here again tonight, he'd need something more comfortable.

Defying his logic, he looked at her. She had come back for him after they had fallen from the tree. She could have run and kept on running but she came back. Hell, he liked it so much about her he found himself smiling. He'd accused her of enticing him because he'd felt lost to desire. He'd wanted to kiss her mouth, her face, touch her, breathe her, have her for one night.

She was as close to being English as anyone could be, damn it! He sickened himself and scowled, turning his eyes away from her.

He couldn't change what was already in motion. Robert knew he was here whether Cain told him or not. The king knew his second in command would not fail.

He ran his palms down his face and groaned. What the hell had he done promising her she could stay? She made him regret taking her home. What the hell was she doing to him, making him feel such useless things as regret, sympathy, and, God help him, fondness?

He'd finally gone mad. He knew it would only be a matter of time, but he'd always believed it would be the things he'd seen and done that drove him over the precipice. Not a lass.

Her vow to never forgive him tore at his guts.

He would write to Robert again and ask the king to allow Miss d'Argentan to keep her holding in the king's name.

But first, he needed to get her to swear fealty to the Scottish king.

It wouldn't be easy.

His gaze involuntarily softened on her hand dangling over the mattress. Palm up, her slim, seemingly delicate fingers relaxed in a beckoning position.

He blinked away from them, remembering those same fingers wrapped around the hilt of a dagger, and pulling the string on her bow.

He flared his nostrils, blowing out a great exhalation. What was wrong with him? He was beginning to worry. Mercy was being given where none would have been given before. He had already proven he would do much for her. His guts seemed to constantly ache. Why?

He had desired women before. But this woman was different. She stirred the ashes.

He shook his head and leaned back in the chair. No. He wouldn't allow it.

"Commander?"

He turned his head to see William standing in the doorway with the other two.

Where the hell was Amish? Why wasn't he keeping an eye on Sir Richard? He was still a damned prisoner.

"William, aye," Cain said, rubbing his belly. "Come in. Father, take Sir Richard to Amish and then return here so that I can get on with the day."

This time, they knew enough not to argue.

"Father Timothy told me about Aleysia. Is everything all right with you, Commander?" William asked when they were alone.

"Aye," Cain assured him, and then slipped his gaze back to her. "She vexes me."

"They all do," William agreed with a shy smile.

Cain cut him a furtive glance. "Och, what would ye know of it, lad?"

He had never pressed William to speak of the lass he called for at night. He wished he hadn't let the conversation get personal now. He didn't share the intimacies of his life with the men, and he didn't ask them to share theirs with him. He was their commander in charge of their lives, not their friend.

But William wasn't a soldier.

The lad moved closer to the bed, his gaze lowered. "I do not know much, save that caring for one can be quite painful." His gaze took on a glazed look as he stared into the past. "And losing her is maddening."

Cain hadn't expected the lad to open up. He shifted in his chair, uncomfortable with such shared intimacies. He didn't know what kind advice to give.

"Father Timothy says that love does not just come once in a lifetime," William said, "but I do not think 'tis possible to love again. Do you, Commander?"

"I dinna know," Cain admitted quietly and looked away. "But if 'tis offered to ye, ye should take it. Ye are not a warrior. Ye should have a wife and some bairns and get old."

"You should have those things as well," William offered, glancing up from beneath the spray of chestnut-colored curls falling over his brow. "You have done much for Scotland. You deserve to be happy."

Cain wasn't sure he deserved anything but soot and ashes after all the battles he'd fought, all the lives he'd taken without mercy, but he said nothing. He should have.

"What vexes you about her?" William asked, breaking the silence.

Cain strangled out a short laugh. He'd hoped the topic had faded. He wasn't sure how to answer without giving too much of the truth away.

"She is…I dinna…" He cleared his throat and began again. "She is spirited and stubborn." He looked toward the door. "What the hell is keepin' Father Timothy?" He didn't want to be here anymore. Once the priest returned, he could leave. It was best if he go.

Why the hell did he send for William instead of Amish? She'd escape a moment after she opened her eyes.

"She's bold for a steward's granddaughter," William said, dragging Cain's attention back to him. "And she does not dress like any lady I have ever seen."

Cain's heart pounded. What did William know? Had he guessed that she was the one they were all looking for? That Cain had lied to them? "I—"

"And Richard and Father Timothy have explained to us that de Bar had put her and many others to work day and night building his traps. It explains her odd behavior." William lifted his gaze and offered her sleeping form a smile. "But I like her."

Cain swallowed and then looked at her. Did he like her, as well? No, he couldn't. She would likely end up dead after she killed even more. He couldn't like her.

He stood up from his chair and forced himself to smile when William shrank back a bit.

Hell, it made Cain want to find the bastard who made the lad this way and beat him senseless for a few months.

"I had planned on goin' huntin' once the priest returned. I know a safe path through the forest, and we have no food."

"Oh," William said, sounding disappointed rather than relieved. "Of course, Commander. She will be safe with me." He took Cain's seat and rested his gaze on her, giving Cain no other reason to speak to him.

Cain looked at the door. He moved toward it. This was how it should be. He couldn't go around liking people and still be the same on the field. He couldn't care. Not again. Never again.

He stopped before he left the room and thought about turning back. But behind him were memories of death and screaming while English soldiers carried his brothers off and took away his life.

He left the bedchamber and shouted Amish's name when he passed the great hall. He didn't think about Miss d'Argentan again while he retrieved his bow and quiver and stormed out of the keep.

CHAPTER TWELVE

ALEYSIA OPENED HER eyes and grasped her head. Oh, why had she guzzled down that devil's brew? "Am I in hell?"

"I hope not, else that means I am there, too."

William's voice startled her nearly out of her skin. It made her head pound all the more. She wanted to scowl at him but it hurt too much to move...or to think.

"Here, drink some water."

She let him feed her from a wooden cup and swept her gaze around the room. No one else was here. "Where is...everyone?"

"Father Timothy stepped out to have a pi—to use the garderobe." He tossed her a sly, knowing look and set the cup down on a small table by the bed, proving he wasn't as innocent as he appeared. "Or is it the commander you are looking for?"

She stared at him for a moment and thought about pretending not to be affected by his boldness. But she gave up quickly and rubbed her aching head. "'Tis the commander. But 'tis not what you think."

It was much worse. She had dreamed of him in her deep slumber, dark, sensual dreams of him atop her, gazing into her eyes, lowering his head, kissing her. He had kept the truth from her. She was going to have to marry someone of the Scottish king's choosing if she wanted to remain at Lismoor.

"I do not trust him," she said as William gave her another sip of water.

William blinked his striking gray eyes at her then set the cup down again. "The commander has never given me a reason not to trust him."

"You are a Scot and on his side."

"He did not know I was a Scot or on his side when he found me."

She remembered the commander telling her about finding him and asked William about it now. "What were you doing on the road?"

He shifted in his seat and remained quiet for so long Aleysia thought he wasn't going to answer. But then, he began in a quiet voice. "Julianna had finally agreed to let me kiss her." He smiled softly, remembering. "We were caught. Her father had me beaten and tossed onto the side of the road outside Berwick. He had beaten me many times before for minor offenses, but he never threw me out. I awoke to find the Scots had taken the village.

"The commander's regiment was leaving Berwick and found me. Father Timothy told me there was nothing to go back to and I would not make it far before I was killed. They had seen the carnage and they would not let me return. But I do not believe Julianna is dead."

Aleysia forgot about her headache and patted his arm. "Then we will find her," she promised. "Do not lose hope. I have already spoken to the commander about it and he has agreed to help."

His eyes looked almost blue in the light as the whites turned red and they misted with tears. He looked away and then back at her. "I am in your debt already."

She shook her head and offered him a tender smile. "As your commander said, there is no debt."

She had many more things to ask him about himself...and others, but the chamber door opened and she looked up instead to see the commander entering the room.

She was completely taken aback by the way her heartbeat accelerated in his presence. She fought to keep from lifting her hand to her messy braid.

"Good. Ye are awake," he said, barely looking at her. "Come with me."

Brute. He didn't ask her how she felt after practically being poisoned by his priest. Did he think her a pet to come at his beck and call? Let William jump to his feet, she would not!

"Lady," he said on a low growl when she didn't move. "Some of the villagers have returned. Father Timothy has taken them to the chapel."

Aleysia didn't consider her aching head or her thrashing heart, but scrambled out of bed. "Why did you not say so?" She smoothed some wrinkles out of her léine and bodice and quickly rebraided her hair. "Take me to them. I am ready."

His hand on her arm stopped her as she moved toward the door. "William," he said. "Amish stands guard at the chapel doors. Go to him and tell him I will be there in a few moments."

When they were alone, he shut the door and finally gave her his full attention. It made her just a tiny bit breathless. "The men knew to expect the villagers' return, but remember, they dinna know who ye are or what ye have done." He clenched his jaw as if he didn't want to continue. "I must tell them, and I will when the time is right. They must not hear it from the villagers."

His eyes held her still, entranced by a single flicker of light somewhere in the deepest shadows. What was it? It drew her in. It made her curious about his past and why, according to Father Timothy, he was a prisoner to it.

She looked away. What good would it do her to know anything more about him? He protected her for his Scottish king's sake.

She stiffened her shoulders and moved toward the door. "I will make certain they understand that, for the sake of our safety, Richard is my grandfather."

"Be brief aboot it," he said, leading her out.

Whatever she thought she saw in his gaze was gone. Good. She wouldn't have her thoughts on what he was thinking or why he was thinking it. She liked the cold, detached commander. It made hating him easier.

She followed him to the small chapel, where Amish stood guard at the door with William at his side.

"From now on," the commander told his second. "Anyone returnin' to Lismoor is to be brought directly to me."

"Aye, Commander."

"Ye and William wait oot here," he told them and let her pass when she pulled open the door, tired of waiting.

She entered the candlelit chapel and spotted Father Timothy chatting with Ronald the blacksmith. She smiled seeing Molly and her husband Walter, the reeve.

There were others, twelve in all, gathered together in small groups until they saw her.

"Miss d'Argentan!" Molly cried out. The rest followed.

Aleysia looked behind her for the commander and found him staying back in the shadows. She was pleased with his decision to let her see to them first.

After she reassured them all that she hadn't been harmed, she asked them to listen to what she had to say. She explained quickly and quietly that she had failed and was not able to defeat the Scots, but that Commander MacPherson was treating her and Sir Richard with mercy.

"He has also sworn on Father Timothy's Holy Book not to cause any of you harm."

"He is a Scot!" Walter the reeve shouted. "Why should we trust him? Our land and our homes now belong to Robert the Bruce! We should have all stayed and helped you fight! Now we have lost everything!"

Aleysia prayed the ground would open and take her down. This was her fault. She'd caused this terror in her friends' eyes and their voices. She had sworn to protect them from this and she failed. Perhaps they were all correct and she had taken on too much alone. What could she say to them now? Nothing.

She remained quiet and dipped her chin to her chest.

She felt the commander come close, demanding silence with nothing more than his presence when he stepped into the light.

Molly and the miller's wife, Beatrice, gasped and stepped back, closer to their husbands.

"Ye could have stayed and fought," he said in his resonate voice. "And ye all would have died. Yer lady fought a valiant fight and her bravery should be commended, not condemned."

Aleysia was tempted to look at him. He was the last person she expected to praise or defend her. She must remember that he was the one who'd set this all in motion. *He* was the reason she had failed. She could have beaten a less skilled warrior.

"I am Commander MacPherson," he continued to the quiet crowd. "What yer lady says is the truth. Ye willna be harmed. Ye have my word. But my men dinna know 'twas Miss d'Argentan who waged war on us. They believe her to be the granddaughter of Sir Richard, whom they also dinna know is a knight. If they discover the truth, there may be trouble." He glanced down at her and scowled as if he didn't understand why he'd kept so much from them. "So from now until I say, ye will address her as Aleysia."

"What does all this mean, Lady—Aleysia?" Ronald asked, slipping his gaze to the six foot four inch Highland warlord when he made the correction.

"It means keep yer—" The commander shot a disparaging look to Father Timothy and then returned his attention to Ronald, correcting himself. "It means that, fer now, as far as my men are concerned, Aleysia is a peasant, innocent of any wrongdoin' besides hatin' Scots."

"You protect her from your own men?" Old John, who'd crafted all her bows and arrows, pointed out boldly when Cain turned for the door to end the meeting. "'Tis unexpected."

The commander looked slightly ruffled for the first time and let his eyes roam around the chapel at the others waiting for his reply.

It was Aleysia who spoke up first. "The king of the Scots does not want to spill the blood of a d'Argentan. The commander is waiting to hear what is to be done with me. He is doing his duty."

If the commander heard the anger in her voice, he made no indication. "I am protectin' ye all," he warned instead. "My men died by her hand and with yer aid, so if ye want to see another sunrise, dinna speak of it and remember what ye were told here today. Go back to yer homes. Prepare fer work tomorrow. Nothin' will change. No one will put ye oot."

Aleysia stiffened when he placed his palm on her lower back. Heat and power, like lightning running through her, made her legs weak and her heart stall. He turned and, without another word, ushered her toward the door.

She moved away from his touch. "You did not have to threaten them."

He reached out and took hold of her elbow. "I told them the truth," he said blandly and pushed open the door.

Amish and William were still there waiting. "The villagers will be comin' oot and returnin' to their homes," he told them. "Make certain they arrive there safely. They are not to be harmed in any way. If they are, the guilty will be dealt with severely."

"Aye, Commander," Amish replied as the commander continued on his way down the hall tugging Aleysia behind him.

"Do you threaten everyone in order to get what you want?" she asked, pulling on her arm to be free of him.

He stopped to hover over her and stare into her eyes. "Instead of bein' grateful fer my protection, however I may offer it, ye stand here flappin' yer tongue aboot me thr—"

She swung at him. She tried to hold her temper but he infuriated her. She knew where there were more daggers, at least two that his men could not have discovered.

"Enough!" he thundered, holding her back without letting her go.

She swung at him again. This time, she hit him in the chest.

In response, he yanked her hard against him, halting her breath and trapping her arms between them in his tight embrace. "I'm beginnin' to think ye enjoy bein' a threat to me, Miss d'Argentan."

She struggled to break free of him, but only for moment. "What?"

"It means I must keep ye close," he said on a soft breath that stole across the edge of her jaw.

Was he going to kiss her? What should she do if he did? She fought to keep her wits about her. If he kissed her, she might find herself lost in a place she knew nothing about, with a man she had vowed to kill.

"Are you mad?" She choked out a forced laugh. "I'm trying to get away from you!"

"Ye want to see me dead."

She didn't deny it, though she was tempted to. "Do you think I can kill you with my bare hands? Fool."

He raised an eyebrow and one end of his mouth. "I dinna know all that yer hands are capable of, lass."

She had no idea why her face felt as if it had gone up in flames, or why her head was suddenly filled with images of her fingertips tracing the hard angles of his body, or touching his lips. Up close, his mouth looked enticing, irresistible. Had he kissed other women before?

Oh, how could she be having these traitorous thoughts about him? Thoughts of his mouth covering hers, dipping to her neck. She didn't think he would stop, as had the other young man in her past who'd kissed her so intimately.

"You know I am no match for you, Commander," she countered, trying to control her wayward thoughts, but barely. "You accuse me of wanting to stay close to you, when 'tis you who has dragged me into your arms as if you have every right to do so."

His smile faded and Aleysia realized once it was gone that it hadn't reached his eyes.

"I wish to continue livin', lady," he said impassively. "Nothin' more."

Nothing more. How could there ever be anything more? They were enemies. One of them likely wouldn't survive this.

She almost trembled in his arms when he loosened his hold on her.

She pulled back the moment she could and swatted his hand away when he reached for her elbow to take it again.

"Crook your arm," she insisted. "I will not be dragged about by my elbow."

Thankfully, he didn't argue. When he bent his arm, she looped hers through it and let him lead her toward the great hall. She ignored the voice in her head telling her how pleasant it was to walk on his arm, to stand so close to him as his equal and not his captive.

She didn't care for his cold, brash manner, but he hadn't actually hurt anyone in front of her and he had sworn not to harm her people. If he wasn't a wild Scot and if he hadn't claimed her home, she might look at him differently.

"Now," he said, "ye will tell me why ye were so angry earlier that ye almost attacked me in front of my men."

She thought about it for a moment and then remembered her conversation with Father Timothy before she drank the poison that set her abed for the whole day. Robert the Bruce was going to name one of his minions to hold Rothbury and her castle in his name.

The truth she'd known but had forgotten for a moment hit her again like a cold, wet cloth across her face. She *was* his captive.

"You said I did not have to leave Lismoor," she said quietly as they entered the great hall.

"Aye," he grunted. "I remember sayin' that."

They reached a table in the middle of the hall, with one man sitting at it. He obeyed without a word when the commander told him to go sit somewhere else.

Was he brooding because he wanted to avoid having to tell her the rest?

"I do not wish to be wed to a stranger," she told him while she sat. "A Scottish stranger, no less."

Perhaps she should not have added the last bit. His scowl deepened and he shouted for someone named Rauf to bring them something to drink.

The ribaldry around them quieted down as the men took their drinks and slowly left the hall.

A man with a long scar running down his face, whom Aleysia assumed was Rauf, brought them two cups of water and stepped away from the table.

"What is this?" the commander demanded after a quick look into the cup.

"We are all oot of whisky, Commander," Rauf regretfully informed him.

"Rauf," she said, causing both men to turn to look at her, each with very different expressions on their faces. "There is an unopened cask of wine in the cellar beneath the kitchen."

Rauf blinked his bloodshot eyes at her and then nodded. "Thank ye, Miss."

Aleysia knew in that moment how easily the commander could frighten the wits out of someone with just his scowl, for he aimed his darkest one on her now. She was tempted to look away, perhaps wipe her own brow.

"How d'ye know where there's untainted wine?" Cain asked in a mild, thoroughly controlled voice. "Did ye serve Lord de Bar?"

Lord de Bar? Aleysia nodded because she had a feeling she should. It took her a moment to remember William mentioning the name and another to realize what the commander was doing. "Aye, I was the...bottler. That is why I know about the wine in the cellar."

The commander seemed satisfied and dismissed Rauf to the task. "Have Richard taste it first," he called out.

To which Rauf called back, "Aye, Commander."

He demanded unquestioned obedience from his men. She understood the importance of it on a battlefield, thanks to Giles' stories. It was up to him to win with as few casualties as possible. She recalled how the commander had ordered his men to travel in a single line, one that had kept them from dying in the field of arrows. He had also gone hunting alone rather than risk his men to her traps. He kept them safe by keeping her close. He was good at his duty.

But they weren't on a battlefield now.

Or were they?

She'd done nothing but try to kill him—or at least, escape him. To no avail. Of course, she had good reasons for wanting to kill him.

She cursed her traitorous heart but, perhaps, there was nothing more she could do.

"I will taste it," she said softly.

His scowl softened. Perhaps fighting with him was the wrong approach. She wanted to escape the future that strangers would make for her and make one of her own. If she lost her home to the Scots, she would leave and live in a village somewhere.

"Where were we?" she asked, not caring if he didn't want to speak of it. "I was telling you I would not wed a stranger."

"A Scot, no less," he reminded her. Surprisingly, his scowl faded.

"Am I so terrible? Would you want to be forced to wed an English woman?"

He shook his head and offered no other comment. He looked into his cup of water.

Never in her life had silence been so deafening. She heard a distant drumbeat and realized it was her heart. Everything he promised, everything he did was all temporary. He didn't want to stay. Would the next Scot honor the promise he'd made to the villagers?

"I will speak with the king aboot lettin' ye stay on yer own."

Her hope rose to the surface and became evident in her smile. "Will he grant what you ask?"

He said nothing for an eternal moment, and then he nodded and smiled as if it were the only thing to do to keep something else from falling from his lips.

CHAPTER THIRTEEN

"YE SHOULD HAVE told her, Cainnech."

Cain moved away from where he stood with Father Timothy in a corner of the now well-lit great hall. His eyes found the reason for his unruly thoughts.

Miss d'Argentan sat at a table with Richard and William, and a few of the other men. He didn't worry about her running. What could she do? More men would come. He'd given her hope of staying at Lismoor without marriage. He knew he should have told her the condition, but he had taken everything else from her.

Most of the time, he was able to remind himself that taking land for the king was his duty. He had done it before without thought of consequence. But no one else had fought so hard for their home, taking on an army alone.

He told himself he didn't care, because caring scared the hell out of him. But when he saw her smile or heard her laugh at something William said, he knew something of cataclysmic importance was about to happen in his life.

He watched her now, leaning in to hear something her knight was saying. He liked looking at her, and he wasn't the only one who did.

He raked his gaze over anyone leering at her. Three men dipped their gazes to their trenchers.

Supper was venison from the deer he'd killed earlier. The wine, thanks to the cask they'd found, flowed freely, and the men, for the most part, behaved themselves.

It was almost…peaceful. He was unaccustomed to it but he couldn't say he hated it.

He found himself moving toward her as if his mind had a will of its own.

He had thought her bonny the first time he saw her face by the light of a single candle in the dungeon, her green eyes sparked with fury. But seeing her tilt her head just enough for the firelight from the hearth to dance across her features while she laughed, made him forget everything else—every dark day of his past.

"When will ye tell her?"

Cain looked Heavenward with a sigh, then at the priest who had trotted up to his side. "D'ye not have a confession to hear, Father?"

The priest shrugged his robed shoulders. "Not unless ye have somethin' ye want to tell me."

Cain flashed him an impatient look and then veered away from her table. Should he tell his oldest friend the things that plagued him? How his enemy haunted his thoughts?

"Ye are particularly sour this evenin'," the priest pointed out. "Is it because ye havena told her the condition to her stayin'?"

"She will never swear fealty to him," Cain said. He sounded defeated to his own ears. It disgusted him. He rubbed his belly.

"Are ye unwell, Son?" the priest asked, concern filling his eyes.

Aye, he was unwell. The one who had attacked and killed his men was sitting with them, drinking, eating fresh venison, and laughing! And worse—so much worse—he found himself attracted to her as if she were a light in the pale gray gloom of death and destruction.

He didn't want to get close to the light. He did everything he could to stay away from it. He was comfortable in the familiar. He knew things here in the gray, like how to remain unseen and untouched.

"I am sorry we came here," he admitted in a quiet, gruff voice.

"Commander," a silken, female voice called out, sending heat through his blood. "Come and try this mead." Aleysia held up a cup and offered him a radiant smile. "I made it myself."

Was she playing with him? Had she poisoned the mead? She tempted him to deliver her over for the punishment she deserved. Or march over to her, pull her up by her arms, and kiss that furtive smile from her lips.

He moved forward, reaching her in three long strides. He took the cup from her hand and kept his gaze on her while he lifted it to his mouth.

From the corner of his eye he saw Father Timothy reach out his hand, as if to stop him. But Cain didn't believe she would poison him. She'd had plenty of opportunities to kill him.

She stared at him while he put the rim to his lips, the challenge unmistakable in her eyes.

He drank, tilting his head to take the entire contents in one long guzzle. When he was done, he wiped his mouth with the back of his hand and offered the cup back to her. "Needs more cloves."

He threw his leg over the bench she was sitting on. He guessed he should be sitting at the higher table in the front of the hall, meant for the lord. But he wasn't one for indoor etiquette. Besides, he wanted to be near her—and she was sitting with the men. He faced her and looked into her fiery eyes. "Ye dinna want to do it, lady."

"Do what, Commander?" she challenged with a quirk of her full, honey-dipped lips.

He couldn't answer with the truth, not with the men listening. They would suspect something if they thought she wanted to kill him.

"Ye dinna want to slap me," he supplied.

She raised a questionable eyebrow.

"Och, dinna slap him, lass," cried Rauf from the other side of the table, clearly concerned for her well-being.

Cain gave him a stern look, though he was not surprised she'd won the poor fool over so easily. Had she won the rest of them, as well?

"'Twould not be the first time I've slapped him, or tried to," she offered boldly.

Everyone at the table, including Sir Richard, grew wide-eyed. The men murmured among themselves about her bravery. They had seen their commander slaughter men for lifting their swords to him. It shocked them to think of her striking him—and him letting her live to smile about it.

Cain saw the admiration for her in their eyes. He let her have her victory. He felt her eyes on him but didn't turn back to her. He took the cup of wine set before him and drank.

Sir Richard's laughter seemed to pull the rest of the men out of their wonderment, for they joined in and then slowly went back to their cups and bowls.

Cain took some bread and meat from the large bowl in the center of the table and began to eat with the rest in silence.

"How long has Lismoor been your home?" William finally broke the uncomfortable silence.

"I came here with my...grandfather twelve years ago," she told him, softening her tone. "I was eight."

Cain knew she was speaking of her brother, not Richard. "What aboot yer father?" he asked, tearing into his bread.

She offered him a curious look, as if she knew joining in on the informal conversation was unusual and uncomfortable for him and was surprised he did it anyway. "Before we came here," she replied more gently, "my parents suffered a fever and died."

"What is Lord de Bar like?" Rauf asked.

"It doesna matter," Amish said, raising his cup. "We'll soon find him and scatter his parts over Rothbury, aye, Commander?"

Cain held up his cup, "Aye, from the trees."

He flicked his gaze to the lass while the men agreed with loud cheers and clanking cups. He hoped she understood the danger of them finding out the truth. Presently, the danger came from her friends.

"How many more people d'ye expect to return?" he asked her.

"Twenty-seven," she said without thinking about it. "And I would like to hunt a nice stag for them since they have been away and will not have much food left."

Cain liked that she knew exactly how many among her people were missing and that she was concerned with their bellies. It was a sign of leadership. If she weren't fighting for the other side, she would make a good commander.

"Then there is the staff, which lives here," she continued, popping a small piece of bread into her mouth and smiling as she thought of the people she named. "There is Matilda my hand—" She stopped and corrected herself. She was the granddaughter of the steward, not the lady of the castle. "And the other maids, Agnes and Sarah, Harry the carpenter, Philip the cook, the seamstress, the laundress, the spinner, the other knights, and Elizabeth." She moved closer to him until he could smell the honey on her breath when she tilted her lips to his ear, "Elizabeth is my brother's betrothed."

He wanted to kiss her. He wanted to carry her to her grand bed and delight in her viperous tongue and her lithe body until the sun rose.

He turned his head just a bit and almost brushed his lips over hers. "Will they keep yer secret?"

A dreamy languor stole over her face. "Who?"

He had the urge to smile at her like a pitiful fool. She hadn't recoiled. In fact, she seemed under the same spell as he. Hell, he found her irresistible when she fought with him, but he grew completely captivated by her when she was being herself and not a warrior with a mission.

Hunger gleamed in his eyes but he did not touch her. He moved back, breaking the hold she had on him. He was afraid of letting himself grow fond of her. Was it already too late? He would not have believed it was even possible.

He turned away and found Father Timothy watching him with a gentle, knowing smile on his face.

What did he know that Cain didn't? Aye, he was attracted to her. Every man here was, and it was beginning to grate on his nerves.

He lowered his gaze and ate his supper in silence, aware of her every move, the slightest touch of her leg against his. Her warm voice seeped through his skin when she answered the men's questions. Her rich, sensual laughter reverberated in his blood.

His head felt light—too light. He tried to stand but stumbled against the table. Was that Father Timothy's voice he heard saying his name, sounding alarmed, afraid. The priest never sounded afraid. Cain looked around at William and Amish, both of them falling into their bowls. He turned to look at Aleysia and glared at the two of her that appeared before him. "Ye did—"

Then he crumpled to the rushes.

CHAPTER FOURTEEN

ALEYSIA WATCHED, HORRIFIED, as one by one the commander and his men fell under the effects of poison.

"No!" someone shouted. A man's voice.

She looked across the table at the only other person still sitting upright, besides Father Timothy, rushing to the commander's fallen body.

"Richard! What have you—" She realized what she was saying immediately and snapped her mouth shut. She had to think. The priest was awake! *Oh, Richard. What did you do?*

"Come, dear lady." He stood up and beckoned with both hands. "We must hurry! Father Timothy," he called out, covering his ears. "Stop your shouting. 'Tis only a sleeping enhancement I put into the wine. They will wake up in a few hours."

Aleysia closed her eyes and held her breath. Why couldn't he keep his mouth shut? He'd done this! The priest was sure to tell the commander *if he woke.*

"Sir Richard," Father Timothy warned after he made certain the commander was still alive. Was he? "If he doesna wake up, I vow before God I will kill whichever of ye is responsible fer this."

"I am," Richard assured him. "I am getting her the hell out of here."

"No!" Aleysia shouted, quieting him. When she had his attention, she softened her tone. "I did not want to go. But now, he's..." Her gaze fell to the commander lying on the floor, guarded by his friend. Her heart skipped beats and she closed her eyes to try to think clearly. "He's going to think 'twas my mead."

"We could be on a ship back to Normandy in two hours," Richard said with more urgency. "We haven't a moment to spare. Come! Please, Aleysia, enough talk! You will be given over in marriage to someone either King Edward or Robert the Bruce choses. Come, for your brother's sake." He moved around the table to go to her. "We must leave! I promised your father, your brother, that I would protect you. This is our only chance to escape. We can go home, dear girl."

She put up her hands to stop him. "Do you know what you have done?" She didn't want to go to back to Normandy. The commander had told her his king would grant her Lismoor without having to marry. It was better than losing everything. Better than Normandy. Better than running.

"Father," she cried, turning her gaze on him. "You must not tell him 'twas Richard. Do you hear? Let him believe 'twas my mead."

"My lady, I—"

"I beg you, please. I will not leave if you vow not to tell him 'twas Richard."

"Aleysia," Richard said sternly. "Absolutely not! If we leave now, no one has to take any blame for anything." He reached for her wrist to pull her away. She snatched it back and shook her head at him. "We will be long gone by the time he awakens!" he argued. "I will not let you do this!"

"'Tis already done, Sir Richard!" she told him. "By your hand. I am trying to save your life. You will be silent and not order me about again."

She turned her attention back on the priest and looked into his doe-like eyes. "Do you vow it?" she asked softly, praying for his agreement. "Richard did this to save me. He would do anything to save me. Just as you would do anything to save him." She pointed to the commander.

Father Timothy turned to Richard. "Do you vow 'twas only a sleep enhancer?"

The knight nodded. "I vow it to you. I did not know you would not be drinking, Father Timothy. I would not harm you. But I will not let—"

"I will not run," she promised, cutting Richard off. "I will take the blame."

"No! I will not let you!" her knight fought on. His eyes were glassy, his voice broken. "Please, my lady. This was not my intention. He will be so angry."

"Sir," the priest said, finally leaving the commander and going to lay his hand on Richard's arm to offer forgiveness and mercy. "If she stays and takes the blame fer what is already done, he will be lenient with her."

"How do you know he will be lenient?" Richard asked.

Father Timothy turned his gaze on her. "He is...fond of her."

Her laughter sounded a bit mad to her ears. "Fond of me? Are you mad? He hates me—" Her eyes darted to Richard. The last thing he or the others needed to know was that she didn't hate the commander. Not entirely.

"No," Father Timothy corrected. "I know him and if 'tis anyone he hates presently, 'tis himself fer what he thinks of ye."

She remembered his lips brushing against hers and brought her finger to her mouth. "What does he think of me?"

The priest shrugged his narrow shoulders. "That, he will have to tell ye himself."

She nodded. All right. There was no time for that now. "Will you promise, Father?"

"Aye, lass. I promise."

She smiled and offered him her gratitude. "Now, what should we do?"

"My lady, I do not—"

"Sir Richard, 'tis decided," she said, stopping him. "We are staying. Lismoor in the Bruce's name is better than no Lismoor at all."

She left both of them and went to stand over the commander. Would he be lenient this time? He'd looked so angry just before…she rubbed her eyes and then let them move over the length of him, from his bare knees to his strong thighs—one of which was exposed by his plaid riding up from his fall. Her face grew warm and she looked at Richard speaking with the priest where she'd left them.

She knew it wasn't a good idea, but she sat on the floor with the commander. What was there to do but wait for him to wake up? While she waited, she thought about what Father Timothy had told her. Was the commander fond of her? What did it mean? What did she want it to mean? She looked down at his sleeping face, his dark hair falling over his cheekbone and the wound she'd inflicted on him with her arrow. She could have killed him. She never missed. Giles had made her practice archery from an early age.

She'd let the commander's stark, deadly beauty distract her. She felt something for him she didn't understand. It wasn't love. It felt more feral, more like she wanted to tear off his clothes and climb all over him.

"You look at him as if you feel something soft for him," Richard said, coming to stand over her.

She closed her eyes to gather patience. Her friend had put their lives in danger by tainting the wine. Would Cainnech still help her keep Lismoor? She wanted to weep. She loved Richard and knew he'd done this for her. She would not let him die for it.

"I feel nothing toward him but hatred," she told him. "But I am not a fool. The King of Scots has ordered these things. If I kill this one, another takes his place."

"You need not kill anyone else," he tried arguing and sat on the bench. "No one will look for you in Normandy."

"And what about Mattie and Elizabeth? The villagers? Do I leave them all to whoever comes here next?"

"No, no," he admitted, shaking his head. "Of course not."

"How long do ye think they will sleep?" Father Timothy asked, coming near them and checking on William and then on the commander again. "His pulse is stronger. He is well."

"As I said, I would not kill him," Richard answered. "He will likely sleep until morning."

"He is goin' to be angry."

Aleysia looked up at the priest, glad to see that he had forgiven her as well. She hoped the commander was so generous. She had no idea what he would be like when he woke. What would she tell him?

Father Timothy sat beside her and touched his hand to her arm. "Dinna be afraid, my dear. All will be well."

She exhaled a low sigh. Would it? "How do you know?" she asked him softly. It didn't matter if he was fond of her, this wasn't the first time she had tried to kill him.

He drank the mead. Even if it was an arrogant answer to her unspoken challenge, he still had to trust her to drink it.

"I canna say how I know," Father Timothy said after she might have groaned. "But I was reminded of somethin' tonight." He paused and turned his tender smile on her.

"What was it?" she asked him.

"Alas, I canna say."

She frowned and blew out her next breath through her nostrils. Why did he say anything in the first place? "Are you trying to be mysterious, Father?"

His smile grew into a chuckle. "No, nothin' like that. I know all will be well because I have seen a slight change in Cainnech for the first time in sixteen years."

What? What was he saying? He'd known Cainnech—the commander for that long? And in sixteen years, the man hadn't changed? And what was the "slight change" he mentioned? She had questions. Lots of them.

She slid her eyes to Richard and then to the priest. "Father, I'd like to confess."

He stared at her, looking unsure and a bit stunned. "Of course."

She looked at Richard and smiled. "You will excuse us, will you not, dear friend?"

Her knight moved his gaze between them. Finally, he nodded and stepped away.

When they were alone, but for the slumbering bodies around them, she turned to look into the priest's large, brown, blinking eyes. "Let us get this out of the way then. I lied."

He sat, waiting for more. When nothing else came, he cleared his throat. "How many times?"

"I do not know how many times, but add to it the one I just told."

A hint of his warm smile returned to his face and emboldened her to continue. "I wanted to speak to you without Richard."

"Ye are fergiven, and aboot what?"

"About the commander," she told him quickly and in a whispered voice.

He inclined his ear and she leaned in to him so that he could hear, poor old man.

"What kind of man is he when he is not killing his enemies?"

Father Timothy drew in a deep sigh and sat straight again. He paused for a moment and then said, "I dinna know. When he is not killin' his enemies, he is thinkin' aboot killin' them."

She sat there staring at him. Did he not understand the question? "But you have known him for sixteen years. What was he like before he became a soldier?"

"My dear," He tried to pat her hand. "Cainnech should tell ye these things, not I."

She shook her head and pulled her arm away. "You tell me. I wish to know."

"Why?" he asked.

She sat back, unsure how to reply.

"I willna tell him," the priest coaxed in his soothing tone. "Ye are still confessin', are ye not?" He continued before she had a chance to reply. "I am not permitted to repeat what I hear durin' one's confession."

She knew that. But could she trust him? And what did she want to confess?

She turned to gaze down at the commander. She hated herself for what she was feeling. "I find him infuriating and arrogant. Part of my heart hates him, but..." Oh, how could she speak it out loud? She was betraying her brother, her friends, her purpose. She closed her eyes when the priest remained silent and patient. "He is not altogether terrible."

"No, he is not."

She opened her eyes and set her gaze on him. "How has he changed? Surely, you can tell me that."

He nodded, his comforting smile returned. "He is sorry he came here."

Six words that set her heart to pounding and insinuated so much she hardly knew where to begin or what to feel. He was sorry he'd taken Lismoor from her. She was glad to hear it. It softened the blow. She had seen fleeting glimpses of regret in his eyes, but she was unsure if she'd conjured it in her own mind. Could she forgive him?

"Why is he sorry?" she asked, settling her eyes on the sleeping commander.

"I dinna know. Truly," he added when she gave him a doubtful look. "But I believe it has to do with ye. If ye and Richard had been anyone else, ye would both be dead, despite King Robert's desired peace. Cainnech is not known fer his mercy."

Her blood chilled. How could one so beautiful be so frightful at the same time? "How many did he kill at Berwick?"

"None. We saw what was happenin', and with no way to stop it, we left. Cainnech doesna raid villages."

The commander had told her the truth then. They had nothing to do with Berwick. Her stomach calmed a bit. He wasn't a complete barbarian. What did it matter? He was going to wake up thinking she tried to poison him and his men again. She couldn't put her trust in the assurances Father Timothy gave her when he wasn't sure of half of them.

"Perhaps I am a fool to stay when I can run."

"Or perhaps ye have more courage than a regiment of men. Not many would be willin' to face his wrath, and fer someone else."

Aleysia smiled. She liked Father Timothy. Did this make her a traitor to God as well? "I imagine the commander's wrath is quite frightening."

The priest chuckled and lifted his eyes to Heaven. "Thank goodness he saves it fer his enemies."

She subdued the urge to tremble. She was his enemy, wasn't she? Especially now. She wasn't courageous at all. She was simply determined not to lose her home or her freedom by running off to Normandy.

Facing this beast of a man at his worst was another matter entirely. There were many more things she wanted to ask the priest but Richard was returning.

"You have known him for sixteen years," she said, "since he was a child then."

Father Timothy nodded.

"How did you meet him?"

"I was travelin' with an unholy regiment of Englishmen," he began and waited for Richard to return to his seat. "They attacked a sleepy village in Invergarry and killed many people, includin' Cainnech's parents. They brought him back to camp and kept him as their servant. They kept him tied him to a tree and struck him often. He was seven." He paused, his smile gone now, his voice lowered to a weighted whisper. "I did my best to keep him safe from their flyin' fists, but I didna always succeed."

Aleysia listened, unsure if her heart was beating or not. They killed his parents and…kept him as a servant? Now it was no surprise why he seemed fond of William. They had servitude in common. She gazed down at him, imagining a beaten, afraid, little boy.

"Where did they take him?"

"They brought him with us," the priest replied. "Fer eight years, he served the English on the battlefield." He paused and looked away to clear his throat. Aleysia knew the memory was painful for him. "They took no pity on the boy."

"You stayed with him?" she asked, blinking away a tear and the urge to touch her fingers to the commander's face.

"I did."

"Thank God he had you."

"I do," he said, back to smiling. "But he needs more than just me."

She looked startled at first and then she laughed. "You certainly do not think that I—?"

"No!" he laughed with her. "Not at all. I have tried to find his two brothers, but to no avail—"

"His brothers?" she asked as a shiver went through her. The English army had left three boys orphans.

"Aye. I was back at the camp when they burned his homestead. He told me of them. Two younger lads, Torin, who was five, and wee Nicholas, who was just two when last Cainnech saw them. I have tried to find them but as ye can imagine, 'tis difficult. I have only been able to learn that Nicholas was sold fer a stone soon after, but I dinna know to whom."

"How tragic to know your brothers might still be out there, alive somewhere and you do not know where."

The priest yawned and shrugged his shoulders. "He doesna seem to think on it often, but I'm sure it weighs on him."

They spoke a little longer, mainly about her relatives in Normandy and why she would not run to them.

When the birds began chirping, signaling the breaking dawn, and the first of the men began to stir, Father Timothy sent Richard to the keep with a vow that he and God would keep Aleysia safe.

"Go to yer room and wait there," he told her. "I will speak to him when he wakes."

"Why did you not drink the wine?" she asked before she left.

"'Twas sour and I prefer whisky."

She smiled and then she left because she didn't want to be the first one the commander saw when he opened his eyes and realized what had happened. It wasn't so much that she was afraid of him, though she was. But her blood rushed through her like waves on a tumultuous sea because he'd drunk the mead. She had somehow gained his trust. If he didn't kill her, he would never let her out of his sight again. She would be forced to be near him day…and night.

But even more than that, her heart ached because if he felt something for her, as Father Timothy had claimed, she'd surely lost it now.

She couldn't believe that her own heart could betray her. How could losing something she didn't want…and likely didn't have anyway, make her so miserable?

She entered her solar and shut the door, then leaned her head against it.

There could never be anything between them. They were enemies. He was the one she and her friends had prepared for so diligently, for so long. She moaned with the pain of it and pushed off the door. It was all for nothing. And worse, she, their leader and friend, had weakened with a hint of warmth in the otherwise cool indifference of a Highland warrior.

She threw herself onto her bed and buried her face in her pillow. What would she tell him when he found her? She'd been prepared to take the blame for Richard. She thought she could convince the commander of her guilt, but she had let her heart go soft after hearing about his past...the past he couldn't move beyond.

Oh, how could people be so cruel to bring a child into war? To kill a child's parents and sell his brothers—it was too much. How could she forget it and pretend to hate him?

She didn't have long to think about it when her door came crashing open and an angry warlord stood at the entrance.

CHAPTER FIFTEEN

ALEYSIA SAT UP in her bed, startled by his entrance, even more terrified by his murderous glare. He appeared larger, more daunting than before. His dark hair fell around his shoulders, adding shadows to his rigid jaw. He didn't move, save to slam the door in Father Timothy's face.

He said nothing for an eternal moment but stared at her with an expression as hard as sleet.

"I—" she began, not sure of what was going to come out next.

"Ye poisoned us," he accused. Beneath the silken words was an unmistakable threat.

"No," she corrected carefully, not really trusting her voice. "You slept. If I had poisoned you, you would be dead."

"Get up."

She blinked. The little boy on the battlefield disappeared and in his place stood a dangerous man with eyes as cold as steel.

She looked away rather than mourn the loss of something she never wanted. His trust. Why did it make her eyes burn and her heart break? "Where are you taking me?"

"Ye dinna get to ask any questions," he said woodenly. "Now get up or I will get ye oot of bed myself."

"Ah," she said, casting him a smirk and getting out of the bed, "so now I get to meet the merciless commander."

"Ye deserve no mercy."

Her legs felt weak. Her mouth felt dry. She didn't want to be afraid of him. He wasn't the ruthless beast she'd feared for four years. "For giving you a sleep enhancer?"

"Fer tryin' to make me suspect the mead when 'twas the wine ye tainted. Ye're clever, and dangerous," he said, taking hold of her arm.

She tried to pull away but he held fast. "You do not have to manhandle me. I've already proven that I will not run."

He ignored her protests and pulled her toward the door without a word.

They entered the empty hall. Father Timothy was nowhere to be found. When he pulled her past the great hall and then toward the outside stairs, she feared he might fling her down them. He believed she'd poisoned them. His patience with her had ended.

"Where are you taking me?" Her heart drummed in her ears when they stepped outside. The crisp morning air felt like a cold slap. There were ravens flying about the gloomy charcoal sky. Was this her last day?

"Cainnech!" she shouted at him, refusing to go quietly. "Where?"

He stopped and turned his storm-filled eyes on her. "Why did ye stay?"

What should she tell him? Her throat felt as if it were closing while she stared up at him. She was afraid he might see the truth in her eyes, so she lowered her gaze and shielded it beneath her lashes. "I was going to run away to Normandy. I only needed a few hours to keep you and the men asleep while I reached the port and boarded a ship for my homeland."

"What stopped ye?" he asked, though it sounded more like a low growl.

"My cousin, Geoffrey d'Argentan. I remembered that he will marry me off a sennight after I arrive. I do not want to leave my home and my friends and live in Normandy with a husband I do not love." It was the truth. Part of it. "So I remained, ready to give you an account of what I did and why. I also remembered that I am a d'Argentan and I will not run."

The commander roamed his eyes over her, peeling away her defenses and seeing her deepest secrets. He curled one corner of his mouth up. "And did ye also remember me tellin' ye that I would speak to the king aboot lettin' ye stay on yer own?"

She had the feeling she shouldn't answer.

He didn't give her the chance to do so. "Ye had no reason to run away…to poison us."

"I did not poison you, Commander. I—"

"Ye are correct. I no longer believe 'twas ye who tried to kill us last eve."

Her heart faltered. What? Had her ears just deceived her? If not her, then the only other person he had any reason to suspect was Richard! "'Twas I, Commander," she insisted. "'Twas I who tainted the wine."

His piercing gaze broke through her defenses. He was furious and…something else. Disappointed? "Ye poisoned William and ye would have poisoned Father Timothy if he had drunk the wine."

"No," she told him shaking her head. He made it sound so malicious. "They were not harmed. Nor were you. 'Twas a simple sleeping draught."

Should she have run when she had the chance? Even if it was just to save Richard? No! "I had simply wanted to ensure that you would not give chase to me. I was rash and foolish and I ask your forgiveness."

He stared at her. Did she see a flash of emotion in his gaze? She watched him while she waited for him to say something.

Finally, he made a deep, short sound from the back of his throat, and then continued walking.

What was that supposed to mean? Was Richard safe or not? She dug her heels into the ground. What more could she say? "I also wanted to prove to you that I could kill you if I chose to," she bit out. There. Perhaps that sounded more believable to his warrior ears!

"When have I ever told ye that I didna think ye could?"

She said the only thing she could remember in this moment. "When you drank the mead."

His jaw relaxed and softened, along with his gaze. He moved closer, hovering over her until she could count each lush, black lash surrounding his guarded, sapphire eyes. "That was to show ye that I didna think ye *would*." He stepped back and turned away. "They are two verra different things."

When he tugged her forward, she tugged back. She didn't know why she did it. She had no idea what to say to him. She believed gaining his trust was a difficult, if not almost impossible endeavor. She'd had it, perhaps to the slightest extent, but she'd had it. "I know that," she said faintly and drew closer. "I regret losing your trust that I would not kill you."

He watched her while she spoke, sending a thread of heat through her when his gaze dipped to her lips. Did he want to kiss her? Would she let him if he did?

"I regret it as well," he answered, and then pulled her toward the rear tower without another word.

He was taking her to where his men were. "You will no longer protect me?" she asked him, trying to calm her anxious heart. Was he finally delivering her to her fate?

He stopped before they crossed the short walkway and turned to her. "I protect ye fer the king."

Her expression grew dark. "Of course."

"Just agree with what I say."

"I can speak for myself."

"Not today."

She wanted to say more but he continued walking.

Anchored to him by the wrist, she had no choice but to follow him across the walkway and up the stone stairs to the narrow door to the tower.

Father Timothy greeted them on the other side and asked how she fared.

"I am alive—for now," she told him, a bit out of breath from keeping up with the commander's long strides.

The priest stopped them and drew his friend down so that he could whisper something into his ear.

The commander turned to her and watched her breathe, then kept his pace slow as he walked her through the short corridor to the massive doors that led inside.

Her heart pounded when she saw Amish and William, Rauf and Richard, standing with the rest of his men. What had Richard and the priest told them? Was her friend safe?

They all grew quiet when they saw her, or perhaps it was when they saw their commander lift his hand for silence.

"Aleysia was just found by me on the floor of her solar."

"I felt sleepy and tried to make it to my bed," she added, pressing her palm to her forehead for good measure. She ignored him when his slipped his gaze to her, but let him continue.

"It seems Lord de Bar tainted all the wine, includin' what ye found in the cellar. And though Aleysia served as his bottler—" he flicked his gaze to Rauf, "—she knew nothin' aboot it."

Relief flooded through her and made her feel lightheaded. She was thankful he was protecting her, but was that it? These men were dangerous. She knew what they wanted to do to the one who'd killed their friends. If doubt was allowed to creep in, they would start drawing their own conclusions.

She had more to say to them, to William and Rauf mostly. Her life and the lives of her friends could depend on it.

"I am sincerely dismayed that you all drank something that was meant for your harm—even if it only made you sleep. I consider some of you my friends." She smiled at William and then at Rauf. "I would not put my friends in jeopardy."

"We didna blame ye, lass," Rauf promised, returning her warm smile. "We knew 'twas de Bar's doin'."

The others agreed and welcomed her back into the fold.

"Ye are convincin', lass," the commander leaned in to whisper close to her ear. "Even I believe ye."

"Thank you," she whispered back.

He offered her a practiced smile and ushered her out of the large gathering hall before she had a chance to speak to anyone else. They left the tower and headed for the main stairs outside.

"Now where are we going?" She looked over her shoulder for Richard or Father Timothy but no one was following. Why was *she* following him? She should have insisted on staying with Richard. How could she betray her friends and her brother by liking this man, by wanting to fall into his arms and kiss him?

"I am takin' ye away from the men."

"You do not trust me with them."

"Or them with ye," he added and picked up his pace.

They reached the long, narrow stairway and began the descent. She paused for a moment to watch him. She told herself she was mad, and then hurried after him.

"You have my gratitude for helping me get out of that," she said, a few steps above him. "Even if 'twas for the king."

"I dinna know how much longer I will be able to keep ye safe if ye continue."

She wanted to tell him that she hadn't done it. He'd been correct. She wouldn't try to kill him. She hadn't wanted to kill him from the moment she set eyes on him. She could have let him move forward into the meadow of arrows. He'd been first in line, but she'd stopped him with her ill-aimed arrow. She could have stabbed him to death in the dungeon after rendering him almost helpless with a kick to the groin. And when they had fallen from a tree, she tried to wake him up instead of swiftly cutting his throat.

She could have, but she hadn't. She hated her weak resolve, but she hated even more the thought of his new misgivings about her.

She could tell him the truth about the wine and regain his trust, but she wouldn't put Richard in danger.

"You do not have to concern yourself with me any longer," she told him. "I may still try to strike or pinch you when you are overly infuriating." She stopped speaking when he turned to look at her with a wind-tossed strand of hair and amusement dancing across the cool surface of his eyes. "But I...no longer...want to kill you."

"That is comfortin' to know," he said with a teasing smile and then returned his attention to the steps.

Aleysia watched him reach the last one and walk toward the grass. She wondered what it would be like to surrender to her desires and set her mind on breaking through his heavy armor. Could she do it? Could she drag him out of his past and into the present? Why should she try? He was still her enemy. But he didn't treat her like he hated her. Even when he believed she'd managed to put what was left of his company to sleep, he still protected her. He hadn't laid his hands on her, and had even begun to trust her.

"Though I must tell ye," he called out, his deep voice wrapping around her like a glove, "the threat of a pinch is not enough to keep me from irritatin' ye."

His error was slowing his pace and waiting for her to catch up.

"Is that so?" She quirked her brow and gave his upper arm a hard pinch.

"Hell, lass!" he erupted, springing away from her. He rubbed his arm and glared at her. "I think I would prefer yer blade."

"I'll see what I can do." She walked toward the stairs to return to the keep but he caught her by the wrist, and pulled her back, gentler this time.

"Why wait?" he asked, giving her a slow half-smile. "With everythin' else that kept ye busy over the last four years, did ye find time to practice?"

"Every day," she told him, a bit breathless when he tugged her toward the grassy inner bailey. "I took my duty to kill the Scots who came here very seriously."

"We shall see." He came to a small area off to the side of the keep, where his men had left their extra weapons, swords and axes, shields and even maces propped against the wall.

He picked up a shield and a sword and tossed both to her. She let the shield fall into the grass but caught the sword by the hilt.

"Ye will be needin' that," he said, smirking at her discarded shield.

She shook her head. "'Tis too cumbersome."

"Verra well. Prepare," he said, pulling his sword free from its sheath and making it dance in the air.

Was this truly happening? Was she going to spar with him? How real was this going to get? What if she hurt him? She watched him swing his blade over his arm and rest it flat over his elbow. He stared at her down the length of it, his eyes harder than the steel. She doubted she would hurt him at all.

"Ready." He was thoughtful enough to warn before he swung.

She threw up her sword and blocked a blow to her neck that shook her arms all the way to her chest. He was holding back and, still, just blocking him nearly brought her to her knees. She blocked another strike to her waist, her shoulder, her knees. Over and over his assault continued, until after only a few moments, she leaped away and held up her hands, too exhausted to continue. Nothing she had trained for had prepared her for the strength and ferocity of his arm. She didn't have the power to hold him off. If she was going to gain a point, she had to make a move swiftly. There was no time for defense.

She straightened her shoulders and wiped her forehead with the back of her hand. "Ready," she said and sprang forward. She caught sight of his smile before she jabbed, stabbed, and thrust. He blocked every strike with effortless ease. She couldn't land a single blow.

A memory of practicing with Giles flashed across her thoughts. He was thirteen years older than she and more like a father than a brother. He made her practice archery every day and commissioned Sir Richard and the other knights to help her learn swordplay when he was away, which was often. She knew she possessed skill. She had even bested Giles once after he'd returned from the Holy Land.

The commander lifted his sword for a swipe to her ribs. Instead of trying to block it, she crouched as low as she could go and swept her leg across his ankles. He went down on his back with a resounding thump. She wondered if his head hit the ground.

She didn't waste time thinking about it now, but leaped atop him and held the edge of her blade against his throat.

Now was the time to win back his trust.

She leaned down, until she could feel his breath on her face and stared into his eyes. "Will I kill you, Commander?"

She had no idea what his reaction would be to her besting him. She could hardly believe it herself. She didn't think it happened often. But he wasn't angry.

His eyes sparked with warmth and humor as they drank her in. His smile washed over her like a gentle caress in the midst of all the ice.

"Nae, lass," he said, his voice, low and rough. "Ye willna kill me."

She felt lost in his smile, swept away on foolish, fanciful thoughts of leaning down just a bit further and kissing him.

"What the hell is this?" someone shouted.

"Has she killed him?" another male voice called out.

Aleysia realized immediately what his men were seeing and tossed her blade in the grass.

Unconcerned with what might be about to happen, the commander continued to smile at her, but the sensual slant of his mouth and the challenging quirk of his brow proved that she was on her own.

"He lives!" she shouted, pushing off him. She looked down one last time and lifted her chin. "We were sparring good-naturedly," she added with a smile.

"And ye bested him?" Father Timothy asked, stunned, and stepped forward from the small crowd of men.

"Aye, she bested me," the commander confirmed, finally rising to his feet. "She swept me off my feet."

The men stared at him, slack-jawed and struck dumb.

And then Rauf winked at the others and they all began to smile as if they understood some secret meaning to his words.

Aleysia was about to correct them but she caught the commander's eyes as he began to look away from her. Their gazes locked for an instant, the residue of amusement...and something else she couldn't define, still shone in his eyes.

She wanted to smile at him, but Richard was watching her and she would not—she could not—let him see her betrayal.

Commander Cainnech MacPherson was a Scot, worse, a Highlander, the most savage of them all and she was supposed to hate him.

But she didn't.

Chapter Sixteen

"**M**ORE OF THE villagers have returned."

Cain stood on the battlements and swept his gaze toward the village dotted with firelight. People had been returning all day, anxious to see their lady. He'd let her greet them all and settle their nerves with her confident smiles. He'd stayed in the background, listening and watching her mostly, until he finally had to leave her alone.

He probably shouldn't have. Who knew what the hell she could plan against him if left to her own devices? But he had to leave. Being near her was driving him mad.

She had asked his forgiveness for tainting the wine and he'd granted it. He worried that he would grant her anything.

If he lived to be as old as Sir Richard, he would never forget the way she looked poised and ready to fight him, her sword held above her shoulder, her long, black braid dangling down her bodice. He never expected her to stand up to his strikes. But she'd braced herself on steady, shapely legs, boot heels to the ground. Who taught her how to fight? Her brother? Of course, Cain didn't use his full strength to strike her blade, but still, she held up. Damn it, but it stirred his blood.

When she ducked low to avoid his next blow and physically swept him off his feet—well, he could have died happily at the edge of her blade, her face, the last thing he saw.

"Has Miss d'Argentan seen to them?" he asked the priest without turning to look at him. He wasn't certain what his long-time friend would see. Just speaking her name brought to mind her viperous tongue and the glory of her face. He liked being around her, but it made him feel uncomfortable in his own skin, as if he were someone else. Someone he didn't know.

"She is with some of her staff that have also returned," the priest informed him. "One called Matilda, whom Aleysia was most happy to see."

Aleysia. Cain wanted to speak it, feel it on his tongue. What had befallen him? He was most likely ill from something. What the hell else had she poisoned? "Where are they?" he asked, trying to keep from spinning around, grasping the priest by the collar of his robes, and begging him for help.

"In Aleysia's solar. William was with them earlier."

Was William safe with her? He knew he was a fool for believing her, but he didn't think she would hurt William.

Still, what did he know of her save that she was headstrong and determined to fight with him at every turn? And she'd already killed some of his men. But she'd been protecting her home—something he wished he could have done when his was taken.

He'd never faced an opponent like her before. When they weren't fighting, or she wasn't trying to kill him, she made him want to smile at her clever wit and seductive smile.

"I would prefer it if William wasna alone with her, and we should put Amish at her door," he said, trying to regain his composure.

"Why?"

"What d'ye mean, why?" Cain finally turned. "The lad doesna know how skilled she is with her tongue *and* with a sword."

"What will she gain by harmin' Will?" the priest asked, his dark eyes tender as always. "Escape? She could have easily escaped last eve, Cainnech. She began this fight to stay here. This is her home. She doesna want to be handed over to Edward and she doesna want to go to Normandy."

"Since when does it matter what any of us want?" he asked, not looking for an answer. His life was his answer.

Father Timothy knew it and looked defeated for the first time since Cain had known him.

"It matters to me," his friend finally said on a quiet voice. "If there is a way fer her to stay, ye must tell her how to do it."

"I dinna wish to involve myself with what happens to Lismoor once I leave it, which will be as soon as I hear from the king."

"Cainnech, ye must help her prepare to swear fealty to—"

"Why do I have to help her? I owe her nothin'. She killed nine of my men, lest ye ferget!"

"God wants ye to help her," the priest insisted.

"I owe Him nothin' either," Cain sneered. "What has He done fer me?"

"He has continued to keep ye alive long enough fer this, I suspect." The priest held up his hands as if he were just guessing.

"Fer what?" Cain asked, stunned. "Fer *her*?" He threw back his head and laughed. "Is that what I get? A lass who wants me dead?"

But she'd proven that she didn't want him dead. In fact, he was sure the fiery spark in her eyes was beginning to burn with a different kind of passion—for his mouth, his touch, and, mayhap, the thing he was most unwilling to give, his heart.

What did she want from him, and why did she want it? How long could he resist her? He had to. His life depended on it. "I dinna want her."

"Cainnech—"

"And as fer keepin' me alive, my battle-arm has done that."

"Careful," the priest warned. "Pride has brought down bigger men than ye, Son."

Cain shook his head. "Nae, Father. I remember the stories ye told, from Adam, to David, to Solomon. Even poor Samson. All taken down by women. I willna make that same error."

He stepped around his friend and left the battlements. He needed to stop whatever Aleysia d'Argentan was doing to him. He didn't know how to stop it, since he had no idea what the hell was happening to him. Was he going soft? He shook with the thought of it. If so, she was the cause. He had to find her and tell her they could no longer practice together—or do much of anything else together, since they always seemed to end up on the ground.

He had other, more important things to see to, like hunting and keeping his men in good condition, and getting a good night's damned sleep.

He marched toward her solar, determined to remain resolute in his decision to stay away from her.

He approached her door and found it ajar. He heard her honeyed voice from the other side and paused to listen.

"The commander is a bit of a brute, but he has not been unkind to me or the others. You have nothing to fear from him or his men. When you meet him, try not to stare for he is both pleasing and terrifying to the eye."

Cain was surprised to hear what she thought of his appearance. He wasn't certain how he felt about it. He supposed it was a good thing to appear terrifying, but he didn't want to frighten *her*. And how did he feel about being pleasing to her eye? He'd never concerned himself with how he looked before. He combed his hair to keep it from knotting and getting caught in things. He washed to keep from stinking.

He ran his palm over his jaw. He should have shaved his face.

Nae. He dropped his hand and reached for the door. He didn't care if God wanted them together. He wouldn't let her change who he was. She'd killed his men. She served the English king. As long as she did, he could never...care for her. Though to be honest, he could never care for her for any reason. He didn't believe he was capable of wanting and forming attachments, which made his reactions to her even more confusing.

"Now tell me of Elizabeth," came her melodious voice. "Are you certain she went back to the abbey? Why did she not stay with you?"

"Oh, Aleysia," cried another female voice, "'twas just awful. We slept in the forest the first several nights. Many of us had nowhere else to go and the ones who had families close by could not take all of us, so we were turned away. Elizabeth could not do it. She decided to return to the abbey in Newton on the Moor rather than live in the woods. I do not blame her really."

"Mattie, I will never forgive myself for what I put you and the others through."

Aleysia's voice broke through his reasoning, his anger, and weighed him down with guilt. Why? He'd done his duty. He'd reclaimed Scottish land. He was loyal to the Scottish throne. Wasn't he? Or was the war more personal for him? Had he had enough killing?

"I would have you know, Mattie," she continued, "I did everything in my power to stop this but, alas, I failed."

Cain's heart raced. Was William still with them? Had she told him the truth? What if he told the men?

Without another thought, he plunged inside the room and looked around.

William was not with them. Aleysi—Miss d'Argentan sat on her bed with another lass, whom he guessed was Matilda. She was younger than Cain had expected. She looked to be about sixteen or seventeen summers, with a fair complexion, and a long, white-blonde braid slung over her shoulder. Her pale blue eyes opened wide when she saw him.

Cain remembered what he'd heard and tried not to look terrifying.

"Welcome back to yer home," he said to the girl. "I am Commander MacPherson."

Her eyes darted to Aleysia, who smiled reassuringly at her. "This is Matilda, my friend and handmaiden."

He nodded then turned his gaze to Aleysia. "I was wonderin' if I could have a word with ye in private."

She turned to her handmaiden. "Do you mind, Mattie?"

The young lass shook her head and scurried toward the door in her tattered skirts. "I have much to do," she called out and left the solar, closing the door behind her.

When they were alone, Aleysia looked up at him waiting for him to continue.

Where should he begin? "I have been…" He brushed a wrinkle out of his léine. "Ehm…thinkin' aboot things—"

"What things?"

He looked up. Hell, why did she have to be so lovely? He could be looking into a room of a hundred lasses and she would stand out among them. It didn't matter. He had to hold to his convictions. What kind of pitiful fool was he that he should lose his nerve when faced with his opponent? He wouldn't let her do it.

"I dinna think we should—" He paused when she slid off the bed and went to her wooden chest to retrieve her comb.

"Go on," she said with her back to him and waving her hand over her shoulder. "I am listening."

"I would like yer full attention."

She sighed and turned to him with her comb in her hand. "Aye, Commander."

He wished he'd kept his mouth shut about having her full attention. It was easier with her back to him. Hell, her large, fiery eyes nearly melted him. What was she doing? Why was she unbraiding her hair?

"Well?" she asked, moving her delicate fingers through her raven plait until it was set free to cascade over her shoulders. "You do not think we should what?"

He swallowed then looked away. He took another instant to remember what he wanted to tell her. "I dinna think we should spend so much time together."

Damn it! It didn't come out correctly.

"That has not been up to me, Commander."

He breathed in deeply, which was an error because the air smelled like her. "Well." He let his gaze fall to her again. She was running her comb through her long tresses, watching him, "From now on 'twill be."

"Why?" she asked with a trace of amusement lighting her eyes.

"Why d'ye find this humorous?"

"Why did you need to come here and tell me if not being around you was up to me from now on? You could have just stayed away. Do you think I would seek you out?"

How had he lost control of this conversation? "Nae, but ye might have a query."

"I see," she said, combing with one hand, stroking with the other. "So you do not want to see or speak to me at all. Why?" she asked softly. The humor in her gaze changed to confusion with a blink of her eyes. "Have I angered you?"

What should he say now? He wasn't expecting to have his decision questioned. "It has nothin' to do with that. 'Tis just better this way."

"I see," she said again, as if she understood. She didn't. She couldn't. "If you wish to be secretive about it, I shall just draw my own conclusions."

He laughed but it sounded hollow to his ears. "And what conclusions will they be?"

She slanted her gaze and her smile as she turned away from him. "Perhaps, you are fond of me and you do not want to be."

"Ye are my enemy," he reminded her, and himself, on a low growl.

"True." She lowered her lashes, shielding her gaze from him. "I can see how being fond of your enemy would be a dilemma."

What? He hadn't said he was fond of her. Had he? She twisted his words with such effortless ease, he wasn't sure exactly what he'd said. "Miss d'Argentan—"

"I thought we were calling me Aleysia, granddaughter of the steward."

"Aleysia," he corrected, and then threw her an impatient look for interrupting again and for making him say her name. "Dinna make things up in yer bonny head, lady. I—" He stopped while her smile softened on him and a slight blush stole across her cheeks. "—I am not fond of ye," he continued in a low, heavy voice. "I mean, I...dinna know ye well enough to be fond of—I do think verra highly of ye. Higher than most, but—"

"I am your enemy," she finished for him.

He nodded and crossed his arms over his chest like a shield to guard his heart when she stepped closer.

"I refuse," she said, close enough for him to reach out and touch her.

"Refuse what?"

She walked around him, causing him to uncross his arms and free them at his sides, ready to fight. It was a reflex whenever someone was close behind him. When she faced him again, she was closer—and he had no shield. "I refuse to stay away from you."

He stared at her for a moment. What was this she said on the softest of breaths? She refused? His belly sank with dread while his blood raced through his veins like fire.

"At least until everyone has returned to Lismoor and things are settled with the Bruce," she finished, stepping away from him.

He watched her go, wanting to reach for her, needing to remain still and let her go.

She hoped to stay here and she thought he was going to help her. He would do what he could but, in the end, Cain suspected she would die fighting.

Damn it! Father Timothy was right. He needed to tell her about the condition, soften the blow, help her understand what she had to do.

"Mi—Aley—" he grit his teeth, "Lady, my wish fer ye is that ye remain here, unwed. But—"

"But?" She turned to him again, her eyes curious and dreadful.

Why had he mentioned it? Why hadn't he left the room? When had he become a coward? "But ye must promise yer allegiance..." She was already moving toward him. He had the urge to step back. He stood his ground and straightened his shoulders. "...to King Robert."

He readied himself for a strike. He wished she would try to hit him, kill him, anything but stare at him as if he'd just pulled out her heart and held it to her face.

"'Tis the only way," he said quietly.

She shook her head. "Never."

Her eyes on him hardened and, for a moment, he hated himself more than he ever had in his life.

"I want you to know that," she continued, tearing away at heavy defenses. "I will never swear my allegiance to him. Not for Lismoor. Not for anything."

He wanted to take hold of her and shake her. "Ye would give up everythin' because ye canna lie to a man's face?"

"And spit in my brother's at the same time! You lied to me!"

"Nae," he said, trying not to shout back at her. "I didna tell ye everythin'."

She looked around for something to fling at him. There was nothing, so she threw herself at him instead. He caught her and held her while she pummeled him with her fists. "Get out! You have your wish! I will stay away from you!"

He should have been happy, relieved by her words. But he felt every slight blow she hit him with like a hammer to his flesh.

Hell, he was in trouble. He wasn't supposed to care.

But he did.

CHAPTER SEVENTEEN

ALEYSIA DIDN'T SPEAK to him again for the next four days. In fact, she did everything in her power to avoid him. Which was what he wanted. She spent most of her time with Matilda, and more time than he would have expected with Father Timothy and William.

Cain didn't mind being alone. The first day. The trouble wasn't loneliness. He'd been alone his whole life. He liked eating alone on the battlements with just his thoughts. But his familiar, comforting reasonings had turned traitor on him, and filled his head with images of her, angry and rebellious, like a wild mare never to be tamed. What fool would ever want to tame her?

Her smile invaded the darkest recesses of his being, shaking him from the foundation. The more he forbade himself to think about her, the more things about her he remembered, like the stubborn tilt of her jaw, the way she looked with her long, black locks flowing freely. Hell, even her damned scent haunted him.

He'd looked death straight in the face from an early age. He didn't fear it. It was nothing compared to what he saw in her eyes when he told her about Robert.

But it was better if she never forgave him—better if she hated him.

Let Father Timothy convince her how to keep her holdings. It was best that Cain had no more contact with her.

He'd put away his emotions as a boy. The loss of his family had been too great. He'd wanted to die more days than he wanted to live. It was Father Timothy who had kept his will to survive alive. He'd never let himself care for anyone since then. Emotions were a soldier's weakness, and love, the most dangerous.

But he found himself seeking her out, watching her from across the hall while she and Matilda rehung the tapestries. She and her handmaiden had also retrieved Aleysia's clothes from wherever she had hidden them, providing the lady of the castle with more breeches and léines to wear while she flitted around, seeing to the daily needs of her home.

In the early morning of the fifth day, someone knocked at the door to the small room he'd chosen for himself while he readied for a day of hunting and staying away from the keep.

When he saw Father Timothy, he waved him inside and finished securing his plaid. "All is well, Father?"

The priest nodded and tucked his hands into the wide sleeves of his robes. "Aye, all is well, Cainnech. As well as can be expected."

Cain gritted his teeth and pulled on his boots. He knew the priest well enough to know something was vexing him. "What is it?" If it had anything to do with Miss d'Argentan, he wasn't sure he wanted to know.

"Ye have not been practicin'," his friend began.

"I have been practicin' alone while the rest of ye are asleep. Ye know I like the quiet."

The priest waved his words away and gave him a frank look. "I mean with the men. They have barely seen ye in four days. They need to see a bigger presence from ye, especially now with more maids in the keep, aye?"

"Aye," he muttered. He hated when the priest was right.

"What is it?" his friend went on. "What has befallen ye? Why are ye hidin' away in—"

"I am not hidin' away anywhere."

"Aye. Aye, ye are, Son. I know ye told Aleysia the truth and I know she has refused to swear fealty to Robert. We will address that later. What concerns me now is why ye are goin' to such lengths to avoid her? I know she is angry with ye but that hasna stopped ye before. Is there somethin' ye would like to tell me? Cainnech," he paused to watch Cain sweep his cloak over his shoulders and then pick up his quiver and bow. "Where are ye goin'?"

"Huntin'."

His friend reached out for his arm. "Be careful."

"I know where I'm goin'," Cain assured him.

"Do ye?" the priest asked. "I think if ye could see clearly, ye would run the other way."

Cain regarded him with affection. He appreciated that the priest cared for and worried about him. But Father Timothy wasn't always right. And this was one of those times. "Soon, we will be away from Lismoor and Rothbury. We will put all this behind us and rest at Whitton, aye?"

"Do ye truly believe 'twill be so easy?"

Cain had had enough of this talk. He needed to stay strong and his friend wasn't helping. "We will speak more later," he said and left the room.

How long would it take him to forget her? Not long, he hoped. The less he had to remember, the quicker it would be.

He thought he heard her laughter ringing through the corridors. It tempted him to go in search of her. He hadn't smiled in four days. Before he met her, he rarely smiled. Why would he miss such a ridiculous thing?

He made his determined way outside and descended the stairs quickly. When he passed the grassy yard and heard the sounds of his men fighting, he went to have a look.

William and Rauf were sparring, as were Amish and Duncan, among others. Aleysia stood off to the side in breeches and a hooded cloak, watching and looking as if she was ready to leap in at any moment.

The sight of her close by, her face drenched in the light of a new day, made his senses reel. He grew nearer to her, pulled by an unseen tether. She looked up from William who'd been laid out flat by Rauf's shield. When she saw Cain, she lifted her fingers under her hood to the wind-tossed tendrils around her face. She lowered her gaze when he reached her.

He didn't know if he should greet her, or speak to her at all. But now that he was here, he didn't want to be anywhere else.

He opened his mouth, though he still wasn't sure what to say.

"Commander," Amish called out, halting his match to greet him. "'Tis good to have ye with us this morn. Practicin' with this bunch is like fightin' the trees."

Cain waited while those men who took insult had their say. He thought about telling them he was just here to have a look and then he was going hunting. But he thought of what Father Timothy had told him about being more of a presence now that the castle staff and the old knights had returned.

And he did enjoy sparring with Amish. The brawny Highlander had sometimes winded him.

He stepped forward, pulling his cloak free and handing it to William in exchange for Will's shield.

"I think a more interesting match," William said in a loud voice, proving he wanted no mercy from Cain when it was his turn to fight, "would be between Aleysia and the commander."

Cain would kill him later. The last thing he wanted to do was end up in the grass with her again.

"I had better not." Her honeyed voice seeped down deep into his bones. "This time, I fear I might kill him."

Her words pulled a smile from him. He was glad she refused, but part of him thrilled at the thought of her ready to take him on. All the reasons he should go hunting and stay away flashed across his mind, but he didn't listen to any of them as he freed his axe from his belt and flipped it over in his hand. "Well then, Amish. Let us be at it then."

The strapping brute lifted his shield and grinned through his fiery beard.

Cain struck the first blow, almost bringing Amish to his knees. But his second would not go down so easily. Cain smiled, glad Amish was on his side. They moved around the small practice field, kicking up tufts of grass and sending wood and sparks flying.

Amish's stamina and powerful arm was difficult to withstand, but Cain had fought men like him in true battle—and he never lost. He could have killed his second twice now, but Amish wanted a fight, so Cain gave him one. He blocked and ducked and finally brought the hulking warrior to his knees.

"Well done, Amish," he said and offered his second a hand up. "Ye've been practicin'."

"Glad ye could tell, Commander," Amish smiled beneath all the fur.

Cain nodded. "Keep the rest of them in line."

"Aye, Sir."

"William," Cain said next, turning to him for his cloak. "Remember, yer shield is a weapon. Dinna just use it fer defense."

"Aye, Commander," the lad was quick to reply.

Cain turned to the men and commanded that they treat the castle staff with the highest respect or they would answer to him.

His gaze naturally fell to Aleysia next. Her eyes narrowed on him, skipping, just for an instant, down the rest of him. "Do you want accolades from me?" she asked, returning her gaze to his.

"Only if ye are compelled to give them."

She looked about to say one thing, and then changed her mind, judging by the sudden fire sparking her mesmerizing green eyes. "You would not be here to spar with Amish if our fight had been a true one."

He stepped closer and then bent the rest of the way, until his breath was filled with the scent of her. "If our fight had been a true one," he said, keeping his voice low, "ye wouldna have lasted longer than two breaths."

She wanted to say something. He could see it in her eyes. But she knew he was correct.

He straightened to his full height, allowed himself to smile at her, and then stepped away.

"Where are you going?" she called out, hurrying after him.

He stopped and looked at her and then at the men all gaping at them.

"D'ye all want to practice with me now then?" Cain called out.

They promptly turned away, pretending interest in anything but the two of them.

"I am goin' huntin'," he told her next.

He took a step to move on, but she bounded in front of him. "How long are you going to avoid me?"

He stepped back, lest a strong enough wind cast her into his arms. "I thought we agreed—"

He would have expected a dagger. Hell, he would have preferred one instead of the pain from her twisting fingers pinching his arm.

"We did not agree! I told you I would not stay away and then I learned you lied to me and told you to get out!"

"Ye said I had my wish and ye would stay away from me," he corrected, glaring at her and holding his hand over his bruised arm.

"I was angry with you! But you, it seems, are more than that!"

"What?" His heart felt as if it had just stopped beating. Were his reactions to her so obvious? Apparently so, for even Father Timothy had accused him of hiding.

"You truly do hate me."

He wanted to laugh with relief but, hell, she was serious! She looked more unhappy than angry. Why would she be? Trying to trick him into agreeing to something was one thing. She would be clever in trying to gain his favor, mayhap keeping him here to join in her battle against his own countrymen. But he didn't believe she was trying to trick him. What he saw in her eyes was real. She didn't want him to hate her.

"My intention is not meant to make ye believe I hate ye," he told her. He wanted to look away—or say more, but he could do neither.

"What is it meant to make me believe then?" she asked, dipping her head and shielding her eyes with her hood.

Hell, what had he gotten himself into? He looked around, wishing for help. None came. "Come," he said taking hold of her arm. "I dinna want to speak in front of the men."

She didn't resist when he pulled her along. He wasn't certain if that was a good thing or a bad thing.

When they stepped beyond the curtain wall, he stopped, having had enough time to prepare himself—as he would for any battle.

"I dinna hate ye," he began on a low rumble. "but—" A cool gust of wind, laced with the fragrance of her hair, blew her hood away from her face. He lifted his hand to a stray lock of hair whipping across her lips. "Ye were correct, lass. I am fond of ye, but I canna—"

"So you lied to me about that, as well," she said accusingly and flipped her hood back up.

He smiled, but he wanted to throttle her. "I dinna see any point in—"

"—saying another word?" she asked tersely. "Since I will not believe anything you tell me? You are correct. I am going back to William and the others." She turned to head back to the inner yard. "At least they—"

He reached out and caught her wrist. He didn't think about any of the reasons he shouldn't, but pulled her back to him, lifting her wrist over his shoulder and snaking his other arm around her waist. She didn't try to stop him when he pulled her in closer, but closed both arms around his neck. When he dipped his head close to hers, she closed her eyes and waited to receive him.

He kissed her with a growl of pure demand, forgetting everything but the wind and the feel of her yielding body melding against his. With a flick of his tongue, he coaxed open her lips and swept it inside her.

She tasted like honey and innocence, intoxicating him and vanquishing his fears.

She moved her fingers through his hair and held on while he devoured her softness.

His hands, so much larger than every part of her, swept over her back, down her spine, drawing her closer. She tugged on his hair, keeping him close, until he breathed her, in and out.

He thought kissing her might be enough to satisfy this need he had of her. But as she answered his passion with passion of her own, he knew he was wrong. He wanted her. Every part of her. He wanted to whisk her away somewhere and...no, she was too dangerous. He wouldn't risk dying a second time.

He broke their kiss, and stepped back, breaking their embrace as well. "I shouldna have done that."

She lifted her fingertips to her lips and looked at him and then away. "Aye, you should not have."

He wasn't sorry that he had. "I fear I may do it again if I dinna go..." He took another reluctant step back. "Now."

She nodded, still touching her mouth, drawing his eyes there again. "Safe hunting."

He didn't want to leave her, but he needed to before he defied everything and carried her back to the keep.

He pushed back his bow over his shoulder, pulled up his hood, and left.

CHAPTER EIGHTEEN

ALEYSIA LET HER hand fall to her side and watched the commander walk away from her after a kiss that made her doubt everything she thought she knew, including her name.

She'd only been kissed intimately twice in her life. She'd been fifteen and curious. It had been nothing like this. Emotions swelled up in her and, for some mad reason, she wanted to weep.

She understood his regret, for she felt it, too. His kiss, his embrace, made her feel too much. This was not some fling with a handsome Highlander. This was more. This warmed her knees and a place below her belly. This made her feel alive and reborn. How would she tell everyone? Richard and the others? Could something grow between them? She knew she was attracted to him and that she sometimes wanted to beat him over the head with something, but she had no idea until he kissed her how much of her he was beginning to claim.

She watched him, his broad shoulders growing small in the distance. He was heading for the trees—to go hunting. She took a step forward, and then looked back at the curtain wall.

She didn't want to return to the men practicing, back to Richard constantly trying to convince her to go back to Normandy with him.

Thank God for Father Timothy always changing the topic and even standing up for her desire to stay. She would have been content to be left alone at Lismoor—after she lied to the Bruce and promised him her fealty. She'd decided to do it last eve. She hadn't prepared for four years only to give it up to some arrogant king. She would feed his ears if that was what it took to keep her home.

But now, after the commander's kiss, she thought about what it would be like to stay here *with him.*

Was she mad? He was correct. They were enemies. But she'd felt like his enemy for the last four days and she didn't like it.

He didn't hate her. No man could kiss her the way he had and hate her.

She touched her lips again and then ran back to the castle, but only to lift one of the men's bows and quiver of arrows. She escaped without even Mattie seeing her, through her tunnel, and came out at the eastern edge of the forest. She'd have to make a half-circle through the woods, but she would find him. The question was, did he hunt from above or on the ground?

And why was she following him?

She smiled, not caring why, and took off up a slanted tree.

ALEYSIA SAW THE roebuck go still. She crouched low in the cradle of two branches and looked around her, knowing the commander was near and finally spotting him in a tree to the south of her, ready to shoot.

She nocked an arrow, aimed, and let it fly. An instant before him.

The buck went down and the critters around him in the bramble scattered.

The commander found her in the trees and stood up. He started toward her, running across branches and planks as if he'd been doing it for four years. If she didn't know him—if he hadn't just kissed her as if his life depended on it, she would have run for her life.

It didn't take him long to reach her. He stopped, a few feet away, settling his boots on a wide, painted plank and his arms on a branch overhead.

"What d'ye think ye're doin'?" he asked in his low, resonant voice. His eyes on her were as still as the buck's had been.

"I'm hunting. Same as you."

He looked as if he were trying to keep from laughing or knocking her out of the tree. "The same buck 'twould seem."

"I have had my eye on it for a good amount of time now," she replied, doing her best to appear unaffected by him and the fact that he was just a few steps away.

"When did ye decide to go huntin'?"

"I believe you will recall me mentioning that I wanted to hunt for the villagers."

Then he cast her a doubtful look. "And ye are just gettin' to it now?"

She chewed her lip and thought about giving him a false reason but, more than likely, he wouldn't believe her. And she *had* followed him. Why deny it? "I decided to go soon after you left."

His smile started at one corner of his succulent mouth and then shone full force on her. He said nothing for a moment, staring at her with a look of acceptance creeping into his eyes, as if he finally realized there was no point in trying to keep her away.

She watched the way his plaid moved around his legs when he left his plank and came to sit on a bough close to where she was.

"Ye're makin' this verra difficult, lass," he said with the residue of his smile aimed at the ground.

She lowered herself into the cradle and sat. He was an arm's length away and a forty foot drop threatened. She wouldn't argue with him about this. Whatever was going on between them was wrong. It went against everything for which they had given up years of their lives. She felt shame over her desires involving him. "'Tis difficult for me, as well. I convinced my friends that I would kill you all. Instead, I find myself—" She snapped her mouth shut and shifted between the branches. She looked at him and caught him looking back. "I find myself drawn to you." There. It was the truth—just not all of it.

"I shouldna have kissed ye," he said hoarsely, turning toward her. "I will be leavin' once I have secured yer place here."

She was thankful for his willingness to help her. But he'd carefully skirted around her confession and made a point of letting her know he was leaving.

"Why did you kiss me?"

The branch he was sitting on cracked and echoed through the trees.

His eyes opened wider but he kept himself still.

Aleysia rose with her heart thundering in her chest. "Come," she coaxed in a quiet voice and held out her hand. "Jump!"

He didn't hesitate, but leaped to his feet, and then straight for her. The bough beneath him splintered and fell away, hitting other branches on the way down.

Aleysia looked into his eyes as he teetered on the edge of one of her forked branches, his hand attached to hers.

She could let him fall. He would likely die.

She pulled him in. He landed in her arms, hard against her. His heart thumped between them. His gaze moved over her as if she were cool, crisp water for his parched body.

"I am tempted to replace Amish with ye as my second."

She smiled at his praise and then let him go. It was better if he never kissed her again, better if he left Lismoor soon.

"Let's be off these branches," she said, turning away. "I do not know if they can hold us both."

She moved away quickly, leading the way over a plank and a few lower branches until it was safe enough to jump. She watched him land with the agility of a cat, appreciating even more his strong, lithe body.

They checked on the buck but rather than take it to the village right away, they decided to leave it where it had fallen and return for it later.

"Who taught ye to shoot?" the commander asked her.

"I taught myself," she told him. "I did not do well." She smiled, remembering. "But when Giles saw my interest, he made certain that I had the best instructors."

"And fightin'?" he asked, walking alongside her on the ground. "Who taught ye to sweep yer leg across yer opponent's? 'Tis a sure way to bring yer enemy down."

She wanted to smile at the lilt of his voice. She was surprised and guilt-ridden that she found the sound of him so pleasing.

"I would like ye to teach it to me, so that I can teach the men."

She gaped up at him as if he were mad. "You would like me to help my enemies?"

He tilted his head just enough for her to look into his blue eyes. She saw the deadly man he could be.

"Are we yer enemies then, Aleysia?"

She wanted to close her eyes and remember how her name sounded on his lips. Aye, he was a wild Scot, but she saw someone else. Someone, perhaps, his men did not see. He'd been patient and merciful despite all she had done. And somehow, he managed to penetrate all her defenses with his reluctant smile and passionate kiss.

She was fully aware of what could never be, but she didn't want to think on it now.

"Let us forget who we are and the war going on around us for a little while and just enjoy the day."

He looked as if he were about to laugh. It appeared that forgetting the war was impossible for him. Well, he was just going to have to do it if he wanted to spend time with her.

Did he want to? She was the one who'd come looking for him, after all.

With a carefree shrug, she continued on, stepping around a few ancient oaks. He followed her to a shady path that was too narrow for them to continue walking together. The commander followed her. She turned to smile at him as the path opened and he paused to let a dragonfly hover before him in a thin shaft of sunlight seeping through the canopy.

Aleysia watched, entranced by the sight of him stepping through the light like some elven king who belonged here.

The path was surrounded on both sides by overgrown wild strawberries. Aleysia picked one and offered it to him. "Try it. 'Tis delicious."

He took the fruit from her fingers and put it in his mouth. She picked another for herself and ate it. They both smiled with delight.

"I would come here every day if I lived here," he said, picking more.

She leaned closer to him and whispered. "I do." Then, with a short squeal of excitement, she took his hand and hurried along the path. "This way!" She pulled him around a bend, toward a small opening in the thick bramble.

Why was she sharing this place with him? She'd stumbled upon it years ago. No one knew of it. It was where she came to rest after practicing all day or building in the forest.

After what Father Timothy had told her about the commander's childhood, she thought, perhaps, he needed a rest, too.

She stepped out into a sunlit glade, carpeted in bluebells and purple orchids, surrounded on every side by plank-free trees and overgrown bramble.

She turned to watch his reaction to her private little paradise and was surprised to see him close his eyes rather than take in the sight.

"This is what ye smell like." He opened his eyes and smiled, first at her, and then at the glade. As he took in the vision before him, he exhaled and something warm—something that came from the inside—filled his gaze.

"'Tis like I stepped into someplace that doesna belong here in this world." He moved forward and then stopped and looked at his boots crushing the bluebells.

"They will spring back up when you move," she reassured him and pulled off her hood. "I sit in them all the time." She looked around at all the flowers and smiled shyly, feeling silly for confessing such a thing to him. "I even lie in them."

She paused for a moment. "Come." She closed her fingers around his much larger ones and tugged him toward the middle of the glade. "Come and sit."

She felt his reluctance and wondered how long he would deny what he was feeling. He was terrified of it. And she should be terrified, too. Why wasn't she? Why was she more afraid of him leaving Lismoor or, God forbid, being forced to wed someone else?

He sat with her in the flowers and stretched out his long legs. He leaned back on his palms and settled his gaze on hers. "Ye seem at peace aboot King Robert."

"I am," she said with a slant of her lips. "I'm going to lie to him. You helped me decide."

"How did I do that?" he asked with a trace of humor racing across his eyes.

"You told me to," she reminded him.

"I would never tell ye to lie to the king," he defended himself, and then laughed when she tossed him an irritated look. "I will help ye."

"Why?" she asked, giving him a candid look. "Why would you help me lie to your king?"

"To keep yer home," he answered easily.

"But why? Why do you care?" She wanted to try to make a little more sense of him—of things between them.

"I…I dinna know." He shook his head and looked up at the sky.

She waited a moment for more and then lay down beside him. "'Tis better like this."

He looked down at her and smiled, then lifted his palms out of the bluebells and lay back. "Ye're correct. 'Tis better."

They lay in silence for a moment or two before he spoke again. "I am not one fer carin' fer things…or people. Things change and people die."

"Aye," she sighed, staring at the peaceful heavens. She understood. She lost her parents to illness and her life changed. She lost her brother to the war and her life changed again. Still, she offered, "My life was easy compared to yours."

He turned his head in the flowers and stared at her. "What d'ye know of my life?"

She didn't realize she'd spoken out loud. She wanted to cringe but he was watching her. "Just what Father Timothy told me."

He scowled and his face went dark. "What did he tell ye?"

The last thing she wanted to do was get the priest in trouble. She feared it was too late. "He loves you very much."

He sat up, shielding her from the sun. He raked his hands over his face and then bent his knees and rested his elbows on them. He inhaled a deep breath, stretching his léine across his shoulders.

"I know he does," came his husky reply. "What did he tell ye?"

Was he angry with Father Timothy or was it love that produced such a tortured response?

She told him what the priest had revealed. When she was done, she felt even more emotion for him.

"That is everythin'," he said, lying back again and staring up at the sky.

"'Tis just the horrific facts," she told him softly. "'Tis not everything."

"What else is there?"

"There is you, and who it made you."

"It made me strong."

"Aye," she whispered, trying with her last ounce of strength not to weep for him.

"It made me angry," he said after a long pause. "Verra angry."

"You are angry still." She stayed silent while he turned to look at her.

He rolled a few words around in his mouth, but said none of them. Finally, he turned again toward the heavens. "I lost everythin' because the English were permitted to raid any village they desired, and do whatever they wished to the people who lived there."

He didn't raid villages. She was glad, and now she knew why.

"Do you remember anything from your life before then?"

"Nae."

He scowled at her, but he should know by now that it wouldn't deter her. "Do you try to remember?"

"Nae." More scowling.

"Forgive me," she said. "I did not mean to bring up difficult memories."

Silence ensued. Then he said, "I dream of them sometimes. But I dinna see their faces."

Aleysia closed her eyes and bit her lip. She could not begin to understand what he must have endured as a boy. "I am sorry that happened to you, Cainnech."

He leaned up on an elbow to look down at her. She wondered if he'd ever heard or thought to hear someone apologize. He appeared a bit stunned and at a loss for anything else to say.

"I was taught to hate the Scots," she continued in a quiet voice. "I did not stop to think about what the English have done."

"We just want to be free."

She reached out and touched her fingers to his cheekbone and the wound she had inflicted to it. "What will free you?"

His expression on her softened and she wondered how it was possible to find him more breathtaking than her glade.

He closed his eyes and tilted his face to her touch. "I dinna know, lass, but I like bein' here with ye."

"I like it, too," she said on a ragged breath, slipping her fingers and her gaze to his mouth. "What should we do about it?"

Oh, she feared her heart was going to burst from her chest and land in the bluebells. She struggled not to lift her other hand to him and pull him in.

"Think aboot it later," he said on a throaty whisper and leaned down.

She nodded and let him brush his mouth over her smiling lips. He didn't kiss her immediately. First, he drove her mad by kissing her cheek, her earlobe, and leisurely working his way down her neck. He stopped at her bosom rising and falling beneath his lips. He turned to gaze into her eyes and then covered her body with his and kissed the breath from her parted lips.

CHAPTER NINETEEN

C AIN SAT IN the great hall with Father Timothy, William, and the men. He looked around, feeling out of place since he'd been eating alone for the past four nights. The priest wasn't helping matters, staring at him as if he were growing a second head.

Why had he agreed to meet Aleysia here and sit with her for supper? Where was she? He'd left her soon after they'd returned from taking the buck to the village.

"What in damnation are ye lookin' fer?" he finally asked the priest.

"Ye look different," Father Timothy told him, his sherry-brown eyes wide and curious. "Why are ye sittin' with us again?"

"Where else would I be sittin'?"

"At the head table."

Cain wanted to sit with her. The men would think it odd if he invited her to sit at the head table with him. But he didn't tell Father Timothy that. "We are all warriors in the same battle," he told his friend instead.

The priest nodded, still smiling. "Where were ye all day?"

Cain thought about the glade and kissing Aleysia in the bluebells and orchids. He could still smell her on him. "Aleysia killed a buck and

I helped her take it to the village. That is all.

The priest's eyes lit up. "It has done ye wonders."

Cain smiled—and then realized what he was doing and lifted his cup to his lips to cover it. He wasn't sure if it was Father Timothy's pure delight, or...something else that made him feel a bit different. As if he'd been shaken from his axis and tilted toward another direction. Should he tell his friend? This forgotten thing he was beginning to feel for her was growing stronger. To be honest, it scared him more than anything else currently in his life.

He set down his cup and put his arm around the priest's shoulders. "Father," he said drawing him in. "I am...I think I..." He stopped. What? What did he want to say?

"She is makin' her way to yer heart," his old friend finished for him.

Cain's blood ran cold with fear. He hadn't faced this demon...not for many years. This one was bigger, stronger than all the others.

He rested his forehead against Father Timothy's and stared into his eyes. "I fear she is already there."

He caught a glimpse of something purple and turned his gaze to the entrance. His breath went still when he saw her, dressed in a fitted overgown, dyed in deep lavender. His heart thundered in his chest loud enough for him to believe Father Timothy could hear it.

He moved away from his friend and straightened on the bench as she entered the hall. He perused her in the way a dying man might gaze upon his heart's desire.

She wore her hair free to fall in black, glossy waves to her waist and topped by a circlet of bluebells.

Her intent was to beguile him senseless and she accomplished it well. He couldn't help but smile at her and stand when she approached him with her friend Matilda close by her side.

"Ladies," he greeted them, then gave William's leg a soft kick to get him to move from his place. He held out his hand for Aleysia to take the place beside him.

She smiled, accepting, and lifted her skirts over her bare calves to take her seat at the long bench.

His blood sizzled in his veins, sending sparks to his heart...his groin. He wanted her. He'd wanted her all day, but he'd refrained, certain that whatever part of his heart she sought to conquer would surrender.

"Ye look better than a summer glade," he told her as he sat beside her.

"That is quite the compliment," Father Timothy teased on the other side of him.

"'Tis perfect," she argued, sharing an intimate smile with Cain. She set her vibrant green eyes on the faces in the hall and said loud enough for all at the table to hear, "I hope that if Lady de Bar ever returns, none of you will tell her that I wore her gown."

"If she ever returns, it will be to collect what is left of her husband," Rauf promised. The others agreed.

Cain watched her captivate them with her radiant smile.

"The only thing missing is dear Elizabeth," she said softly.

"Why is she not here?" he asked. He already knew Giles d'Argentan's betrothed had gone to an abbey rather than stay in the woods, but he didn't want to let Aleysia know that he had eavesdropped by her door.

"She went back to the St. Peter's Abbey where she spent much of her time growing up. She does not know 'tis safe to return to Lismoor. She would not consider it safe with any Scots here. I will likely never see her again."

"Ye were close friends?"

"Aye." She leaned in closer and lowered her voice so that only he could hear. "She was closer to my age than Giles'. We became friends while she waited for him to return from his ridiculous adventures. I miss her."

Cain's gaze roved over her. She was loyal to her friends, to Richard—the people she cared about. He liked it. Loyalty was a highly favored trait.

She blushed when she realized how close she was and straightened in her seat.

"Why did she take shelter at this abbey? Was she an orphan?" Cain asked. He thought he might think a little more highly of Giles d'Argentan if he had taken an orphan for his promised bride.

"She is not an orphan. Her father is Lord Hugh FitzSimmons, Baron of Richmond. He hardly ever sees her though. He tried to marry her off and when that didn't work, he didn't send for her back but left her with barely a word for five years." Her eyes grew round and soft, filled with mist. "I guess you can be an orphan even if your parents are alive."

"We sound like a band of misfits," William said, hearing the last part of the conversation. "We all lost our families."

Cain looked away, not wanting to think on such things after so pleasant a day.

"I was thinking," she said, smiling at everyone, and then at him, "of riding to Newton on the Moor tomorrow."

He might have nodded but, thank goodness, he almost choked on the whisky he was swallowing instead. "What?" he asked, bringing his hand to his throat. "What is in Newton on the Moor?"

Her smile remained. "Elizabeth. Would you care to escort me? 'Tis but a short distance away. You would not be leaving your post for very long."

Cain held his cup to his lips and drank to keep from nodding again and giving in to her request. What else would he do for her? Escort her to Newton on the Moor? He had better things to see to than ride to an abbey to bring back a lass who likely hated the Scots for killing her betrothed.

"If you would prefer not to come," she continued when he said nothing, "Rauf can escort me. Mayhap William, as well." She turned to offer William her most radiant smile.

"Of course we will escort ye," Rauf hastened to assure her then almost withered in his seat when Cain glared at him.

"No one is goin' anywhere," Cain ground out. "I dinna know how many men they have guardin' the place. I dinna—"

"There are no guards there, Commander," she informed him with a little smile he wanted to stare at for the rest of his life. "'Tis an abbey." She looked past him at Father Timothy for a moment, as if he might know why Cain would say such a ridiculous thing.

"Still, I—"

"'Tis perfectly safe," she continued quickly. "I could go myself, but I would rather have your company on the road, or the company of friends."

From the corner of his eye, Cain could see William and Rauf squirming in their places on the bench. They wanted to grant her request. Hell, so did he.

He glanced up at her bluebell circlet and remembered her face in the sun, her soft, yielding body beneath his.

He nodded then blinked out of his reverie. He realized quickly what he'd done by the smile widening on her face and the fire burning from his hand when she laid hers atop it. He wanted to take her and lay claim to the fire, be consumed by it.

"Thank you, Commander."

She made him want to cast his fears to hell and smile back. He wanted to kick away everything in his life and run toward her. But his heart clanged too loudly in his ears, like an alarm trying to wake him up before it was too late.

He moved his hand away and was horrified to find it shaking. Had she felt it? What was she doing to him?

"William and Rauf will accompany ye."

"I will go as well," Father Timothy offered.

"No, Father," Aleysia told him. "The abbess would not take kindly to a Scottish priest. If she sees Will and Rauf, she will not speak to them. But she will speak to you, and when she hears your speech, she will have you dealt with."

"Dealt with?" Father Timothy echoed in a hollow tone. "A nun?"

"A reverend mother," Aleysia corrected him then turned to Will and Rauf. "If you meet her, she is not to be touched."

"Ye sound as if ye know her well," Cainnech noted.

"I spent some time at St. Peter's. She's a mean-spirited woman who fears nothing. She possesses some sort of power many speculate is given to her by God, but I believe 'twas the devil."

"What is this power?" Father Timothy asked, engrossed in the tale.

Aleysia met the priest's troubled gaze with wide eyes of her own. "She can fell a man with a single touch. Just a touch and he goes into a deep slumber."

"Fer how long?" Rauf asked, looking worried.

"Not long."

Cainnech's short burst of laughter restored everyone's good mood.

"And you?" Aleysia asked him, crushing the stones of his thick walls with her soft voice. "Will you not join us?"

"Nae, I willna."

She looked as if she wanted to say more, but did not. When she turned to William again, Cain breathed in her hair, and then turned to find Father Timothy was back to staring at him.

She made him regret his decision while they ate and pretended there was nothing between them, no spark when they reached for the bread and their fingers touched, no racing heartbeat when she caught him staring at her and a blush stole across her cheeks.

He ate until he could no longer stand sitting with her and not taking her in his arms. Finally, he pushed away his cup and rose from the bench. "Ye will leave fer Newton on the Moor at sunrise." He settled his attention on Will and Rauf. "I want ye both back before sunset."

He told himself to just walk away. He didn't need to say anything else to her. But he bent to her and said against her ear, "Thank ye fer today."

He left the hall without looking back. He needed to be away from her to clear his head. It seemed when he was near her he had little control over his tongue. Why had he thanked her? He didn't know whether to laugh at himself or groan. She must think him a fool. He *was* a fool.

He didn't go to his room or to the battlements. He wasn't used to living inside, sleeping in a bed, or pissing in a bucket. He preferred it outside, and with the platforms in the trees...he smiled. He liked it here at Lismoor.

He left the keep beneath the soft glow of moonlight. He had to think about what he was doing. He wasn't staying at Lismoor. Soon, Aleysia d'Argentan would no longer be his responsibility. He told himself that he couldn't wait. He'd had a good day with her at the glade. So what? Would he abandon everything he'd learned throughout his life for one good day? For a lass who would very likely bring love into his life? He closed his eyes and breathed a deep breath. He didn't want to pursue anything with her, but when she was near, his mouth and his body didn't give a damn what his head told them to do.

When he made it to the trees, he looked around to make certain he was still alone, and then began climbing an old, sturdy oak.

Now, he was sending her off the Newton on the Moor with William, who was no warrior, and Rauf. What if they were attacked?

He carefully made his way over thick branches to a wider plank and sat on it. He dangled his legs over either side and leaned his back against the trunk with a sigh of contentment. Here was what he knew, sleeping under the stars—not high in the trees—but under the stars nonetheless.

He relaxed and tried to think with a clear head. How had he allowed someone to penetrate his armor? Father Timothy was no help. He was delighted that Cain was losing his damned mind. He didn't understand that caring for her scared the hell out of Cain.

He had to deny it, defy it, resist it. Not because she was his enemy. He didn't believe she was his enemy any longer, but she was still just as deadly. She could do more damage to him than any army. She'd made him think about his family today for the first time in many years. He hadn't wanted to. He'd fought it, not ready to look that demon in the face yet. The truth was he couldn't remember anything about his parents or his brothers before that day. Nothing. Not a smile, a habit, or even a word. When they left, they took love and the memory of *being* loved with them. He grew up in the madness of his anger. But he could not be sad for something he did not miss.

Mayhap it had been the serenity of the glade, or her voice beside him, like a soothing stream against his ears, that compelled him to speak of things he preferred to leave unsaid. Strangely enough, he found that the telling wasn't so terrible. She seemed to understand him.

Kissing her afterward had been even better. He could have continued all day, but he knew it was dangerous. He knew it would lead to more affection for her—possibly love. He wanted to pray for strength to resist her but, according to Father Timothy, God was in on this.

He sat alone for a few hours, nodding off for a bit and dreaming of crying faces, pleading, unrecognizable voices, his mother screaming, Torin running, and Nicholas being lifted up by his trews. It was always the same, and it left him wide awake and ready to fight.

It was the best time to practice.

He'd done it often over the years while the men, including Father Timothy, slept. He swung his legs to the plank now and pushed up to his feet. He couldn't practice in the trees, though, he thought, it would be quite a skill to master.

First, he had to master moving through them in the filtered moonlight. There was one good thing about the dark though. It didn't make him lightheaded when he looked down.

A rush of admiration washed over him for how Aleysia had used the forest to her advantage, for learning to walk up here—to run. He remembered the tunnel in the dungeon and how she'd come through it, ready to fight.

She was vivacious, fearless, and well trained. She stirred his blood like no lass before her. He doubted he would meet anyone like her again.

He left the last tree, dangling first from its lowest branch to let his muscles stretch. Once done, he went quickly to his room and retrieved his sword. It didn't matter if he didn't practice with a flesh and blood opponent. Practicing alone let him devise new combinations.

He walked to the grassy field, rolling his wrist and making the long blade dance in the night air. He pulled his axe free from its place in his belted plaid, and gave it a good swing.

And almost cut Aleysia in half.

She stepped back on lightning quick reflexes and swung a sword of her own at him.

Before he had time to take in what was going on, he sent his blade chopping down on hers, imbedding hers in the ground.

He gave her a moment and stepped back while she pulled her weapon free. She'd changed into her hose and léine, with a dark bodice laced up the front. She'd also cast off her bluebell circlet and wore her long hair braided down her back.

"What d'ye think ye're doin', Aleysia?" he demanded, tossing away his axe and walking back and forth before her.

"I want to practice with you," she told him, stepping back with her freed sword. "Is that so terrible?"

"It could be dangerous," he answered. "Our sight is poor."

"William says you are the Scottish king's finest soldier." She raised her sword, ready to spar again. "I want to practice with the best."

Moonlight caught her smile as it flashed off her blade. It held him captive long enough to slow his reflexes and he barely dodged a swipe intended for his throat.

"Are we fightin' fer blood then?" he asked, eyes gleaming.

She shrugged her dainty shoulder. "That depends on how well you block me."

He gave out a short, surprised laugh at her boldness, and then readied his sword and braced his feet in case she thought to knock him on his arse again.

He thought he heard her laughter in the midst of swiping and plunging at him. Her blade kept him on his toes, but he soon adjusted to her movements and found himself looking at her while he blocked.

Tendrils of her hair had escaped her braid and blew across her face like war paint in the pale moonlight. She met his hungry gaze through the streaks and faltered in her defense. He used the opening to grab hold of her sword wrist, hold it up, and move in close for the kill.

"I would hate to cut such a bonny throat," he whispered with a warm breath as he held the edge of his blade to her neck.

Her chest rose and fell hard against him. When she spoke, her breath fell upon the flat of his blade. "You beguiled me."

Moonlight glinted in her eyes, promising delights in which his soul could bask. He dipped his gaze to her mouth, dropped his sword, and dragged her closer.

"And here I thought I was the one bein' beguiled."

She let go of her sword and clung to him as his mouth descended on hers. She wanted this, he thought as his lips molded and teased. His blood seared through his veins, making him burn for her. He felt her heart thumping in unison with his and, though he rejoiced in their equal measure of delight, he feared she would be his undoing.

He was losing fast with every stroke of her tongue against his, every touch of her fingers in his hair, down his back. Falling with every inhalation of breath, filled with sweet orchids and bluebells. She had managed to knock him off his feet yet again. Off his axis. Spiraling downward into the darkness. He held her closer as they kissed, not wanting to let her go.

But too afraid to hold on.

He broke their kiss and stepped back. "Lass, I—"

"Do not say it, Cainnech." She held out her fingers to his lips. "I will not be such a fool for you again!"

She ran off, back toward the keep.

Cain did not follow.

CHAPTER TWENTY

ALEYSIA SECURED HER saddle outside the stable as the sun came up. She looked over it at Sir Richard standing on the other side.

"I do not understand why you do not simply send a missive to Miss Elizabeth," her old friend said. "Why must you go to Newton on the Moor and why must I wait here?"

"You know the nuns will not give Elizabeth my letter. I took her from them for five years."

"What makes you think they will let you *speak* to her?" Richard insisted.

She shrugged. "Whether they want me to speak to her or not is of no concern to me. I will see her and I will speak to her. And you are staying behind to keep Father Timothy company. I thought you were friends."

"We are friends," he argued, "but my duty is to see to you, not a priest."

"And you have done your duty well, dear friend. But I will be fine." She secured her water pouch and her bow and some borrowed arrows to her saddle.

"Why is the commander not going with you? Who will protect

you if you are attacked on the road? You know how dangerous—"

"I will protect myself, Richard," she told him, growing frustrated with his fears.

"Besides, have you not watched William practice with the others? What he knows, he has learned from the commander. I'm certain if we were attacked, he would do quite—"

Her mouth snapped shut when she saw Cainnech approaching. Had he come to see her off?

She grinded her teeth when Richard spotted the commander next and hurried toward him. "Speak to her!" the old knight insisted. "Why are you allowing this?"

She moved to interject. She didn't have to.

"Her mind is her own, Richard," Cainnech told him as they neared. "Or have ye not noticed that in all the years ye have known her?"

And how was it that the commander had known her for a sennight and knew it already?

Knowing he was correct, Richard gave in and stormed off.

Alone with him, Aleysia watched him from over her horse's back. He didn't wear his plaid, but breeches of undyed wool cut snugly over his long, muscular legs, and a léine beneath his long, gray cloak. He looked tired but still wonderfully fit.

She remembered being held in his arms the night before. What a fool she had been for him. She didn't care if nothing in her entire life felt as good as kissing him; she would never let him do it again. She understood he'd had a difficult past and he hated the English because of it. She didn't need reminding that they were enemies—especially after he kissed her.

"What are you doing here?"

"I am comin' with ye," he muttered. He moved past her without a word and disappeared into the stable.

She smiled, turning to Rauf and William heading toward her.

"Is he coming then?" William tossed her a knowing smile, but she had no idea what he thought he knew.

"It seems so," she shrugged, pretending not to care. She didn't look at them again while they entered the stable.

Though Cainnech was first into the stable, he was the last one out. By the time he finally sauntered out, leading his mount by the bridle, she tossed him an irritated glance. "I could have slept a little longer had I known you would take so long."

"Ye slept?" he asked, gaining his saddle.

Two words. Two words were all it took to tempt her to forgive him anything, to wait for him forever.

"Let us be off!" He called out, then slid his gaze to her and said more quietly, "Which way is clear of yer traps?" When she pointed east, he flicked his reins and rode away.

She caught up with him and cantered her horse at his side. "What made you change your mind and come along?"

"I havena *come along*, Aleysia," he told her, sounding mildly annoyed. "I'm here to lead this wee adventure of yers. What that means fer ye is that ye will do what I tell ye."

She laughed softly, refusing to let him goad her. "Now, Commander, you know that I will not be ordered about, but I will consider any request you put to me. So, are you going to tell me what made you change your mind about coming?"

He looked as if he might be considering turning back. She held her ground, waiting. She didn't think he would let her go to Newton on the Moor alone, now that he was here. She hoped she was correct. It was dangerous beyond the castle walls, especially for a woman traveling alone.

"I was worried fer the nuns," he drawled. "And if ye met any English soldiers along the way, I wanted to be here to kill them."

"Can you not control your lust for English blood? We are going to a holy place, Cainnech."

He set his bloodshot blue eyes on hers. "Ye sound like the priest."

"Good! At least one of you has sense in his head."

She thought she caught sight of his elusive smile as he flicked his reins and led his horse away at a steady trot.

She watched him go. What kind of brute was he to always think about killing? One raised on the battlefield, surrounded by death, she reminded herself. One who had forgotten the faces of anyone he ever loved.

She thought about riding to him but stopped herself. No more. She'd promised herself. She wouldn't go back on it. She waited instead until William and Rauf caught up to her and rode with them the rest of the way.

"Is he always so distant?" she asked them when they stopped just outside of Newton on the Moor for some bread and honey, and water for their horses from a nearby stream. The commander had claimed he wasn't hungry and went to have a look around on foot.

"Aye, fer as long as I have known him," Rauf told her.

"How long has that been?" she asked, taking a bite of her bread.

"Four years. Most of us know little aboot him, fer he prefers to be alone when we are not fightin'."

Aleysia wanted to know what they knew about him, even if it wasn't much. She hadn't asked them before because Richard was always around. She hadn't wanted him to know she was curious about what kind of man the commander was...when he wasn't fighting.

"Everyone seems to fear him. Has he given you a reason?"

"We dinna fear him," Rauf answered. "We respect him. He has brought us oot of battle safely more times than any of us can count."

"No one wants to fight with him on the practice field when he's angry though," William told her.

"Or when he is not," Rauf laughed. "We all know the tales though," he said a moment later, sobering.

"What tales?" Aleysia asked.

"The tales of how when the commander was just a lad ten and five he massacred an entire squad of men."

"'Twas half that," William corrected. He didn't lower his gaze when they turned to stare at him, but continued. "I asked him and he said 'twas half the squad."

"Still," Aleysia said in a quiet voice, "that is a lot of men to—"

"They were the ones who killed his kin and held him captive," William was quick to defend him. He knew Aleysia was aware of the commander's past. They'd spoken of it briefly during Cainnech's four-day disappearance. "They deserved what he did to them."

Aye, Aleysia thought, perhaps they did. But it hadn't changed anything for him, had it? He still hated the English. He could never have his parents back, and his brothers were likely dead.

He would always see her as his enemy.

"He seems to like you though."

She turned to William sitting closest to her in the grass. "Why do you say that?"

Her handsome young friend looked at her with his penetrating silvery eyes and gave her a skeptical look as if she shouldn't need him to tell her.

"He smiles when he's with you. He does not smile often."

"I have seen him laugh a time or two when he was with ye," Rauf agreed with a sly wink cast at her.

She blushed and was about to rise to her feet, when the commander returned and gave them a disgusted look.

"Would we like to reach Newton on the Moor today?" he asked in a wry tone.

The men tossed away their bread and leaped to attention. Aleysia decided to move a little slower.

"I would like to get there today," she answered pleasantly and tossed him a playful smile. It was difficult to remain angry with him when, according to his men, she made him smile.

He looked as if he were fighting one from forming right now. "Then mayhap," he said, trying to sound angry, and failing, "ye can all quit flappin' yer tongues aboot—"

He ducked, but her honey-soaked hunk of bread hit him in the shoulder.

She wasn't sure what made her laugh harder, the bread sliding down his arm, leaving a sticky, glistening streak behind, or Rauf and William's exclamations of disbelief.

When a moment passed and Cainnech didn't demand that they all pick up their bags and head back to Lismoor, her friends exchanged knowing smiles.

"Are ye done then, lady?"

Oh, he was angry, calling her lady instead of the more tender lass. She really should stop laughing but it felt too good. She hadn't laughed so hard in a long time.

Finally, he gave in and crooked a corner of his mouth up at her. His smile, subtle though it was, sobered her faster than his anger. He made her laugh and even though it was at his expense, he didn't grow angry. He smiled.

They stared at each other across the small clearing, their eyes saying what their mouths would not.

He lifted his hand and swatted something away. When he waved his other hand in front of his face, Aleysia gasped and then covered her mouth. Bees! He took a moment from fighting them off to glare at her, and then unclasped his cloak and pulled off his léine.

He wore nothing underneath but skin, muscle, and scars. Aleysia watched, captivated, as his dark hair fell over the broad flare of his shoulders. The filtered sunlight caressed his long, lean waist and fell across his washboard belly.

She stopped paying attention to the others and remembered what it felt like to be pressed so snugly to him, to be caught up in his strength and the passion of his kiss.

She fought the urge to take a step forward when he strode to the stream and bent to it. He dipped his léine into the water and looked over his shoulder at her, as if he simply couldn't believe she'd thrown her bread at him.

She adjusted her bodice—not realizing what she'd done until his gaze dipped to it—and then marched over to him. "You are fortunate 'twasn't a dagger."

He slanted his mouth and turned back to his léine. "Not as fortunate as ye that I dinna toss ye into the hive."

She tried to think of something to say but her gaze was fastened on the play of muscles in his shoulders and arms as he scrubbed. She tore her eyes away and looked around the clearing. She found Will and Rauf standing by the horses. They still appeared stunned by her boldness and looked away quickly rather than meet her gaze.

She glanced down at the commander again and then sat on her weak knees beside him. She wouldn't let him frighten her off. "Your men are afraid of me."

He angled his head and gave her a pointed look. "They should be. And ye dinna have to sound so pleased aboot it."

She couldn't help but smile. She knew the men weren't afraid of her, but she couldn't tell him what they truly thought. "I should help," she said softly instead, and reached for the wet bundle in his hands.

He covered her hands with his and when he looked at her, his gaze went altogether soft. "Ye are not a fool, lass."

She could have stared into his eyes until her last breath if he would always look at her the way he was looking at her now, as if he knew her and liked who she was and wanted to know more about her.

He found her beautiful, more beautiful than the glade. He'd said so himself.

He wrung out his léine and rose up above her. "But there can be no..." he continued, and then paused as if the words tasted foul coming from his mouth. "I must keep my head clear to my duty."

Her heart sank as she straightened. "And what is your duty, Cainnech?"

He stared into her eyes and clenched his jaw, as if he were trying to keep whatever he wanted to say inside.

After a moment, he blinked away and glared at the men. "Time to go!"

He was running again. Father Timothy had told her that the commander was fond of her. His men believed it, too. She thought of being with him at the glade and how serene he had been, how his mouth had worked slowly over her flesh, her lips, awakening parts of her she didn't know existed. She hadn't wanted to leave the glade—to return to who they were and what they were supposed to feel.

She wanted to be angry with him for always running, always pulling away, and keeping a "clear head", but she couldn't. She was quite suddenly sad, in fact. He was so angry and filled with hatred for the English, and for those who swore fealty to King Edward, that he was blind to his own heart.

What should she do about him? When he'd first come to Lismoor, she'd wanted him to leave. It was all she had wanted. Now, the thought of him going made her ill. What had changed? He'd kissed her and changed her dreams and desires.

She watched him return to his horse and pull on his wet léine. It clung to him, outlining the muscles defining his chest. He shoved his cloak into his saddlebag and mounted in a single leap.

She would have to think on it later. Elizabeth needed to come home.

ST. PETER'S ABBEY was an old structure in the southwest end of the lovely village of Newton on the Moor. It wasn't overly large, as far as abbeys went. Its high bell tower and two corner towers rose up over the quiet village.

Aleysia recalled the last time she was here five years ago. Giles had been with her. They had come to take Elizabeth to Lismoor. The abbess had been angry and had argued with Giles. It seemed Elizabeth's father had been paying handsomely to keep his daughter here while she was away from home and the abbess didn't want to lose his donations. But Elizabeth had written to her betrothed telling him how much she hated being there, so they had come and brought her home. But it had been a harrowing visit.

Aleysia stopped Cainnech and the others before they rode any closer. "We cannot simply knock on the abbey doors."

"Why not?" Cainnech growled, staring at her from his saddle. He brought his mount closer until his leg brushed against hers.

Aleysia found it difficult to keep a clear head, staring straight at him, their legs touching. It made her want to curse him for being so untouchable. "The abbess does not care for me that is why not," she replied tersely. "Now, are we going to discuss my plan to get to Elizabeth, or remain here all day and ask questions?"

William and Rauf remained quiet.

Cainnech's expression darkened. "Why did ye not tell me this before?"

"I am telling you now. Also, I have been thinking."

He actually sighed.

Truly, sometimes she believed she could happily kill him.

"Elizabeth does not know you and your men were not defeated at Lismoor. I fear she will not return if she discovers the truth."

He stared at her for a moment then blew out a short laugh. "So I am to let ye go inside alone? Is that what ye have been thinkin'?"

The poor man *still* had no idea who he was talking to. She narrowed her eyes on him. "I do not belong to you, Commander. You do not *let me* do anything. You should feel privileged that I even *let you* in on what I'm thinking!"

"Och, look at them apples!" Rauf said, pointing to a vendor when her pitch grew to a shout.

Will smiled and looked away.

"Fergive me," the commander said, giving her his attention with a hint of warmth in his gaze to go with it. "I do feel privileged. Go on."

She stumbled around a few words until she found the right ones. She wasn't expecting his reaction to her outburst. Apparently, neither did William or Rauf, for they gaped at him as if he had appeared before them from thin air. She wasn't sure how to respond.

"Thank you," she said first. She kept her voice low so that only he could hear and let herself smile. "I forgive you."

She thought he didn't hear her at first, for he leaned closer. His smile began in his eyes and it was as if the shutters blew off a hundred windows. Was that a glimpse of his heart she saw in the deep blue fathoms?

"Lead the way, lass," he said hoarsely, quietly. "Fer 'tis clear I will follow anywhere ye go."

CHAPTER TWENTY-ONE

"THERE IS A graveyard behind the small church," Aleysia told them while they secured their horses to the trees. "'Tis gated, but I know how to get in. Once inside, I can get to Elizabeth's rooms. I will go get her while the three of you wait for us in the cemetery. If you see any of the nuns, do not speak to them, do you understand?"

"Nae." Cainnech said, looking uneasy. "Tell me again why we canna enter through the front gate. Why are we sneakin' aboot? 'Tis an abbey. There are nuns inside. They willna stop us from—"

"You do not know the abbess," Aleysia insisted. "She is frightening."

He smiled indulgently. "Lass, I have faced mighty warriors in battle. An abbess doesna frighten me."

She closed her eyes and prayed for patience. "Still, why face her if we do not have to? Aye?"

Without waiting for him to respond, she hurried past quacking ducks to a wall behind the second tower. There, she found a small door curtained by vines.

It looked as if no one had used the door in years. The vines sprang free when she pulled it open. She smiled, looking over her shoulder at

Cainnech, and led the way into the cemetery.

She saw the narrow, stone stairway that led inside the abbey and turned to tell the men that she was heading inside when William stopped and went deathly still.

Aleysia followed his gaze to a young woman standing alone at one of the gravestones. Who was she? Probably another poor girl orphaned or abandoned by her family.

"Will," Aleysia said gently to get him moving. They shouldn't stop and speak to anyone.

"'Tis her," he managed, not taking his eyes off her. "'Tis Julianna."

The girl heard her name spoken and turned to see them. She stepped back and pressed her slender hands to her chest.

"William?" she asked with a stunned, hesitant breath.

She wore a full white kirtle and a yellow silk overgown with a fur-lined mantle and a golden coronet over her brow and long, red tresses.

"Hell," Aleysia heard Cainnech groan next.

"What are you doing here?" Will rushed to her like a man just given back his life.

Julianna backed away and cast a nervous look around him at the commander standing close by and Rauf moving about.

"I was sent here after...Berwick." Her large, dark eyes shimmered with tears and she dabbed them with her dangling sleeve. "It was terrible. Where were you?" Instead of waiting for an answer to her current question, she asked more. "Who are these people? Why have you come here?"

"I...I am here for..."

"We are looking for Elizabeth FitzSimmons." Aleysia stepped forward and smiled, though wanting to stay and needing to go tore her heart in two. "I am Aleysia...d'Argentan." She added her surname in a low voice.

"Giles' sister!" Julianna smiled and Aleysia was tempted to look over her shoulder at William or Rauf to see if they had heard.

"Elizabeth has told me all about you and your brother. Did the Scots ever come for your castle? Did your traps kill them all?"

Aleysia felt William go stiff beside her and step away. She wanted to turn her gaze to Cainnech. She needed his help. She also needed to say something to Julianna to shut her up.

Aleysia turned to William first. "Please forgive me. I will be killed if 'tis found out."

When he flicked his diamond-hard gaze over her shoulder, she turned to see Cainnech coming toward them. Rauf was keeping watch at the stairway and was thankfully out of earshot. For now.

"If what is found out?" Julianna asked her, her wide eyes moving from her to Will. "Killed by who?"

"Aleysia?"

She turned to see Elizabeth step outside from the side entrance to the abbey.

When Elizabeth took off running toward her, Aleysia met her in a long embrace.

"What are you doing here?" Elizabeth finally pulled back and asked her. "Is it safe to return to Lismoor? Did you kill all the—"

Her gaze skidded to a halt on the commander and the two men around him. "Who are these men?"

"Elizabeth," Aleysia said, trying to keep her voice light. This wasn't how she wanted to tell her friend about the Scots. "We've come to bring you home. These..." She closed her eyes, knowing the moment Elizabeth found out who they were could likely be the end of their friendship. She'd sent delicate Elizabeth away into the woods and back to the abbess for nothing. Not only did she not keep her promise to kill them all, she was losing her heart to one and had brought him here. "These are my friends."

"Where did they come from?" Elizabeth asked, leaning in so the men wouldn't hear. "I've never seen them at Lismoor."

"Dearest, come now." Aleysia tried to usher her toward the hidden exit. "We will discuss everything on the way. The abbess will be angry if she finds me here unannounced."

"Aye," Elizabeth finally smiled. "But I do not have my things."

"Everything you need is awaiting you at Lismoor, and we can send for the rest later."

She was almost sure she heard Cainnech expel a long sigh when they finally began moving. Still, Aleysia thought thankfully as she led her friend to the door, this was easier than they thought it would be.

"Julianna." Elizabeth suddenly remembered her and broke free of Aleysia's arm. "You must come with us! You will love it at Lismoor."

"Where is your father?" William asked turning to the striking redhead.

She pointed to the gravestone close to where she stood. "He died at Berwick."

"Who is this?" Elizabeth smiled at him, tall and handsome, and not nearly as dangerous as Cainnech.

"He is William Stone, my father's servant," Julianna told her.

"The one you told me about?" Elizabeth's smile faded and her flesh paled. "The Scottish boy?" She turned to Aleysia with confusion and betrayal in her eyes. "What are you doing with a Scot, and who are these men?" She looked warily at Cainnech and Rauf when the latter made his way over.

"I heard women's voices," Rauf informed them, reaching for his sword. "We need to hurry the hell oot of here."

Elizabeth staggered backward and cast Aleysia a horrified look. "You brought the Scots here?"

Aleysia tried to tell her they were safe and Lismoor would soon again be hers, but Elizabeth hated the Scots for killing Giles and, like them all, she couldn't see beyond it.

"You betray your brother by befriending these murderous, treasonous outlaws!" she shouted.

The voices from inside the abbey grew louder, closer.

"Elizabeth, if you will please listen," Aleysia tried to no avail.

"Here!" her friend called out to the nuns now entering the cemetery.

When the sisters saw the strange men in their yard, they scrambled back and made the sign of the cross.

"These men are Scots!" Elizabeth shouted. "Get the abbess!"

"Please, Elizabeth," Aleysia tried again. "Just come home with me. Give them a chance. They are not even staying."

"You called them your friends," Elizabeth said with tears staining her eyes. "They killed Giles. How could you, Aleysia?"

What did Aleysia dare say? That she might be falling in love with one of them? She turned to look at him, wishing Elizabeth would just give him a chance the way Mattie had.

"Miss d'Argentan, I should have known."

Aleysia slid her gaze to the entrance and scowled when she saw the abbess. She hadn't changed. In fact, she hadn't aged in five years. "Reverend Mother," Aleysia said impassively, "we were just leaving."

Swathed in stiff wool, the reverend mother's face was a mask of utter composure, save for the rage in her stormy gray eyes.

"Before you go, why do you not introduce me to your companions?" From within the long wide sleeves of her white robes, the abbess extended her hand toward Cainnech.

He looked down at it, not sure what he was supposed to do, and then reached out to accept her offering.

"No!" Aleysia shouted, but she was too late.

Cainnech pulled back his hand after barely touching the abbess and looked at it. His eyes opened wide and then he turned to Aleysia. "She jabbed me with some—" He collapsed in a heap at Aleysia's feet.

Instantly, Rauf and William drew their swords, but Aleysia leaped in front of the abbess and held up her palms to hold back the men.

"Stop! Do not touch her!"

"She killed the commander!" Rauf shouted, but did not try to move past her.

"He is asleep," the abbess corrected him blandly.

William fell to his knees to check. Rauf didn't seem convinced and tried to move forward.

"She did not kill him, Rauf!" Aleysia told him, making certain her heard her. "He only sleeps. Remember, I told you about this? The commander will awaken. What will you tell Father Timothy if you kill a nun, a woman?"

Rauf finally nodded and stepped back, out of range of the abbess' touch.

"If I wanted him dead," the abbess told them in a strict but serene voice, "he would be dead." Her eyes sparked with fire when she met Aleysia's gaze. "I do not know what you want, but Elizabeth will not be going with you this time. Now, take your men of war away from my abbey before I truly lose my temper."

She turned on her heel and swept away in her long robes, with her nuns behind her.

Aleysia crouched and had a closer look at Cainnech. His breathing was strong, his skin, wonderfully warm.

She followed him upward as Rauf scooped him up, thought better of it for a moment, and then agreed with his first decision and hefted his commander over his shoulder.

"Let's get the hell oot of here," Rauf ordered and led the way, slowly, and huffing at Cainnech's size as he went.

"Come away with me, Julianna," Aleysia heard William say.

"Are you crazed?"

Her heart broke at Julianna's reply.

"Come with you and live among the Scots? They ravaged our entire town—"

"Not these men," Aleysia told her. "They had no part in Berwick."

Julianna looked as if she might be reconsidering but then shook her head. "You are a servant, Will. We were never meant to be together."

"I am changing my life. Things will be better for me."

"No," Julianna said and turned her alabaster face away. "No. I am here until the man to whom my father promised me—a man of means—arrives. I will be married and have no more time for childish fancies."

"Let's go!" Rauf commanded.

Aleysia met William's tortured gaze and urged him to come. He didn't move.

"Julianna, I have loved you my whole life. I will never love anyone but you. Do not sentence me to such a lonely life."

"Go, William." A whisper, but it boomed throughout the grave-yard.

Aleysia pulled his sleeve. "Come, we must go."

This time, he followed.

They rested in the shade of an old oak until Cainnech opened his eyes. They didn't have to wait long. Aleysia was relieved to see him well, even though she didn't doubt he would be. She was also glad to have him to speak to because, with Rauf around, she couldn't speak to William about him knowing the truth.

"She has no powers given to her by God," Cainnech groaned sitting up. "She stuck me with something." He looked over his hand and wrist for any sign of a wound. There was none.

"She gets her power from darker forces," Rauf said while Aleysia took the commander's hand to examine it.

Almost immediately, she quit thinking about the abbess, the other men with her, or anything else, and became excruciatingly aware of Cainnech's large hand in hers. She studied his long, broad fingers, moving each with a delicate, curious touch of her own. She ran her fingertips across his rough palm and trembled at the power he possessed when he rubbed his thumb over her flesh.

"Or mayhap," she said, noticing a tiny red spot on the inside of his wrist, "she cleverly coats a thin needle, or even an insect stinger with poison, and then stabs her victims."

She pointed out the tiny wound to the rest of them and then scowled at Rauf when he suggested going back and killing the abbess.

Soon, they were back in the saddle and heading home. Rauf rode with William up ahead while Aleysia told Cainnech how the abbess had felled Giles when she and her brother had come for Elizabeth. "I could not carry him out of the abbey so I had to sit with him while he slept and the abbess kept watch. I never took my eyes off her, my sword always pointing at her. I had never killed anyone before and I certainly hadn't wanted to kill an abbess, but he did awaken. And I knew you would as well."

"Ye saved Rauf from eternal damnation," Cainnech said, smiling. "And worse, Father Timothy." She laughed with him, forgetting for a moment all that was lost today.

"I am sorry aboot Elizabeth," Cainnech said, as if reading her thoughts.

She shook her head. "She made her choice. 'Tis William who tears at my heart. Julianna cares for him. I know it."

"Dinna give the lad false hope," he warned gently.

She nodded and sighed, knowing he was right. "I would like some words with him."

Cainnech winked at her, and then rode ahead and sent William back to her.

Aleysia was sad that Elizabeth wouldn't come with them but her heart broke for William. She knew he was angry with her. He had every right to be. She was Giles d'Argentan's sister. Lismoor was hers. The traps and the arrows that killed his friends were hers.

"I was trying to protect my home," she told William, riding up close to him.

"Does the commander know?" he asked softly, averting his gaze from hers.

She looked at Cainnech riding with Rauf ahead of them. "He knew the men would kill me if they knew. Father Timothy convinced him to speak to your king about it first."

"You attacked us on your own," he said after a pensive moment. "The villagers were away."

She nodded.

He finally looked at her from beneath his soft curls. "You are very courageous."

"Lismoor is my home. The villagers are my friends. As are you."

His smile was slow and quite heart wrenching. "I see why he likes you."

Her happiness faded, remembering what he'd left behind. "I'm sorry she didn't come with us."

He nodded, but said nothing else. He didn't want to speak of her. Aleysia wouldn't push.

"I did not know your family name is Stone," she said with a lighter smile. "Do you know anything about them?"

He shook his head. "Stone is not my family name. The governor called me Will Stone because he paid a stone for me when I was a babe."

"Oh." She swallowed. What was she supposed to say to that? She wanted to weep, not speak.

Thankfully, Cainnech came riding back to them. "Will, we should speak."

"I already spoke to Ale—Miss d'Argentan," William told him.

"Aleysia," she corrected with a smile.

"I understand why she did it, Commander. I will not tell the others."

Cainnech smiled at him and then at her. "All right, go ride with Rauf fer a wee bit."

William left without another word. Aleysia sniffled.

"Ye have a good heart, lass," he told her with a deep-throated purr. "And ye are faithful to yer friends."

She looked at him, no longer wondering how this Highland warri-
or had won her heart. She smiled, her spirits lifted. "Thank you. Those
are good traits to have."

He nodded, looking as enchanted by her as she was by him.

He pulled a pouch from his saddlebag and offered it to her. "Drink
slowly," he instructed when she accepted. "Take a wee sip."

The Scot's deadly whisky. She could use a wee sip. She held the
spout to her lips and drank. Her hand shook as she handed him back
his pouch. She could feel him smiling at her. She could no longer see
him through the fireballs that had once been her eyes.

She held on to her reins as the flames passed, then looked at him.
"'Tis potent."

He laughed, a deep, rich, beautiful sound. "Aye, 'tis." He took a
small sip for himself and then replaced the pouch. "Tell me, how did
ye become who ye are? What kind of life did ye have with no parents?"

"I had a happy life," she told him as a wave of soothing warmth
washed over her. "I feel warm."

"'Tis the whisky," he said, still smiling.

"At first, 'twas difficult, losing my parents and then the traveling
with my nurse from Normandy to Cambridge. But I grew accustomed
to things."

He nodded, listening and keeping his horse at an even canter with
hers.

"Giles left soon after I arrived to go jousting on the Continent.
While he was away, I got myself into various sorts of trouble until my
nurse could no longer care for me. I was sent to St. Peter's for a year.
Giles' lands were seized by Edward I, and he was sent to Lismoor to be
kept safely until further order. He brought me with him. 'Twas the
longest time I had with him. After he was pardoned by Edward II, I
saw much less of him."

"Who raised ye?"

She shrugged. "The villagers, and the knights."

His smile was wide, his gaze as warm as the whisky.

He made her forget that she'd lost a long-time friend and William had lost his beloved. He made her think of a different future. One with him in it.

Now, she just had to figure out a way to get him there. She thought of his past and the demons that haunted him. She rolled up her sleeves. She would drag him if she had to.

CHAPTER TWENTY-TWO

A LEYSIA RAN HER hands down her emerald green silk kirtle. The snug fit accentuated her bosom, small waist, and hips. She had a wee bit of enticing to do.

"Now remember," Mattie said, holding up her matching over-gown. "Use caution around candles with these flaring sleeves."

"I will try to remember," Aleysia promised, stepping into the over-gown as if it were a coat. It did not close all the way around and there was no train. They were too cumbersome. "Though 'tis difficult to think when I am around him."

Mattie's smile was every bit as dreamy as Aleysia's when they faced each other in the candlelit solar. "He is very handsome. He reminds me of an older, harder version of William."

Aye, there were times when William reminded her of Cainnech, in a certain way he turned his head, when he practiced with the others and the sunlight caught a glint of death and destruction in his eyes.

Something else about him tugged at her memory, but she couldn't put her finger on it. Poor William, and poor Mattie for being so enchanted by him.

"Oh, Mattie, how many times must I tell you?" she said as gently as she could. "William is in love with Julianna Feathers. She broke his heart yesterday. I fear 'tis going to take some time for him to forget her." She didn't tell her friend that she'd heard William tell his beloved that he would never love another.

"How much time do we have, Aleysia?" her friend asked with wide, worried blue eyes.

"I do not know," she answered truthfully.

"Well, until then," Mattie replied, back to smiling as she reached for a wide, gold embroidered belt. "I will not give up. If you could win the commander's heart, then I can win William's."

"The commander is fond of me, Mattie," she said, sucking in air when her friend wrapped the belt around her waist and yanked on the laces in the back. "But I am far from winning his heart."

She couldn't believe that she wanted to win it. She wasn't sure she could. Or that she should. She might be betraying her brother, but she hadn't seen Giles in years. It was the villagers and her knights that concerned her. What if they all reacted the way Elizabeth had?

And what if there was nothing to react to? The Highland commander hadn't proclaimed his love for her. If she couldn't break through his defenses completely, he would leave and she would never see him again. And he would take William with him.

She thought about these things while she combed her own hair. She left it free to fall in a cascade down her back.

She might not have much time to convince him. Of what? To stay? To defy how circumstances would have them feel and give in to something greater?

"Hmm," Mattie said thoughtfully. "Which circlet should you wear tonight?"

"The gold with the emerald-encrusted glass," Aleysia decided. "But I can do the rest myself. Go and prepare yourself in the gown I gave you. We will tell the men that we raided Lady de Bar's trunks. You might not be able to win William's poor heart yet, but you can look pleasing to the eye while you are practicing."

They both giggled and then Aleysia watched her leave the solar. She was thankful that Mattie understood what she was feeling and didn't hate her for it.

She placed her circlet on her head and adjusted it. Oh, was she wrong for caring for him? What was she to do about it if she was? She hadn't seen him since they'd returned from the abbey and she missed being with him, hearing his voice, seeing him try not to smile and fail.

She hurried into her slippers and left the solar. She met Father Timothy on the way to the great hall.

"Ah, I was just on my way to yer door." He greeted her with his usual kind smile. "Cainnech grows impatient fer ye in the great hall. When he sees ye, he will understand the delay. Ye look lovely, my dear."

"Thank you." She smiled and accepted his arm.

"It pleases my heart to see this change in Cainnech," he remarked as they walked. "He returned from huntin' this morn smilin'."

"It pleases me, as well," she admitted. How much should she tell the priest? He knew Cainnech better than anyone else. Perhaps he could help her reach his friend. "I do not hate him anymore."

His smile softened. "I know."

"In fact, I am coming to care for him."

"Are ye?" He didn't look surprised.

A thought occurred to her and she offered him a frantic look. "You do not think he knows, do you?"

He shook his head and patted her hand. "I can assure ye, my dear, he is completely unaware."

"How do you know? What has he said?"

"Nothin'. But that is not unusual," he muttered and then waved his hand in front of him as if he were trying to scatter those thoughts and get back on topic. "I know because he knows so little of love."

"Has he...never loved a woman before?" she asked hesitantly.

"Nae. Nor has he been loved by one."

She thought it remarkable, but then remembered that he spent most of his time fighting for Robert the Bruce—which he would likely be getting back to soon.

"I confess, Father, I do not know if I have time to help him battle his hatred."

He stopped and set his lambent eyes on her. "My dear, the battle he fights is not hatred, 'tis love."

"What do you mean?"

He sighed and began walking slowly again. "'Twas hatred that took his kin from his life. But 'twas love that drove them from his memory, and the pain of love that came closest to making him lose his mind. He made himself forget his family so that he could survive the life he had withoot them. He hasna loved, or even attempted to love anyone in the years I have known him. In fact, my dear, 'tis the only thing that frightens him."

This was a whole new battle. Aleysia wasn't sure she was prepared for it. "He loves you," she argued hollowly.

A wistful shadow passed over his gaze. "As much as he is able, I imagine."

Her heart thundered in her chest. What if he could never love, or if he continued to deny it? Why was she wasting her time? No, she couldn't give up on him. It was too late for that. She cared for him. Besides, she'd never fled from a challenge before. She wouldn't begin now. "Do you truly think I can break through all those defenses, Father?"

"Ye are the only lass I know with the courage to try."

Aye. He was correct. He—

"Priest!" Cainnech stood at the other end of the corridor, blocking the torchlight. "Did I ask ye to fetch Aleysia or delay her?"

Aleysia widened her eyes on him and tightened her lips. How dare he bark at Father Timothy and treat her like a favored pet?

She straightened her circlet, pinched her silk skirts above her ankles, and strode toward him. "Just exactly who do you think you are?" He didn't look like he was going to answer quickly enough, so she continued. "The next time you want me, come to me yourself. Or better yet," she said, reaching him and tilting her head to look into his eyes, "learn to wait. I will not be rushed to please you."

"Fergive me. What?" He blinked his gaze away from her snug gown and then seemed to catch his breath when he looked into her eyes.

He was utterly serious. He hadn't heard a word she'd said. She wasn't back to hating him for it just yet though. She had wanted to entice him, after all. He certainly looked enticed.

"Apologize to Father Timothy!" she demanded and waited for him to step aside and let her pass.

He moved out of her way and she proceeded toward the great hall. "Truthfully, Cainnech," she said over her shoulder as she came to the small stairway, "just when I think you are not so irritating, you go and shout at a man of God."

She felt his eyes on her like a wolf that had just spotted its mate. And then he was there, behind her, bending his nose to the hair at the nape of her neck.

"Ye look ravishin'." His voice was a deep-throated growl that made her knees nearly give out.

"What about your clear head?"

"I have already lost it."

He stepped around her like liquid smoke. His eyes danced over her features in facets of blue and gray. "Ye are goin' to gain much attention when ye go in there."

"Oh?" she asked lightly, hoping it drove him mad. "Will it make you uncomfortable?"

He laughed, startling Farther Timothy behind them. "Why would it?"

"Why would you mention it?"

"To prepare ye."

She walked up the steps and turned to stop him with a smile. "I'm already prepared. If any unwanted hands come near me tonight, I shall cut them off."

He slanted his sensual mouth into a challenging half-smile. "With what, lass? Yer sharp tongue?"

She leaned down so he could hear her when she whispered, "A dagger. I found a few that your men missed in their search."

His smile widened, his gaze roved over her boldly. "Where d'ye have it hidden, Aleysia? I see no imperfection."

She didn't answer but led the way into the great hall, letting him take his fill behind her. As she walked to her table, she paused to look around the crowded hall. She liked the ribaldry of the men, the sounds of their laughter and swearing, the clanking of their cups. There was wine, thanks to Rauf who purchased six jugs on the way home from Newton on the Moor.

He stood with William by the table. When they saw her they stared and smiled, along with the others, but all the men remained respectful as she sat on the bench.

She looked for Richard but didn't see him.

Cainnech slid in beside her, and Father Timothy took his place to the right. Soon, the rest of the men joined them at the tables and shouted for the food to be served. They all came to a spluttering halt for the second time that night when Mattie stepped into the hall on the arm of Sir Richard. Why, even William, sitting at Aleysia's left, turned to have an appreciative look.

Aleysia's gown fit her dear friend perfectly. She looked breathtaking in a yellow kirtle beneath a lovely saffron overgown embroidered with a thin vine of small golden leaves around the scooping neckline and elbow-length sleeves. Tiny yellow flowers were entwined into her thick, flaxen braid draping one shoulder.

"Who gives yer friend wings?" Cainnech leaned in to ask her.

"William," she answered on a wilting whisper.

"And that troubles ye because he's a Scot?"

She shook her head and eyed him, wondering if he truly thought her so double-minded that she would begrudge her friend the same thing she wanted. But, according to Father Timothy, Cainnech didn't know she cared for him. Should she tell him? No, she thought, let him discover it on his own.

"It troubles me because his heart is lost to Julianna," she corrected him on a hushed voice, and then watched the men stand when Mattie reached their table.

"I think," he said, raising his cup to her and then to Mattie, "the two most bonny lasses in the three kingdoms reside at Lismoor."

The men agreed, but William had already gone back to his cup.

"You see?" Aleysia asked, turning to Cainnech. "There is beauty in no one else when your heart loves another."

"Pah! What drivel!" He laughed, bringing his cup to his lips. "Love doesna last. Sadly, he, too, was taught its cruel lesson."

His battle was with love. He hated it, rejected it, and was afraid of it. How in blazes was she to fight this? She was confident in many things, but not this.

She crooked her finger at him and when he came close, she whispered, "The cruelty was not love, Cainnech. 'Twas a heart tainted by prejudice. True love lasts. You cannot hide from it forever. You know that."

He put down his cup and stared at her. She had no idea what he was about to say but he didn't look pleased.

"Commander." Amish hurried into the hall with a folded parchment held high in his hand. "A messenger arrives from the king!"

Cainnech stood up and waited while a tall man dressed in dark clothes and mantle entered behind his second.

Aleysia thought she could hear his heart pounding, but realized soon that it was her own.

Whatever it was, it couldn't be good news for her if it was from the Scottish king.

The messenger reached Cainnech and greeted him with a familiar smile. Cainnech did not smile back.

Unfazed by the commander's aloof regard, the messenger reached under his cloak and produced a folded missive stamped with a royal seal. "From the hand of the king of the Scots, Robert the Bruce to ye, Commander MacPherson."

Cainnech took the letter and offered the man a place at one of the other tables. The messenger declined with good reason. His wife was at home ready to have his second child.

After he left, Cainnech broke the seal and opened the parchment. He read silently for a moment, and then glanced at her with a scowl that made her want to demand to know what it said.

"Is it about Lismoor?" She couldn't wait another moment.

"Let us go somewhere else to—"

"No." She shook her head. "You will tell me now, please."

He looked as if he might refuse or tear off someone's head. Finally, he said in a lowered voice. "The king advises that ye are to be wed."

"To whom?" she heard herself say, her blood beginning to sizzle in her veins.

"To one of the English noblemen who have already sworn loyalty to him. He has taken it upon himself to invite them here to…court ye. Once ye are wed, yer husband will be rewarded with Lismoor."

Wed? Her home was to be a reward to an English traitor? "Do you think I will abide by your king's rule?" she asked acidly.

Cainnech didn't answer but crumpled the parchment into a ball and flung it into the hearth. He rose from his chair and stormed out of the great hall.

CHAPTER TWENTY-THREE

"WHERE IS HE?" Aleysia hurried through the halls after not finding Cainnech in his room. She wasn't about to let him run from this. He'd promised her she would stay and without marriage if she swore fealty to Robert. What was he going to do about it now? Was he going to abandon her to a stranger? An Englishman?

"Father!" she called out, stopping the priest on the way to his room. "Where is he?"

"I was asked to tell ye that Cainnech will speak with ye in the mornin'."

She crunched her hands into fists at her sides. "Thank you for telling me. Now where is he?"

He turned his doe-eyed gaze upward.

Aleysia looked up and then shrugged her shoulders, frustrated by his silence. "What does that mean, Father? Are you trying to tell me you hope he goes to Heaven when I kill him?"

"Not that far up, my dear," he said with a furtive smile and then left her alone in the hall.

She looked up again. The battlements.

She hiked her skirts over her knees and hurried for the stairs. He wouldn't escape this time. She wanted answers. Not about standing by while she was wed. She'd kill any bastard put beside her in her bed. She wanted to know how long he was staying now that he'd heard from his king. She wanted to know if she meant anything to him.

What if she did? Would he run from it?

She stopped before the last few steps to the battlements and put her fingers to her lips. She couldn't tell him how she felt, that she was falling in love with him. He would run. He'd leave Lismoor and her to whatever future she had left.

She almost turned back but a desire to be near him pulled her forward like an unseen tether.

She stepped through the doorway and into the night. This was one of her favorite places to come when she needed to think clearly. Was he here for the same reason? What did he need to think about? She walked to the edge and then around it until she found him looking out over the north, toward the distant mountains of Scotland.

She observed him in the moonlight, his hair dancing around his deeply pensive face and his shoulders from the roiling wind. He looked like a man with the weight of the three kingdoms on his shoulders.

He heard her approach and turned just for a moment to look at her.

"Do you want to go back?" she asked, coming to stand beside him.

"I wish I was there now," he answered in a voice as cold as the gale blowing in from his land.

Her heart sank. "Then you will be returning soon?"

He inhaled a deep breath and took his time releasing it. "I dinna know when I will see my home again."

"Why?" she asked so softly that she was sure her question was lost on the wind. But he turned his head to look at her.

"I must stay and hand ye—" He caught himself and grinded his jaw. "—Lismoor over to—"

"Commander," she cut him off. Her heart broke. He was going to hand her over. She meant nothing to him. "As I have told you from the beginning, I have no intention of taking a husband. I will lie to your king to keep my home, but I will not take a husband."

"Ye will lose Lismoor."

She hated him for speaking those words. He'd lied to her, given her false hope. She would not weep over it now. She squared her shoulders and tilted her chin. "I will prepare myself for that."

And perhaps he could visit the villagers and tell them one of the Bruce's dogs would soon be ruling here without her.

"If I must leave, I will forever hold you responsible for this," she told him and left the battlements.

She was a fool! A fool to fall for the man who raided her land and took her home! He'd kissed her and made her feel things…things he knew he would not feel in return.

It no longer mattered. He wasn't going to help.

It was up to her to make certain none of her suitors wanted her.

She smiled as she tore her golden circlet from her head and tossed it aside, and then she wiped her eyes and headed for her room.

CAIN HAD NEVER been so miserable in his life. The last two days had been hell. Aleysia avoided him at every turn and when he *had* seen her, he couldn't help but notice her unhappiness. All the men had remarked to him on it. They'd also shared their confusion as to why the king would trouble himself in the affairs of a steward's grand-daughter.

Finally, this evening, he knew it was time to tell them the truth, who she was, and what she had done. It was long overdue. They trusted him and deserved to know why he had lied to them.

He went to the tower to speak to them alone, without Richard or the castle staff hovering about.

He sat with them in the gathering hall, watching their familiar faces in the light of the large hearth fire. He knew what to expect from them on the battlefield, and which of his men fought best. And during the many nights when they all slept beneath the stars, he knew which of them cried out in their sleep.

"At first," he concluded, "I protected her fer the sake of peace, and because I understood that she had been tryin' to keep her home, as any of us would have done, and then finally…" He paused. What he was about to say was even more difficult than the previous truths to which he'd admitted to them. "…because, as ye likely already suspect, I have come to care fer her."

Father Timothy, William, and Rauf grinned at him, tempting him to smile back. But he continued soberly, "I understand that I broke yer trust, but I couldna turn her over to ye. If any of ye wishes to fight under a different commander, I shall make the request on yer behalf to the king."

The men were quiet. Most appeared stunned. A few were angry.

"She waged war on us," someone muttered.

"She fought alone from the trees," Amish pointed out, shaking his head in astonishment. His eyes opened wider and he stared at Cain when he remembered. "She almost killed ye."

"Aye," Cain agreed with a slow smile aimed at the man who'd fought by his side since the Battle of Loudoun Hill. "Who else can say such a thing, eh, Amish?"

"No one, Commander," his second replied. "I admire her fer her bravery."

"As do I," William said boldly, "She shouldna be scorned because we lost men in the fight or because we were bested by a lass."

The men all finally agreed. She had won them over with her many rare, if not odd, qualities, her loyalty now that she knew them, and her radiant smile.

What was Cain to do? Was he willing to defy the king and send her suitors away? Was it too late to stop this madness in his head? He didn't want to love her. If he did and she was taken from him, he would lose his soul this time.

"Stay and have a drink with us, Commander," Amish said and offered him a cup. "'Tis whisky Rauf and Duncan brewed in the kitchen."

Cain accepted. He didn't do too much talking, but he laughed with the men, and he listened and learned more intimate things about them.

For instance, William found no interest in the bonny Matilda when her name was brought up. The lad was miserable. His heart was lost to Julianna Feathers.

Love made men weak and Cain had made certain his whole life that he would never be weak again.

"What will ye do aboot her, Son?" Father Timothy asked quietly, sitting beside him. "The suitors will be arrivin' soon."

What could he do? Prepare for the day when she would be out of his life for good? Or prepare for war? One scared the hell out of him. One did not.

THE SUITORS BEGAN arriving early on the third day. Dressed in their fine wool tunics, fur-lined mantles, and brightly colored hose, they paraded through the front doors like a plague set loose on Lismoor. Bearing gifts of silks and spices and other nonsense, they waited patiently with Richard and Father Timothy in the great hall while Aleysia prepared herself to meet them. Cain's men guarded the entrances.

Two cushioned chairs, one a bit larger than the other, had been dragged from the other rooms and placed at the head table in the center of the hall. Cain sat in the larger chair.

He didn't know what to expect when she arrived. Hell, she could have done anything if she had put her mind to it. He looked into the cup he was holding and put it down without taking a drink. She could have one or more of her handy little daggers hidden wherever the hell she'd hidden them. He would stop her if he had to. If anyone was going to kill any of her suitors, it was going to be him.

Cain eyed them, hating them all, hating being this close to them. The more they looked at him, sniveling little peacocks that they were, the more he thought about killing them.

When the guests stood, Cain knew she had finally entered. He didn't have to turn around. He knew she was breathtaking.

When those closest to the entrance stepped back and whispered, Cain finally turned to see what they were seeing.

She wore a plain brown tunic, belted at the waist, and black breeches. Her beautiful raven hair was pulled back in an unkempt tail trailing down her back. Her face, including her lips, was pale, ashen white, and around her eyes were dark circles.

She looked deathly ill. She even coughed into her hand.

Cain hurried toward her. "What ails ye, lass?"

She stepped around him without acknowledging him and sat in his slightly larger chair. "Let us get this over with," she barked out and then yawned.

"Lady," one of the peacocks addressed her, looking a bit confused. Cain kept his eye on him while he sat in her chair. "Are you ill? Is it something that should concern us?"

She opened her eyes and glared at him. "What kind of men does the King of Scots send to court me that they fear a harmless..." She paused and looked off to the left. "...at least I think 'tis harmless, condition?"

Cain realized what she was doing and couldn't help but smile. She wasn't ill, or even pale. She was wearing some kind of powder on her face and her lips. 'Twas clever.

"Ye didna cough up blood again this morn, did ye?" he asked, wanting to help her.

She swung her head around to squint her eyes at him and held her thumb and index finger a bit apart.

She severed their gaze, though he sought to hold it. What did he want to tell her? Something! He liked being around her more than anyone else he had been near in a very long time. He thought she was the bonniest lass he'd ever come across, even looking like death was at her door. Would this work? What would Robert do if no one wanted to wed her? What if he wed her?

The thought rushed through his mind before he could stop it. He looked away and scowled at the men looking at her.

She didn't want to marry, and she sure as hell wouldn't want the Highland commander who took her home from her.

"I do not care if you are ill!" Some about-to-be dead peacock called out.

"Oh?" Aleysia said and coughed into a small cloth she pulled from her belt.

"I am Sir James Woods, Governor of Bamburgh." He stepped forward in his wrapped hood and presented thin, outstretched arms. He looked to be at least twenty years older than her. "I have brought you some perfume from France and fine silk from the Far East. I have much more to offer once we are wed."

Cain wanted to spring from his chair and tear out Sir James Woods' heart from his chest.

"I do not fear if you are ill, my dear lady," Woods continued, oblivious to the rumbling mountain beside her. "I see the strength in your eyes to recover. I would be a fool to leave once I laid eyes on you."

She smiled behind her cloth and coughed again, then leaned forward for Cain's cup. After a long sip, she leaned back and swiped her knuckles across her mouth, smearing off some of the powder from her lips. "Thank you, Sir James, you may—"

"Look at that!" he smiled, showing a row of yellowing teeth. "You are looking better already! Why, your lips are like ripe—"

"Governor Woods," Cain cut him off with a warning glare. "Take yer bow and move on. The lady has more suitors to greet."

He didn't want to go. Cain could see it in his eyes. He wanted to stand up to the primitive-looking Highlander who'd taken this castle and a dozen before it, but he didn't.

The next worm to step forward was Sir Andrew something-or-other from Doddington. He was tall and thin with timid eyes and a sharp nose. "Commander MacPherson, thank you for inviting us into Lismoor to—"

"Why are you thanking him when 'tis my castle?" Aleysia asked with icy contempt. "You are not off to a grand start, Sir Andrew." She waved him away. "Who is next?"

Confident that none of these peacocks could win Aleysia's heart, Cain smiled as more English noblemen from everywhere in Northumberland came forward. He even recognized some of the faces from various castles he'd stormed.

He listened while she methodically discouraged every suitor, either with her fits of coughing or her sharp tongue. So many times, he wanted to smile at her, proud of her courage and determination to avoid what she didn't want. But she barely spared him a look the entire morning.

When the last courter of the morning left, Cain finally turned to her. "Ye were a nightmare."

She finally smiled at him and it felt as if he could breathe again. He hated that she held such command over his moods, but he didn't know how to stop it.

"Do you think I frightened any of them away?"

"All of them, no doubt."

"Good," she said and stood from his chair. "Well, 'twas nice seeing you—everyone today."

Hell, what was this warmth seeping into his muscles, his bones, his gaze? It made him ache to hold her, kiss her, tell her…what? What could he offer her? There were days he felt like a tortured soul in a living grave. Days he prayed to Father Timothy's God to let him die on the battlefield so that he could have this peace he'd heard so much about. But he lived. Every time.

He watched her turn to leave. He reached out. "Aleysia." His voice stopped her. She turned her pale face to him.

I must help ye find her first. Father Timothy's words at Bannockburn came rushing back at him. *Something to do with love.*

He swallowed and his heartbeat accelerated. He looked toward Heaven. He didn't want love in his life. He couldn't love her and watch her marry someone else, or watch her give away her home because of him. He couldn't stop any of it without betraying the king. "There is nothin' I can do, lass."

"You mean, there is nothing you *will* do," she accused him and left the hall.

CHAPTER TWENTY-FOUR

ALEYSIA STOOD ON the battlements and watched Cainnech leave the castle. She let her tears fall freely, leaving streaks down her powdered face. She deserved this misery for losing her heart to a Scot.

Still, as infuriating as Cainnech was, she would rather spend the day—or the night with him than any of those noblemen. She'd almost fallen asleep twice. In fact, she believed she had taken a short nap when Lord Kendrick of Brampton went on about his lavish home and all of his riches. He may have said something about liking beautiful things and her fitting right in. Or she may have dreamed it. Either way, she didn't like him. She didn't like any of them. She made a note to tell Rauf and the men all about Lord Kendrick's lavish home.

Why couldn't the man seeking her hand, pledging his life to her and her happiness, be the man who was letting her go?

She would like to run away as well. But she had people depending on her. What was she to do? If Cainnech was leaving, and the Bruce took over her land, who would look after everyone? Shouldn't she be at least trying to discover which of her suitors would treat her friends the best?

She closed her eyes and said a prayer. She didn't want to marry any one of those men. They cowered to her, and if not to her, then to Cainnech. They looked like pretty little flowers all lined up in a row, ready for the picking.

"My dear?"

She startled at the sound of Father Timothy's satiny voice behind her. She wiped her eyes quickly and tried to steady her voice. "Forgive me, Father, I did not hear you," she said without turning around.

"That's quite all right. Here now." He put his hand on her arm and gently urged her to turn. "Why d'ye not come sit down and tell my why ye weep."

"I should confess first," she said, sliding down the short wall and sitting on the cold ground.

"If ye wish." He looked down at her and then at the small bench a few feet away. Finally, he shrugged and bent to sit beside her. When his knees popped, she looked at him and he smiled sheepishly.

Oh, what was happening to her? She was beginning to love Father Timothy…and William. All of them!

When she felt her eyes begin to burn again, she refused to weep or beg him not to go. She didn't know what tomorrow would bring, but she wanted to confess just in case.

"I thought about killing today," she began, and then stopped again. "In truth, I have thought about it often. Ever since Cainnech arrived. I do not know if he has told you, but I took a dagger to him many times. Father, I do not see the humor in this."

"Fergive me, child," he said, his smile not altogether fading. "Go on. Who did ye think aboot killin' today?"

"Oh," she threw up her hands. "I do not remember his name. They all looked the same, spoke the same, smelled the same. I thought I was dying, and there are still more arriving for me to see this afternoon! Father!"

He covered his smile with his hand and gave her an apologetic look.

"Cainnech was the only thing that made it bearable," she confessed. "Every time I think about someone else kissing me, it makes me want to weep." She swiped a blasted tear away from her eye but another one fell in its place. "He has done something to me, made me feel things I thought I would never feel—like loving the man who took my home and then left me to the whims of his king—Father Timothy, if you are going to continue to smile at everything I say, I will no longer say anything at all."

"My dear, ye love him."

What? No. That wasn't what she said. Was it? She nodded and gave up wiping her eyes. "Aye. Aye, I love him. I confess the treachery of my heart for it. I am sorry for those I have betrayed because of it. But if I must share my days and nights with someone, I would prefer it be him. But I fear I cannot break through to him. He runs from me over and over again, even though I do not think he wants to. He will never love me."

He took both her hands in his. "Oh, but ye are incorrect, my dear lass. That is why he is more afraid now than before. Ye have made him speak things I never thought I would hear him say. That is why he is runnin'. Nae." He stopped and put his hand to his mouth. "I shouldna be tellin' ye any of this. 'Tis not my place to—"

"Father!" She almost pinched him. "You must tell me everything!"

He thought about it for a moment and then looked into her pleading eyes. "All right, but I dinna know much."

She groaned impatiently.

He cast her a furtive smile and looked around, making certain they were alone. "He cares fer ye, lass. He has admitted to it, even to the men." He paused when her eyes widened with surprise.

"When did he tell the men? And what exactly did he tell them?"

"Last night. He said he protected ye from them because he cares fer ye."

Her heart quickened and her belly knotted and made her feel

queasy. "Father, why was he telling the men that he protected me from them?"

The priest didn't have to say anything else. His large, fretful eyes spoke for him.

"He told them?" she asked, wanting to run and never face any of them again.

"He had no other choice, lass. Their suspicions grew when the king involved himself in yer future."

She nodded, understanding, but—"They hate me."

"They admire ye," he corrected. "Ye were ready to die fer yer home."

She lowered her gaze. "How can they forget what I did in the forest?"

"There are some who understand the necessity fer battle, great or small. Some who admire the courage to see it through. Those are the men who already care fer ye." He smiled and, for a moment, she believed that all would be well.

"But the difficult part now lies before ye."

"This has not been the difficult part?" she asked softly, holding her hands to her chest.

"Nae. Gettin' Cainnech to tell ye…and himself, how he feels will be the hardest. But ye must or I fear he will go, and then there will be nothin' left to salvage."

"What do I do?" she asked, praying he was right and he could help her.

"Well, it seems to me, but I dinna know much aboot courtin', so I could be wrong, but, if he is doin' the runnin', perhaps 'tis time he do the chasin'."

She leaned in closer and listened to his advice.

When he was done, they sat against the wall and the strong wind and spoke of other things for a little while, like her brother, King Edward, and William.

"He needs our help, Father," she said of the young Scot. "His heart is broken over a girl whose father purchased him for a stone and then…" She looked at Father Timothy. It hit her. The thing creeping around in her head about Will, not making itself known until now.

The priest wore the same look on his face she must be wearing on hers. "William was purchased fer a stone?" he asked on a shaken breath.

She nodded. "He told me so himself." She felt lightheaded at how hard her heart was beating. "Has he never told you?"

The priest shook his head. "He has never spoken of his past and we thought it best not to push. So we didna ask."

William! Was it possible Cainnech's brother had been living with him for the last few months?

"Did he…did he say when he was purchased? Where?"

"No, but how many people do you know who were purchased for a stone?"

The priest scrambled to his feet. "Come. We must find William and ask him."

"Oh, Father, do you think 'tis possible?" She was afraid to hope for such a wondrous thing. "I'm certain William is his brother. Mattie and I even spoke of how they share expressions, and look how they get along."

"Aye," Father Timothy agreed as they hurried toward the guard's tower and through the heavy doors. "But we must be as certain as we can be. Cainnech would go mad if he lost his brother twice."

Was Cainnech truly going to get his brother back? She wanted to shout with excitement.

They searched for William and found him in his room. Aleysia noticed a quill and parchment on a small table beside the window. She was surprised a servant could read and write. Had Julianna taught him? The instant Aleysia looked at him, she saw Cainnech in the depths of his angry gaze. Was he writing to Julianna?

"William, what do you know about your birth, your kin, any-thing?" asked Aleysia.

"Nothing really. Just what I told you. Why?"

"Where did yer purchase take place?" Father Timothy asked him, staring into his eyes, searching for the answer.

"Invergarry, I think," William answered. He waited while the priest held his hand to his forehead and used the other hand to guide himself into the nearest chair.

"How old were ye when ye were sold?" he asked. "A babe? A boy? Which was it? Do ye know?"

William nodded watching them, seeming to sense that these insignificant questions were about to usher in something new in his life. "A babe. I—" He closed his eyes as if he were trying to remember. "I was told I was two winters."

"And how old are ye now?" Father Timothy asked, his breath held, his dark eyes filled with tears. "You canna be more than a score. Nicholas would have been—"

"Two and twenty," William answered softly.

"Two and twenty," the priest echoed and stood up from his seat.

"Is there anythin' else, lad?" he asked, stepping forward.

William looked off to the side, trying to remember and then finally did. "I may have had a brother or a sister, but I do not know for certain."

"Ye have two," Father Timothy told him. "Brothers."

William stood still in his place, only his eyes moved from Father Timothy to Aleysia. "I have…" He shook his head, not understanding. "How do you know this?"

"Cainnech had—has two brothers," Father Timothy told him, "who were taken by the English a score of years ago after they killed the boys' parents and burned down their home in Invergarry. One of his brothers, called Nicholas, was two winters old when he was sold fer a stone."

William said nothing for a long time. His eyes filled up with tears that sparkled like diamonds in a summer stream. "The commander is my brother," he said as if he needed to say it, hear it coming from his own mouth, to believe it. "My brother."

"Aye," Father Timothy said, his smile turning into laughter. "He is yer brother."

The priest turned to Aleysia with his luminous, sable eyes going warm. "Ye found him, my dear lass." He reached up and took William's stunned face in his hands. "Ye found Nicholas."

MORE SUITORS HAD arrived, along with some returning lords. Aleysia made them all wait for her in the great hall while Mattie helped her change her gown and clean her face. They took their time. There was much to do and, besides that, Cainnech hadn't yet returned to the castle.

Aleysia needed him here. She couldn't go through another hour of listening to these men speak as if they knew her, loved her on sight. Oh, she lamented, this afternoon was going to be so much worse.

Now, there was a different plan altogether and Cainnech needed to be here for it. Where in the blazes was he?

She hadn't told Mattie about William being Cainnech's brother. That was their tale to tell if they chose to.

"Aleysia, you are shivering!" her friend pointed out and finished pinning the last pearl to Aleysia's hair. "There! You are ready!"

Aleysia's hair was loosely plaited into a side braid clasped at the shoulder and then left to cascade in rich, lustrous locks over her breast. Mattie had interwoven pearls throughout the plait and dusted her skin with crushed pearl powder.

"I dried some of your bluebells and then crushed them with a bit of water, and then I added a small smudge to the corners of your eyes," Mattie said, smiling, proud of her work. "You can hardly notice it, but it makes your eyes look more vivid green."

Aleysia stood up and ran her hand down her white velvet gown. "I cannot delay this day any longer." She turned to her friend. "Will you come with me?"

"Of course!" Mattie said emphatically and stepped in behind her. "Remember to watch your sleeves."

Aleysia nodded. The damned things practically hung to her knees.

With no other reason to wait, she led them out of the solar.

When she stepped inside the great hall and saw her suitors seated and waiting at the tables, she felt a little ill and pressed her hand to her belly. Was she truly going to have to marry one of these men in order to remain at Lismoor? Who else would see to her friends, the people who raised her?

She smiled at Father Timothy, and then she saw William behind him, armed with at least six different weapons in his belt and behind his back. He no longer looked like he couldn't use them.

She eyed Cainnech's slightly larger chair and was about to sit in it when all eyes turned on the doorway again and the towering Highlander standing in it, his dark, brooding eyes on her.

CHAPTER TWENTY-FIVE

ALEYSIA FORGOT ABOUT being the most beautiful one in the hall when Cainnech stepped inside. He moved with leashed power toward her, keeping his eyes on her alone. Her heart both broke for him and prepared to stand strong against him. She had to. She had to in order to snatch him from hatred's cold hands and win his heart.

He took in the sight of her like a dying, angry man. She stared right back. If anyone should be angry it was she! He was allowing this!

Finally, he broke their gaze and raked it over Father Timothy and William.

"Ye brought two women here in the midst of twenty men," he said in a low, dangerous voice. "With only the two of ye to protect them?"

"I can protect myself," Aleysia reminded him stiffly. She glared up at him as he stepped around her. He smelled of the forest.

"And who would have protected Matilda?" he asked before he fell into his chair, "the priest or the lad?"

"Perhaps, if you had been here instead of—why are you looking at me like that?"

"Ye have recovered nicely," he murmured, flicking his gaze over the pearls in her hair.

She caught Father Timothy's eye and remembered their plan. "I am feeling much better." She took her seat and turned her most radiant smile on her guests.

"Who among these handsome gentlemen would care to speak to me first?" she called out.

Even with all the men rising to their feet together, she could feel Cainnech's eyes on her. Hot, dreadful, burning eyes, which she successfully ignored for the next hour.

An hour. He let it go one for an *hour*. She could have killed him. Aye, he could barely sit still and his mumbling was beginning to frighten the suitors. He had many opinions about them, none of which should have been spoken out loud, but were. His challenging, murderous glare stopped any from replying. But he hated them because they were English, not because they were here to take her from him forever. If so, he would have stopped this. They were all wrong. He didn't care for her. Even after his smoldering kisses, his curious touch, she meant nothing to him. He cared only for fighting, evidenced in his eagerness to kill every man who stepped forward.

"Sir John de Granville of Avranches," the next guest called out, moving forward. He wasn't as tall as some of the lankier men there, but beneath his quilted doublet, snug hose and shiny boots, he appeared nicely fashioned. He wore no hood, wrapped or otherwise, on his golden head.

"Welcome to Lismoor, my lord." Aleysia graced him with a perfect smile as he reached for her hand to kiss it. The flat of Cainnech's sword stopped the Norman knight when he held it between Sir John's lips and her knuckles.

Was he jealous? All the men had flattered her, but none had been so bold as to reach for her hand. Aleysia turned to look at him, the first time she had in an hour. She shouldn't have. Her heart immediately warmed toward him. He was so masterfully made, coiled and ready to spring into action. Oh, but she didn't want anyone but him. She wanted *him*.

"Get on with what ye intend to say before I lose what is left of my patience," he warned in an icy tone. His lightning-streaked eyes never left Sir John's.

"Pardon me, Commander," the Norman said, straightening and turning his full attention on him. "I should have made my intentions clearer to you. I am not here by invitation from your king, like these men."

"I do not understand," Aleysia said with a sinking feeling in her belly.

"You will." Sir John's smile on her was more like a sneer, turning his handsome face into a homely one.

He put his hand into his doublet and Cainnech leaped to his feet. His sword was first against Sir John's neck. William and Father Timothy had swords pointing to his throat before anyone blinked.

"Easy, my friends," the knight held up his hands and laughed. "'Tis just a letter I wish to present."

Cainnech reached into the doublet and pulled out the letter. He opened it, read it, and then threw it in Sir John's stunned face. "I dinna give a damn what her cousin demands. He is not gettin' Lismoor, nor are ye. Get oot! All of ye, get oot before I start cuttin' ye to pieces!" With the hilt of his claymore clutched in his hand, he turned his dark, deadly eyes on her. "She is mine."

When no one remained but Father Timothy and the others, he told them to leave as well.

Finally alone, he turned on her. "What d'ye mean by lookin' the way ye do and smilin' at that cocky Norman bastard?"

"Why should I not look pleasing or smile to find a husband?" she countered.

"Is that what ye want now, a husband? This morn, ye tried to scare them away and now ye want a husband?"

"I cannot abandon my friends," she told him. "If becoming the wife of one of these noblemen is the only way to keep Lismoor, then aye, I will marry. Who is there to stop me?"

"Me," he told her, rushing forward and taking her in his arms. "There is me."

CAIN COVERED HER mouth with his and drew her slim body closer to him. He kissed her with merciless desperation and longing, lifting her feet off the floor in a crushing, yet tender embrace.

Whatever he felt for her, whatever he tried to deny, followed him wherever he went. He'd tried to outrun it, terrified to open himself to love again. But he no longer wanted to run. He'd never met anyone like her. No woman had ever made him feel what she did. So what if it scared the hell out of him? He'd kicked fear in its teeth before. He'd do it again. He'd do it for her.

When she coiled her arms around his neck and let him have his way, he teased her with his tongue and ran his hands over her dips and curves. She felt good in his arms, as if she belonged there, fitting perfectly against him and making him whole.

"Fergive me fer bein' a fool," he broke their kiss to tell her. "I will face anythin' fer ye. I canna let ye go, lass."

"I do not want you to let me go," she whispered.

He loved the sound of her, the scent of her, the memory of her laughter leading him through the wild strawberries to the glade.

Should he tell her about the demons he fought? The ones he wouldn't let out? They were fighting for release even now. He held fast.

"I came back and found ye lookin'…hell, beautiful and all yer suitors pantin' at the bit. 'Twas difficult not to kill them."

"You were jealous?" she asked, slanting her glance at him.

"Aye, I was jealous."

When he lowered his head to kiss her again, she pressed her palms against his chest and pushed away. "Just so we are clear. You have been known to run from me. I will know what this means."

He smiled and dipped his mouth to hers. "Ye mean this?" he asked and planted a series of soft, sultry kisses on her mouth.

"Aye," she said breathlessly. "This." She let him kiss her again.

"Stay right here," he told her and stepped away. He was going to do this. He couldn't run any longer. He was going to lose her forever if he did. And that frightened him even more than loving her did. He'd taken away her home and claimed it from under her. He was going to make right the things he had done wrong to her.

Finally, his belly stopped aching.

He had no idea what he would tell the king. He'd fallen in love with the lady of Lismoor. He almost didn't believe it. He hadn't been sure it *was* love until the threat of losing her to someone else stirred up the darkest parts of him.

If anyone was going to marry her, it was going to be him.

When he reached the entryway, he called out for Amish. His second, Rauf, and William appeared almost instantly, apparently listening by the door.

"Gather the men," he told them. "Bring them here."

"What are you doing?" she asked him with laughter in her voice when he asked her to sit in her chair.

"Showin' ye what this means." He went to stand by the tables at the far end of the hall, alone but for her watching him.

The men began filing in, following his instruction. They sat on their benches and waited, whispering under their breaths, curious why they had been called in.

Finally, Cain quieted them with a look and strode forward.

"I am Cainnech MacPherson, second commander of the elite Highland warriors under Robert the Bruce, King of the Scots." He reached her chair in a few strides and bent before her. "I come seekin' yer hand in marriage."

Everyone behind him went utterly still. The collective silence of their stunned disbelief was proof that he'd truly just asked her to marry him. Her smile was resplendent, or mayhap she glowed like a beacon of light only to him.

He moved his hand to her face and swiped his thumb over a tear on her cheek. "Ye have met many suitors, fair lass. Which one of us d'ye choose?"

"I choose you," she replied without hesitation. Her voice was a silken melody to his ears. Her face, the most breathtaking face he'd ever beheld. His heart thundered against his léine.

The men cheered and demanded that she offer him her hand. She did, and he took it in his rough, callused one and brought it to his lips. His touch, his kiss was his promise made before God and his priest, who rushed forward and pronounced a blessing. But he pulled her into his arms anyway and kissed her.

"Come away with me to the glade," he groaned at her ear. "I wish to be alone with ye."

"Aye," she agreed, nervous about what exactly would happen between them.

"But first, Cainnech," she leaned in to whisper to him. "there is something you must know that cannot wait. Send the men away. All but William and Father Timothy."

He did as she bid him, sending the men away with wine and a warning to stay out of trouble.

"'Tis already too late fer that, I'd say," the priest remarked when they were alone.

"I dinna care," Cain told him. "If someone wants to contest our betrothal, let him fight me on the field."

"'Tis Normandy," his old friend reminded him, lowering his voice.

"King Robert is in secret talks with the Normans. Did ye ferget? He wants them on our side."

No he hadn't forgotten. He didn't care. He hadn't agreed to her being married off, put on display like some prized chattel. Now was not the time to argue. She waited for them with William at her side.

Cain was glad she was friends with William and had gotten him to open up more. She had a way about her, a fearlessness to step right into one's hell and kick up some ashes.

Something to do with love.

To wake him up, to breathe new, cleansing life into him. If he didn't run.

His eyes gleamed on her. He could feel the fire rising in him. Fire he hadn't felt in years, save when it came to killing.

"Cainnech," she started as she held out her hand and put him in front of his chair. "Why do you not sit?" she suggested and then pushed him down.

"What is goin' on?" He laughed and looked at William and Father Timothy. They remained silent.

"Cainnech," Aleysia began and sat beside him. "Father Timothy and I discovered some things about William."

Cain smiled at the lad and then back at her. "Good things, judgin' by yer excitement."

"Aye, they are good things," she agreed.

What did good things about William have to do with him? "Well, tell me what they are, woman. Ye keep me waitin'."

"We found out that he was born in Invergarry a two and twenty years ago."

Cain slanted his gaze at the lad again. Two and twenty years ago? He appeared younger.

"He was two when—" She stopped and looked at William. "Why do you not tell him?"

Cain's heart beat a steady hard drumbeat against his ribs. Two. He was two when…

"I was two when I was sold to Governor Feathers," William finished. "For a stone." He paused when Cain's face drained of color and he sat up in his chair.

Cain thought he might be dreaming. But no, in his dreams, Nicholas didn't have a face. Was this Nicholas standing before him now? His brother was alive? He'd never dared hope. The ghostly echoes of a crying babe filled his thoughts. He looked away—toward the door—from the terrible pain of that day. He ran his hands down his face and left his chair.

Unexpectedly, Aleysia reached out her hand and fit in into his, lending her strength, keeping him still.

He looked at the lad again, this time with glassy eyes. He didn't ask more questions of him. They didn't have many facts save for the ones the lad matched. Could it be that he had his brother back? In William? Hell, he liked the lad. He closed his eyes as if doing it would keep his heart from reaching out, and going back.

"I think you are my brother, Cainnech," William told him, his eyes holding the same startling potency as Cain's.

"Nicholas," he said, choking on the word. It was too much to ask for, to hope for, so he never had. "Nicky." They moved together into a long, tight embrace.

"Here," Cain held his brother's face in his hands, "Let me have a good look at ye."

Aye, he saw traces of their resemblance, with hints of deep-rooted anger within the quietness of his servitude. "I would kill Feathers if he was alive today," Cain told him, remembering the condition in which they'd found him.

"'Twould not fix things," his brother said. "Knowing who I am—knowing you, will."

"Aye," Cain agreed, drawing him in again and holding on to him as if he'd been waiting twenty years to do it. Hell, he had been. How would Cain help him discover who he was when he had no idea about himself?

"Tell me, Brother," he said, pushing off and then pulling him in under his arm again. "What should we call ye? William or Nicholas?"

"Brother sounds nice," the lad said, grinning. Aye, he looked happier than Cain had ever seen him. "But I choose Nicholas. My whole life I knew my name was not William Stone. I often wondered if I had been born with a name. Now I know that I was, and I know what 'tis." He stopped for a moment to wipe his eyes with the backs of his hands. "I never want to be called Stone again, for it always reminded me what I was worth."

Cain pulled him close again and rested his forehead against his brother's. "Ye are a MacPherson, worth more than any sum, worth more than any sufferin'. Havin' ye back feels like a part of me has been reborn."

He felt another arm coming around him and turned to see Father Timothy between him and Nicholas when they withdrew.

"God is good," his friend said with a joyous smile.

"Aye, God is good," he agreed.

He turned to look at Aleysia, sitting in her chair with her hands to her mouth. He smiled and went to her. "Thank ye, lass."

"Thank me in the glade."

She heated his blood and tightened his muscles.

"Tonight we will celebrate!" he announced to the others. "Father, see to the details. Nicholas, I will see ye tonight, Brother."

He turned to Aleysia again and took her hand, content for the first time in twenty years.

CHAPTER TWENTY-SIX

LATE MORNING SUNSHINE formed glistening columns throughout the forest, lighting their way. This time, it was Cainnech who led Aleysia past the strawberries and around the bend to the narrow opening in the thick bramble.

He waited while she stepped into the glade first. She'd changed her clothes quickly back at the castle. She wore her léine, bodice, breeches, and boots, but still, she felt his eyes on her when she passed him as if she wore her thinnest chemise. It made her blood go warm and her skin feel too tight for her body.

She looked before her and let her eyes bask in the splendor of a colorful palette that made her heart rejoice.

She turned to watch Cainnech enter, then went to him and fell into his arms. His arms molded her supple warmth to his body until she could feel every inch of his strength.

"Are you happy about William?"

"'Tis the best gift anyone has ever given me."

She heard his heart beating fast within the deep rumble of his chest when he spoke.

Something was troubling him. "But?"

"There is no but," he assured her with a smile and ran his thumb across her bottom lip.

"But you do not remember him," she reminded him, loath to take his mind off kissing her. When his muscles stiffened beneath her fingers, she knew she might have gone too far. She patted and petted his chest and then pressed her cheek against it. "I want you to be happy, my love."

He stopped breathing for a moment and then cupped her face in his big hands and tilted her face up to meet his. "D'ye love me, lass?"

She smiled at his handsome face. "Aye, Commander, I love you."

He looked a bit stunned, but how would he know if she loved him or not? He had nothing with which to compare it. He didn't question it though. Instead, he scooped her up off the ground and cradled her against him. "What have I done to deserve a heart like yers, lass?"

He kissed the answer from her mouth and carried her to the plushest part of the glade.

She felt weightless in his strong arms, lost in his passionate kiss. When he set her down in the bluebells, she clung to him, not willing to let him go.

He sat beside her and they laughed as they continued kissing. He took her lip between his teeth and gently pulled. She felt something burn below her belly and fought not to blush. Except for her experience with Cain, she hadn't been kissed in years. There hadn't been time. She knew nothing of intimacy and, yet, instinctively, she knew the way to angle her head and kiss him more deeply, until he groaned. She knew that if she tugged on his léine, he would remove it. She was correct.

She could have gazed at him all day, lost in his raw, rugged, male beauty. His dark hair fell over his sun-kissed shoulders, drawing her gaze there…and lower, to his belly, tightly knitted with sinew.

He caught her admiring him and smiled. "My scars dinna offend ye?"

"Offend me?" She ran her fingers along his chest. "They are signs of your courage." She looked up and touched the small scar over his cheekbone. The scar she had put there. She had almost killed him the day he arrived at Lismoor. The thought of it turned her blood cold. "I would prefer it if you never got so close to a weapon again. Just because I did not kill you, does not mean someone else will not."

He pressed his forehead to hers with a paralyzing sweetness that drew the breath from her trembling body. His deep voice resonated in her veins, setting fire to her blood. "I will live, Aleysia."

How had this happened? She wondered about that, tilting her head to press her mouth to his. How had she fallen in love with a man she was supposed to hate? Every moment she was with him or away from him, her need of him grew. She loved watching him move, tasting his desire, touching him.

She flicked her tongue over his with confidence born from independence and with passion born from loving him.

He moved his fingers over her face like a light, tender caress, touching her while he kissed her. He pushed her down gently, his hand slipping to her neck, and lower. Her nipples grew tight and erect when his fingers brushed over her breast. She tried to remember to breathe while he kissed her and worked the tight laces of her bodice. He fumbled and she gazed at him, loving that he wasn't deft at working the laces of ladies' bodices. She helped him and closed her eyes when it was loosened.

He glided his arm beneath her and pressed her to his hard angles, kissing her mouth with exquisite thoroughness. "Lass," the word left him on a raspy whisper when he slightly withdrew. "Ye dragged me oot of the ashes and into yer fire."

She curled her lips and smiled against his mouth. "My heart would allow no less."

She didn't stop him when she felt his fingers on her belly beneath her léine. His touch was like a flame, burning a path up the side of her body to her left breast. She gasped when he cupped her in his hand.

"Dinna be afraid," he whispered above her.

"I am not afraid," she promised, despite her shivering. Perhaps she should be afraid. He was a Scot, after all. But she trusted him. He'd been protective from the first few days and never anything but gentle with her.

When he began to push her léine up, she thought she might die of embarrassment. He meant to undress her here in the open! But there was no one here to see. After Cainnech's threat to kill them all, her suitors had left Lismoor. The villagers never came here, and Cainnech's men certainly had no reason to come.

Oh, her heart thrilled at the thought of being even more intimate with him. When he bent to kiss her bare belly she stopped caring about her clothes and helped him undress her.

Finally, she lay bare beneath him, modest and untried, afraid to look him in the eyes, lest she see disappointment. Afraid also to look at him, for he was bare, as well—atop her. That is, he was leaning up on his splayed palms, keeping himself above her.

"Aleysia," he groaned deeply and waited for her to meet his gaze, "ye are perfect, lass."

He made her skin feel tight and her heart thud in her ears. She didn't know what to expect. She should be afraid, and she was. But she'd somehow managed to capture the heart of this warrior. He might not be known for his mercy, but he would not harm her.

He looked down at himself and his heavy erection growing between them. When he returned his gaze to hers, he appeared a bit worried. "I hear this hurts if ye are…"

Her eyes opened wider, due both to the beast getting closer to her and Cainnech's warning. "I am," she told him quietly, suddenly not so sure she wanted to do this.

The long, grueling days of preparing for the Scottish army had strengthened her to many things, but she wasn't sure taking a man, especially one like him, into her body, was one of them.

No. She could do it! She wasn't afraid of some little—oh, but there was nothing little about any part of him! What if he smothered her? How would she breathe with all that muscle on her? He knew it would be difficult, that was why he hadn't let himself down yet.

"I can do it," she promised him, tilting her chin just a bit, unsure who she was trying to convince.

He lowered himself and then shot back up when he touched her and she nearly leaped out of her skin. "I canna do it." He shook his head and pushed off. He landed in the bluebells and pulled his plaid over his lap when he sat up. "I dinna want to hurt ye and I fear I will. I know nothin' aboot—virgins."

She nodded. "We will need some help."

He paled and then scowled. "Nae! I willna—"

"I would not feel right about asking Father Timothy for advice about this," she said, pulling on her breeches.

He turned even whiter. "The priest? Advice?"

"We cannot ask any of the men," she pointed out while hurrying into her léine. "They would give terrible advice. We cannot ask Mattie. She is but a child."

"Aleysia, I am sure we can—"

"Of course!" She smiled thinking of just the right woman to ask. "Beatrice, the miller's wife! She will know. She was always like a mother to me." She smiled to herself, remembering, and then looked at Cainnech.

He was not smiling. In fact, he appeared quite horrified. She laid back and pulled him with her. They stared up at the sky for a moment, and then he turned toward her and pulled her close against him. "We will do as ye suggest, lass," he said, as if his agreement in this truly mattered. "I willna see ye hurt."

If anyone would have suggested to her that one day a Scot would vow not to hurt her, or that this fierce, angry man would go soft and give in to her whims, she would have called them mad. But Cainnech proved her wrong.

She stared into his eyes. "I love you, Cainnech."

Instead of the reaction she expected, he looked pained. She realized, suddenly, that he hadn't said he loved her yet. Her heart sank. She had just assumed... "Is it so difficult for you?"

"Aye," he said quietly. "'Tis. Love is..." He stopped to think about it. "...'tis worse than death when 'tis lost."

Oh, he couldn't feel this way! Love was so much more than that. How would he ever heal? She realized that was what she wanted. Not for herself, for she wanted it for him since Father Timothy had told her about Cainnech's life. But what could she do? He had his brother back. Was that not enough?

"'Tis true," she said, her soft breath making a strand of his hair move over his jaw. "Sometimes love can be painful, but we need it in our lives, Cainnech. We need it to live because, most times, 'tis fulfilling and wonderful."

"I have done just fine withoot it," he argued quietly.

Rather than reply, she gave him the look such a preposterous statement deserved.

"I have," he insisted.

"Are you happy?"

"Aye," he said with a smile that made her forget everything else. "I am."

She was happy to hear it. "I mean if you never met me. Were you happy before?"

"Life is not always aboot bein' happy, lass. Things need to be done. Ye know that."

"Cainnech." She stopped him. "When is the last time you were happy?"

He didn't answer. He bent his head to hers, but he said nothing. Not for at least fifty breaths. She closed her eyes and prayed she didn't just ruin his time in the glade.

"I have been dreamin' aboot her more," he said, finally shattering the silence.

"Who?" she prompted, knowing every word brought him closer to healing.

"My…mother."

Aleysia waited, feeling his heart beating against her…or was it her own heart?

"She is…" He shook his head against her, not wanting to think on it.

"She deserves her place in your heart, Cainnech."

He began slowly, hesitantly, telling her first about his dreams, the screaming, and the flames—a babe crying. There were some things he admitted to remembering lately, like flashes from someplace deep of his brother Torin's dirty face and his mother smiling when she saw him.

The more he told her, the more memories came rising like molten lava to the surface. He tried to resist for a while, but she was there, holding him, there with him in his anguish and helping him fight through it.

Later, they lay entwined in the sun-soaked, tear-drenched field of bluebells, kissing and smiling like fools, and kissing some more.

Finally, just before the sun set, they rose and set off toward the miller's house. No one was home. The village was empty.

CHAPTER TWENTY-SEVEN

C AIN LOOKED ACROSS the great hall to where Aleysia stood with a small group of women from the village. He thought of her body beneath his, naked and sublime. He hadn't wanted to hurt her. He knew whores, not virgins. She'd wanted to do it, of course. She was brave and bold.

But what they did was intimate, no less. She came for him. She broke down his defenses stone by stone until she breached his inner core and dusted off his heart.

He found himself remembering things, like a flash of a face or the sound of a voice. It had nearly driven him mad once. He didn't want to miss them again.

But remembering didn't hurt. In fact, it felt wonderful.

He smiled at her when he caught her eye. She blushed and tempted him to go to her.

"So ye are not angry that I invited everyone from the village to the celebration?"

Cain sipped the last of his whisky and looked down at Father Timothy. "Nae, I am not angry. They are her kin."

"Aye," the priest agreed. "Is it not odd to think that now ye have kin, too?"

"Aye," Cain turned his eyes toward his wee brother, who was not so wee anymore. "Nicholas!" he called out and gathered the lad in his arms when he reached him. He had his brother back because of the two people who loved him.

"Has the announcement been made aboot who ye are?"

"Hours ago," Father Timothy replied for his brother.

"Come," Cain said, urging them to their chairs. "We have much to discuss."

"Oh, what is it, Brother?"

Hell, would he ever grow accustomed to hearing the lad he'd called William for a pair of months now call him brother?

He smiled into his cup and thought for a moment about how much Aleysia d'Argentan had changed his life.

"There is somethin' I would tell ye," Cain said, taking a seat beside him. He finished off his whisky and called on the nerves of steel that aided him on the battlefield to help him now. "I...ehm...I have been tryin' to remember things."

"Son." Father Timothy placed his hand over Cain's larger one. Once it had been the other way around. Cain remembered that, too.

He smiled at his old friend and then returned his gaze to his brother. Nicholas had lost much. They all had. He wanted to give his brother something back. "I remember our mother holdin' ye." Tears gathered at the rims of his eyes as the memory played out before him as though it happened yesterday, bringing with it waves of emotion. "She carried ye with her while she did her work and called over her shoulder..." He had to stop and remember to breathe. "...as Torin and I wrestled in her carrot patch."

"Torin." Nicholas repeated the name, as if needing to hear it on his tongue. "Tell me about him, and our parents."

Cain looked across the table and found Aleysia watching him, knowing what this meant to him, for him. He would thank her for it all later.

"He was five when last I saw him," he told his brother. "He was fairer than ye and I, more like our mother and he enjoyed when mother told him stories." He shared what he remembered of their parents, their mother especially—the one whose love he remembered most.

Aye, it had been painful at first, almost maddening—going back and finding her in the ashes. But in the end, her smile and gentle voice was worth the search.

He hadn't been alone on the difficult journey. Aleysia had been with him. It wasn't over, but she would be with him for it all. She was more courageous, more determined than any man he'd ever known. He wanted to spend the rest of his days with her. He wanted to go to sleep beside her each night and wake every morning to her bonny face. He wanted to watch her belly grow full with his bairns and be there to help them grow. Hell, he loved her. He hadn't told her yet. He wanted to tell her now.

He rose from his seat just as someone called out a toast. He raised his empty cup and smiled with his men. Someone else rose up with another cheer for him and Aleysia, more for him and Nicholas. Before he knew it, everyone was gathered around his table, patting his back.

His eyes found Aleysia as the cheering settled down. She was speaking to an older woman with her back to him. When his be-trothed looked up, he smiled and moved to go to her. The woman turned to have a look at him—from his boots to the top of his head. Beatrice. Hell. He averted his eyes from her the instant she looked at him.

"Ye look...happy."

Cain turned to the warm, salient eyes of his oldest, only friend. "I am."

"I am glad to hear that, Son."

Cain knew he spoke the truth. Father Timothy had been the only comfort Cain knew in the cruelty of his world.

"Withoot ye and God lookin' after me," he said. "I might have died and never seen this day. Thank ye, Father."

Father Timothy scrunched up his face and his large eyes filled with tears. Cain drew him in for an embrace he wished he hadn't waited so long to give.

"In case ye didna know, I love ye, old man," he managed and then patted the priest on the back and released him. "We will require ye in the chapel later. Just us."

Father Timothy raised his brows. "Ye will marry her before ye speak to the king?"

"Aye," Cainnech didn't hesitate to tell him. Why wait? Nothing would stop him from having her. "I willna lose her."

"Ye will need witnesses," the priest reminded him gently.

Cain nodded, looking toward Aleysia and moving instinctively toward her. "Bring Nicholas and Richard."

Beatrice was gone and his betrothed wore a smile touched by an inner light, radiating outward. She loved him. He still could not believe it. How had she fallen in love with such an unlovable heart?

"You are not rubbing your belly," she noted, stepping into his arms.

"It no longer pains me," he told her and dipped his mouth to hers. Their kiss was brief but she tasted of honey mead and desire.

"I spoke with Beatrice," she told him quietly, stepping out of his embrace. "All is well. The pain is eased by a tender lover. Will you be tender?"

Her eyes were so green, so round with anticipation of his reply he couldn't do anything but nod his head. He would do his best.

She moved in closer. He inhaled the top of her head. "She said we should do pleasurable things to each other."

"Oh?" he asked. "Like?"

She laughed softly. "I did not ask her."

"Good." He took her hands in his and gazed into her eyes. "We will learn as we go." He pulled her hands up behind his neck and leaned down close to her ear. "I am eager to begin."

"As am I," she whispered along his jaw and set his blood on fire.

"Father!" he called and pulled her toward the priest. "To the chapel!"

They couldn't find Richard, but picked up Nicholas and Mattie on the way. Mattie wept and stared at Nicholas while Father Timothy gave his benediction. Cain tapped his foot and the priest kept it brief. He and Aleysia gave their consent. Father Timothy made the sign of the cross, and told them they were husband and wife.

Cain's heart leaped for the first time in—well, for the first time.

Eager for each other, they bid good eve to the priest and their witnesses and hurried out of the great hall. When they reached the solar and opened the door, they found the hearth fire, along with a dozen candles, lit, and Aleysia's bed sprinkled with rose petals.

She turned to cast him a surprised, delighted look. He shook his head. It wasn't he, but now he knew something she enjoyed…besides fighting and lying in bluebells.

"Oh, it must have been Mattie!" she sang out, smiling. "She is always so considerate."

"Aye." He smiled, entering the room behind her. He bolted the door and turned to look at her standing before the bed bathed in the soft glow of candlelight. His heart beat madly against his chest. She was his. She had braved the battlefield for his heart and won it. It was hers. It would always be hers.

He walked to her tall wooden chest and took her comb in his fingers. He brought it to his nose and smiled at her behind it. "Ye are hauntin', lass."

Her eyes followed him as he moved nearer and pushed his plaid off his shoulder. Her gaze dipped to his belly after he lifted his léine over his head.

He watched her unlace her bodice and slip it off. His body hardened for her.

"The first time I had ye in this bed," he told her, his voice thickening as he reached her. "I knew I wanted ye there always."

She tilted back her head and laughed softly. "Do you mean the night I almost killed you?"

He snaked his arm around her waist and brushed his lips over her exposed throat. "Ye didna want to kill me even then."

"I was a coward. Nothing more." She laughed when he gently bit her neck. "I hated you!" She squealed when he tickled her and pushed away from him. She fell back on the bed and he fell with her.

He grew serious looking down at her against a backdrop of rose petals. He picked one up and brushed it over her cheekbone. "Ye are everythin' to me, lass," he told her, his voice a deep-throated rasp. "Yer heart calls out to mine and I answer—" he looked into her eyes. "I love ye."

Tears gathered at the rim of her inky lashes. She didn't have to speak, for he could see her heart in her eyes. "Oh, Cainnech, I love you, too."

He kissed her, taking her full, lush mouth with measured control. He swept his tongue over hers, and she answered by joining him in his sensual exploration. Her body felt soft and warm beneath him. His, on the other hand, was as tight as a drum string.

He moved his hands over her and liked that she had the boldness to do the same to him. Her fingers running down his arms made his muscles tremble. She asked him modestly to turn his head while she undressed.

Doing as she bid, he waited on his knees facing the head of her rose-covered bed. He felt her moving behind him and closed his eyes to pray for control, to be a tender, gentle lover with his untried wife.

She came up behind him slowly, placing her hands on his shoulders. Her body was warm at his back. He turned his face toward her when she dragged her bottom lip up his arm. He inhaled her, aching for more of her. She came around slowly, tantalizing him with her breath, each fluid movement of her body. He'd wanted her in the glade. Even more now.

He unclasped his plaid from around his waist and unwound himself from it. He heard her gasp and, reaching out, he pulled her around and set her down on the bed. He took in the sight of her long, lithe curves, the tight tips of her breasts beckoning to be kissed, the sensual slope of her belly, the sweet tuft of black hair below.

He lay beside her, leaned on his shoulder and faced her. "Everythin' will be well," he promised on the tenderest whisper he could manage. "I will see to it."

"I am not afraid, Cainnech," she assured him, her warm, honey-scented breath falling on his face. "I wish to join with you and bring you pleasure."

What had he done to deserve such a wife? "Lookin' at ye gives me pleasure."

She stared into his eyes and ran her fingers over his smile. "I feel the same way about you. Still, I want more. Do you not?"

He bent in close to her lips. "Aye, I want more."

They coiled their limbs around each other, unable to get close enough.

"Does it pain you?" she asked of his heavy cock resting between them. "May I touch it?"

She ran her fingertips along his length, stretching his control to its limit. He groaned and grew even harder. When she closed her fingers around him, he grazed his teeth over her erect nipples and moved over her. They explored and enjoyed each other's bodies with their fingers, lips, and tongues.

Taking his time at such pleasures was a new experience for Cain. Each kiss, every moan he pulled from her would be forever emblazoned on his memory. He would never forget this night with her. He loved her. He *loved*, and it didn't hurt.

He told her while he kissed her body, tasting the sweet fruit of her breasts, the tight nub between her milky white thighs. His brave, beautiful woman didn't flinch at his scandalous exploration and delight. No. She writhed in his mouth and drove him mad with the need to have her.

When he lifted himself above her, she smiled, ready to take him.

I will be tender. I will be tender. He chanted the litany over and over in his mind.

"Thank ye fer takin' me as yer husband," he said against her mouth as he lowered his body and rested himself on her.

Her warmth and inviting arms were nearly his undoing. He slipped his hand between them to guide himself to her entrance. He closed his eyes, afraid of hurting her, but her long legs parted for him.

"My love," she whispered on the sultriest of breath, "thank you for taking me as your wife."

He pulled her legs around him and pushed forward.

Tender.

He pushed a little more, leaning down to kiss her face, her neck, and to tell her he loved her. He moved slowly, grinding his teeth with the effort not to thrust into her. She held him as he pushed deeper, breaking her veil. At times, he paused and spoke softly to her when it seemed too painful, but she would not release him and, finally, she began to move under him.

Burying his face into her neck, he groaned and kissed a fiery path to her ear. He pressed her hands to the bed on either side of her and twined his fingers through hers.

He pushed forward on his knees and lifted her up with the force of his thighs. He almost withdrew, and then thrust himself deep into her.

She was sleek and tight around him. When he lifted his face from her throat, her languorous, sensual gaze captured his. They shared an intimate smile and then she closed her eyes and arched her back.

He took her nipple into his mouth and sucked until she undulated like a wave beneath him.

She grew tighter, wetter, hotter around him, gripping his shoulders. He released her nipple and clenched his jaw, watching her surrender all to him. She cried out. He sank into her again, surging against her slowly and with scintillating purpose until they both found their sweet release.

Chapter Twenty-Eight

ALEYSIA OPENED HER eyes to the morning sun shining through her unshuttered window. She felt Cainnech's heavy weight on her and looked down to find him sprawled across her belly, asleep. Both of them dusted with rose petals.

He wasn't so heavy that she could not breathe—at least he wasn't last eve. She tried to move. He let out a little snore and snuggled deeper into her.

Oh, her heart swelled with love. She would not have believed it was possible to love anyone the way she loved him. She settled her gaze on his big, broad hand resting on her arm. He'd been careful with her, tender—and he'd pulled from her a part of herself she didn't know existed. A wanton, scandalous side she discovered she liked and wanted to explore.

Beatrice had been quite right. The pain hadn't lasted long before it was replaced with pleasure. And oh, Aleysia had never felt anything like it! Everything he did to her felt charged with fire, driven by pure male demand, and tempered with love.

She was happy, happier than she'd ever been before. Cainnech loved her and the villagers still loved her, as well. The men didn't hate her. She looked down at the man in her arms. If she must bow to his king, she would. She would do anything for him.

He moved atop her, waking from his slumber. She ran her fingers through his hair while he kissed her belly and then lifted his head to smile at her.

"You slept well, Husband?" Her body believed he was her husband, but her mind still had difficulty.

"Aye," he told her groggily. "I did."

She decided she loved how he looked in the morning, his languid lids and sleepy smile, the first things she saw. She ran her palm down his corded, scarred back and then blushed when her gaze fell on his firm, naked bottom.

Could she take him again? She felt a bit sore...there. How many times did a married couple join together? Every day? She hoped so.

He leaned up on his palms and gazed down at her. "What is that smile aboot?"

"I was thinking about joining with you again."

He arched a brow and quirked his mouth at her. "Oh? Ye liked it then?"

"Aye," she laughed softly and looked away.

He moved up her body, wedging himself between her legs. "Ye will find me ready, Wife."

Someone rapped at the door.

Her husband growled like an angry bear. "What is it?"

"Cainnech," Father Timothy's voice came through the door, a note of urgency staining his voice. "I must speak with ye at once."

The instant Cainnech pushed off her, Aleysia sat up and pulled the bed coverings to her chin. She watched her husband lumber out of bed and snatch up his plaid. He went to the door, tying the plaid around his waist, and yanked open the door.

Aleysia listened as the priest spoke.

"King Robert has arrived. With him are Sir John de Granville of

Avranches and a section of Norman soldiers."

"No!" Aleysia cried out.

Cainnech said something to the priest in a low voice and shut the door. He didn't stop her when she bolted from the bed and began dressing.

"What does he mean to do?" She was glad he didn't ask whom she meant. She didn't know. Both. What were the Normans doing with the king?

"Dinna fear, lass," Cainnech tried to comfort her. He came close to where she stood and took hold of her frantic fingers trying to braid her hair. "I will go see what this is all aboot. Ye stay here. I will send Matilda in to ye."

"Cainnech," She pulled on his arm when he moved for his léine. "What if the king—"

He came back to her and took her in his arms. He leaned his fore-head against hers and said in a low, rough voice that seared across her soul, "Aleysia, I will never be taken from ye, my love." He kissed her, a promise, and then broke free, pulled on his léine and boots, and left the solar.

Aleysia listened to the door close and shut her eyes. Sir John had returned for her. What could he do now that she and Cainnech were married? Would he try to contest it? She would kill him if he did. She'd need a dagger or two. She knew just where to find them.

She hurried into a fresh pair of black breeches, a woolen léine of dyed blue, and a black bodice. She had no intention of luring Sir John into a fight he would lose.

Bastard! Was this the man her cousin had chosen for her? One who couldn't take no for an answer?

Why was he with the Bruce? She would soon find out. Her heart thrashed wildly in her chest and she had to redo her braid three times, but she sent Mattie away when her friend arrived with no further news.

She set off soon after to fetch her daggers from under the cupboards in the kitchen.

THE GREAT HALL was swarming with men. Cainnech's men mixed with the Bruce's, who had not joined them yet, and the Normans eyed them all while they gathered together near the hearth fire, whispering amongst themselves.

Aleysia found Cainnech standing with his men. The King of Scots hadn't graced them with his presence yet.

She entered alone, her head held up, shoulders straight. She took a step toward Cainnech, but Richard blocked her path. She smiled briefly at her old friend. "Where is the Bruce?"

"He is speaking with Sir John, I believe. Aleysia," he said. Something hard in his voice stopped her when she would have moved toward her husband. "What did he do to you to make you agree to wed him?"

She blinked. "Cainnech?"

"The Scot, aye. Am I to believe he did not coerce you? Perhaps using Lismoor to gain—"

"Stop it. Has it not occurred to you that I love him?"

His eyes grew as hard as his tone. "No, it has not. They killed your brother. They took your home. You have been planning their deaths for four years!" He shouted the last and Cainnech and some of his men turned to see what was going on.

"And you want me to believe you have put that all to the side because you love him?"

"That is enough," Cainnech appeared beside her. "Amish, take him to the keep."

Aleysia didn't question his decision, but called his men to gather around the table. Her hands shook. She could hear her heart thumping in her chest. Every part of her screamed not to do it, but it was long past the time they knew the truth.

"You are all my friends," she told them, trying to calm her nerves. "I have not had a chance to tell you that I am sorry for everything that took place in the forest when you arrived. I am no longer the person I was that day—or four years ago."

"We understand why ye did it," Rauf told her.

The rest of the men agreed. Her relief was overwhelming. Perhaps things would turn out all right, after all. Save for Richard, who would come to his senses once this was all over.

She moved under Cainnech's arm when the King of Scots was finally announced. It took three men and a trumpet. Aleysia rolled her eyes. When she saw Sir John enter after him, her gaze went cold. She instinctively felt for one of her daggers tucked inside her bodice. Her eyes slanted to her husband and she found him watching her.

"Commander MacPherson!" Robert the Bruce's boisterous voice filled the hall.

Cainnech turned toward him with a smile and released Aleysia to bow to him.

"Yer Majesty," he called out. "Welcome to Lismoor Castle."

Robert the Bruce wasn't overly tall, but she remembered Giles speaking of him once during one of his visits. His size didn't matter when it came to his skill and his courage. One did not have to be a Scot to hear the tales.

His dark eyes drifted to her, and then sized her up from boots to braid. "Miss d'Argentan, I presume?"

She nodded, suddenly caught speechless that Robert the Bruce was standing in her great hall, believing he was here to decide her fate. That was why Sir John was here with him. Pity he didn't know it had already been decided the moment Cainnech MacPherson set foot in her forest.

"What brings my lord here?" Cainnech asked rather boldly.

If the king, who reached Cainnech's shoulder, took offense, he did not let it show. "I was leavin' Fife when I received word from Sir John here," he turned toward the Norman, standing close by, "that there was some sort of dispute between ye and him over a woman. When I met with him, I told him that 'twas I who ordered she be wed."

"Yer Majesty," Father Timothy interrupted with a smile. "There is some—"

"Ah, Father Timothy, 'tis good to see ye!" the King of the Scots greeted him with open arms.

After a tight embrace, the priest stepped back and bowed, losing his nerve to continue.

"Sire," Cainnech tried to take up where his friend left off.

The Bruce held up his hand to cut him off. "Sir John has already been promised to Miss d'Argentan by her cousin, Lord Geoffrey d'Argentan of Normandy."

"Aye, Sir John showed me his letter," Cainnech agreed.

"So then?" the Bruce asked, holding up his hands. "What is the dispute? Hand her over."

No! Aleysia took a step back. Cainnech stepped in front of her.

"Sire, she is my wife."

"Yer—" the king worked the word around his tight jaw. "—wife?" He turned to Father Timothy. "Ye married them. When?"

"Yesterday, Sire," the priest told him. "They are in love. Meant to be by God's own hand!" He shouted when the king would quiet him.

"Do ye want to be removed, Father?" the king asked.

Before anyone moved, Aleysia stepped forward and did her best to smile. "Sire, I do not want to marry Sir John. I love Cainne—the commander. What difference does it make which of them I take as a husband? My castle and my land will still be yours."

The Scottish king's face was unreadable. His tone, when he spoke, was sweet and condescending. "Miss d'Argentan, it doesna concern ye what difference it makes to me. If 'tis not I who stands behind this agreement, I will send Sir John off to yer King Edward and ye will see who he chooses fer ye. Aye?"

"He wants Norman allies," Cainnech told her boldly facing his king. "That is why he wants ye to wed Sir John."

"I see bein' here hasna had a good effect on ye or the priest," the king said, holding up his hands. "Ye will take yer men and leave after the ceremony."

"What ceremony?" Cainnech demanded. "She is my wife before God and witnesses. Ye canna—"

"I will never swear my allegiance to you!" Aleysia swore as four of the king's men stepped forward. "I want to make my plea before *my* king, Edward."

"Yer Majesty," Sir John stepped back when Cainnech reached out for him. "This is a volatile place. I wish to take Miss d'Argentan away tonight. I will take her to England."

"Robert," Cainnech said, commanding the king's attention. "I have fought many battles in yer name, was willin' to give my life to yer cause. Dinna repay me this way. I love her."

Tears filled Aleysia's eyes until her vision was blurred. She swiped her tears away and moved closer to him.

"Cainnech, if this were anyone else," the king said regretfully. "But what ye say is true. I need this alliance. Imagine our force with the Normans on our side!"

Cainnech shook his head. "Nae. I can never give her up."

"I understand there is a dungeon here. Dinna make me throw ye in it," the king warned. "I canna let ye stand in the way of this."

Cainnech ripped his sword from its sheath. "Let the Norman meet me on the field."

"Nae," the king warned again. "Put yer sword away."

"Sire," Cainnech pleaded. "Dinna make me do this."

"My love," Aleysia placed her hand on his arm. She didn't want him to fight the king's men. Some were men he knew and he might not make it out alive. "Please, put your sword away."

He looked at her with his heart in his eyes. He wouldn't lose her. He would do anything but lose her.

"Ye will leave tonight," the king told him once his sword was sheathed.

"Then I will leave with my wife."

"Take him away," the king ordered. "And relieve him of his sword."

Father Timothy held out his hand as if to stop them. "Sire, please."

Cainnech fought six of them off before Nicholas and some of the others leaped into the fray. Once Cainnech saw his brother in the fight, he stopped and commanded Nicholas to stop as well.

Aleysia watched them push him away. He looked over his shoulder at her and then smashed his forehead into the next man who pushed him. The man fell to the floor as if dead.

When he was gone, the king gave the fallen man a pitied look and then turned to Aleysia. "Ye will leave with Sir John at once. Ye are England's problem. Not mine. And ye," he turned to Sir John, "will remember who 'twas who helped ye today."

"Who betrays his friend," Aleysia bit out. "I will not remain at Lismoor while you are king. Let Sir John wed one of your other puppets."

"Our time is done here, Miss d'Argentan," the Bruce told her. "I suggest ye go make ready fer yer trip."

Oh, she felt for her dagger, she was ready.

CHAPTER TWENTY-NINE

C AIN WAITED ALONE in the light of a single candle in the depths of
Lismoor. Put in the dungeon by the man he'd served for more
than a decade. The betrayal cut deep and Cain would never forget it,
but now was not the time for such thoughts. Now, he had to find a
way out of Lismoor's dungeon. He knew there was one, for Aleysia
had escaped. Unless she'd already had the key with her.

He searched the cell for over of an hour but, in the dark, he could
find nothing. He shouted for someone to come and then continued
searching for the key. He was surprised to see Richard step into the
torchlight by the entrance.

He rushed to the bars. "Richard, help me get oot of here!"

"'Tis too late," he said, coming closer, looking drained and miserable. "He took her."

Cain threw himself against the bars. "Sir John? Where?" he demanded when the old knight nodded.

"To England. He denied my company. Oh," he lamented. "This is
not what I wanted when I wrote to Geoffrey d'Argentan. I only meant
to protect her."

"Ye wrote to him?" Cain asked, stunned. That was how Sir John knew to come here. "'Tis too late now fer regrets, Sir Richard. But 'tis not too late to protect her. Help me get oot."

"There's a key in the waste bucket. There is a false bottom," the old knight told him. "The tunnel leads to the woods."

Cain immediately dumped the waste bucket and tore apart the bottom until he had the key. Clever lass. No one *she* put in the dungeon would happen upon the key, or think to look in such a place. "How long ago did they leave?" he asked Richard as he unlocked the door and ran out of the cell.

"About a quarter of an hour ago. She tried to come to you but the Bruce's men stopped her."

Cain nodded. "Dinna fear. I will bring her back and settle this with the king."

"Commander?" The knight stopped him before he entered the tunnel. "Do you love her?"

Cain nodded. "Aye. Aye, I do."

"Then hurry."

Cain smiled and disappeared through the small hole in the wall.

He hadn't gone this far inside the last time he was in here chasing her, he thought as the walls closed around him. He closed his eyes and kept on going, breathing in the air and searching for something fresh.

Finally, he came to the end of the tunnel and made his way out into the open. He climbed into the trees, hoping to see better from the high vantage point.

What he saw surprised him. Norman knights. Was Aleysia still here? No, there were less than a dozen of them. What were they still doing here, lingering about? He watched them, following them through the trees back to the castle, where they snuck inside.

What were they up to? Why were they sneaking about?

He hurried out of the trees and sprinted back to the keep. He nearly knocked over Nicholas on his way back in.

"Brother! The men and I were planning to break you free!" Nicholas greeted him.

Cain told him what he saw and suspected and they rushed toward the stairs for the solar.

They found two of the king's guards dead in the corridor. Cain helped himself to one of the soldier's swords. They looked inside the solar with hesitancy. The king was not there. They practically ran into four Normans on the way to the great hall. Cain swung his sword across two of the men's throats. The other two died just as quickly as their guts spilled out across the rushes.

"Hell, Brother," Nicholas stood still and pale with the dead around his feet. "I heard you are savage with a weapon. I see the tales are true."

Cainnech patted him on the back and continued back on their path.

When they entered the great hall and saw that most of the men were still there and oblivious to what was happening, Cain informed them. "Find any Normans and kill them, no questions."

They found more dead men, some Robert's, some Cain's, strewn across the rushes leading toward Cain's room.

When Cain and Nicholas approached the room, they saw shadows by the bed, where the king lay napping.

Without a thought about what the king had done to him earlier, Cain sprang forward. After a short scuffle, he emerged the victor, with the hilt of his bloody sword in his hand. He put it into Nicholas'.

"Take it. Tell the king ye killed those bastards."

"No. I will not take the credit for saving the king's life when 'twas you who did it."

"I must go," Cain argued. "I must find Aleysia. Dinna tell Robert I am gone. Vow it."

"I vow it," Nicholas agreed quietly and did not call him back when the king awoke and called out.

ALEYSIA DIDN'T CARE about alliances, or Normandy, or the damned King of Scots. She wasn't going to England with Sir John. She would escape the Norman knight and return to rescue Cainnech from the dungeon. She had tried, but Robert's men wouldn't let her see him. She'd visited Richard instead and begged him to promise to go to Cainnech and show him where to find the key to the cell. He had to escape. She had to get back to him.

She'd never agree to annulling their union and marrying anyone else.

"You are even more fair by the moonlight, Aleysia," Sir John said as they trotted along on their horses.

"Why are we going south? Are we going to England?"

He tossed her an impatient look with a sigh to go with it. "You are not going to ask questions the entire time, are you?"

He needn't worry. He wouldn't be alive long enough to answer them.

There were twelve men in her company. Where were the rest of them? She was sure she could take down two with her daggers. One being Sir John. But then what was she to do? The rest of them would kill her.

Her traps were useless since she was on the ground and they were leaving the forest.

"Are you going to answer me?" she asked.

"We're not going to England, dear Aleysia," he told her impatiently. "We do not have to. Edward will do what I want now that I have disposed of the Scottish king."

"What are you saying?"

"I am saying, Robert the Bruce is likely dead by now."

Aleysia's eyes opened wider. "You are in league with King Edward." Now it made sense that Sir John had sought out the Scottish king. He planned on killing him quietly in her castle. Cainnech would never let it happen. But he could still be in the dungeon.

Amish would stop it. But it was an ambush. Father Timothy, Nicholas—Mattie!

She reached for the dagger shoved behind her bodice. She had to get back to the castle! She looked around at Sir John's guards. Which one looked the most daunting? She found a man who sat tall in his saddle. He looked like a mean one, with a black patch over his eye and at least four hilts that she could see sticking out of his belt.

She pulled her dagger free and flung it all in one motion, aiming for his heart. Her blade landed in his chest with a thump. She moved swiftly, pulling another dagger out of her boot. She pointed it at Sir John and addressed his men.

"The next man to move ends his life!" she warned in a loud, clear voice.

"You will never get away," Sir John warned. He smiled and it was so unlike Cainnech's resplendent, patient smile that she nearly wretched thinking about life with this man.

"What do you care?" she asked him, oddly calm. "You will be dead. Now, tell your men to—"

Something dropped out of the trees and took down two guards before Aleysia realized it was Cainnech. His sword flashed in the filtered sunlight. Blood splashed a nearby tree. A guard came at him on his horse but Cainnech stopped him with a brutal blow from his axe. He whirled around in a deadly dance that was both captivating and terrifying to watch. Even Sir John could not tear his eyes away from the carnage Cainnech wreaked havoc upon his men. He didn't stop swinging and jabbing until every man save Sir John, was dead.

Aleysia thought about what he must be like on the battlefield. She shivered in her spot.

Thunder reverberated beneath her. Horses were coming.

Cainnech came toward Sir John and Aleysia, his léine pulled free from his waist and stained in blood, his eyes glittering like the northern sky. He dropped his axe and held open his arms, a dripping sword in one hand. "Come!" he roared at Sir John.

Her would-be betrothed, and possibly the Scottish king's killer, wilted in his saddle. He held up his shaking hands and surrendered.

Cainnech still came forth. Aleysia held out her hands to stop him, forgetting the dagger she'd held on Sir John.

The Norman leaped for her, knocking them both from the saddle.

Cainnech was there instantly, lifting Sir John off the forest floor by his collar. When Cainnech had him on his knees, he pulled the Norman close, letting Sir John see her as he pressed the edge of his blade against the knight's throat.

She met Cainnech's cold gaze over Sir John's shoulder. He was going to cut his throat.

The thunder beneath her grew louder. They looked toward the sound to see the king and Amish, everyone coming into view. She darted her gaze back to Cainnech. She didn't want him to kill Sir John. His king would not forgive him.

"Let him go, my love."

He smiled and kissed the top of Sir John's head and then let him go, sending him forward on his knees before the king with a kick to his backside.

Aleysia didn't care about what was going on around her. Her eyes were on her husband. He looked up and their eyes met. This savage, merciless bloody Highland warrior was hers. Hers.

She ran into his arms, where she ached to be, where she belonged. No damned king was going to take her from him again.

THEY SAT WITH the king in the great hall as night fell. They drank and cheered Nicholas, who had saved the king's life. Mattie was especially happy. She hadn't stopped smiling all night.

For attempting to kill the king, Sir John was shipped off to Normandy in three separate crates as a message to Aleysia's cousin.

Aleysia was afraid this would make them enemies, but the Bruce assured her that was not the case. He was sorry for sending her off with a killer.

He was not so forgiving to Cainnech. "How did ye get out of the dungeon?"

"Does it matter?" her husband asked him, in between sips of wine. "I told ye I wasna leavin' withoot her."

"Cain, I have known ye since ye were a lad. I fergive much from ye because of yer past. But yer insolence is gettin'—"

"Sire," Nicholas interrupted, rising from his seat. "Cainnech is—"

Cainnech set his steady gaze on his brother and Nicholas sat down, saying nothing else.

This piqued the Bruce's interest. He eyed them both. "When did ye escape that dungeon, Cain? Before or after the Normans infiltrated the castle?"

Cainnech blinked slowly, his gaze still on his brother. "After."

"Brother," Nicholas said and then looked at the king. "Sire, he saw the Normans coming inside."

"Nicholas," Cain said again.

"Nae. Let him speak," the king commanded.

He told the king what had happened and when he was done, the Bruce commended him on his honesty. Again, he wasn't so forgiving to Cainnech. "Ye saved my life, so I canna toss ye back into the dungeon—not that it would do any good. Instead, I will grant ye whatever ye ask. Insolence or not, I want no one else by my side in battle."

"Thank ye, Sire," Cain said. "But I willna be fightin' fer awhile. I want to start a family with my wife. I also want Lismoor—"

He stopped when Aleysia leaned up and whispered in his ear.

"Are ye certain?" he asked her.

"Aye," she told him softly and without hesitation.

He took her hand and turned back to the king. "I want Lismoor and Rothbury to be given to Nicholas. I am goin' home to rebuild my life."

Aleysia closed her eyes. She would be there to help him, for as long as he needed her. Images of him killing ten men to save her flashed across her mind. She would never tame him.

"Cainnech," she whispered to him, leaning in close. "Tonight, I do not think we need to be overly concerned with being gentle."

He looked at her and then laughed. It was a deep, rich, beautiful sound. A sound she was growing to love. She said a silent prayer and looked across the table at Father Timothy. They both smiled.

The End

Made in the USA
Lexington, KY
04 April 2019